OF BETRAYAL

Within minutes, the sky was lit with a dreadful orange glow as more of the druchii timber stores went up in flames. A wild exultation gripped Eldain as he shot yet more druchii, but the strategist in him saw that they would not be able to keep this momentum going for much longer. Soon, the druchii would organise themselves, and if he and his warriors were trapped within the shipyards, it would only be a matter of time before they were hunted down and killed. – *from* **Kinstrife** *by Graham McNeill*

He felt the teeth – fangs – plunge into his neck, biting deep, hard. The old man's body tensed, every fibre of his being repulsed by the intimacy of the kill. He lashed out, twisted, flopped and finally sagged as he felt the life being drained out of him. – *from* **Death's Cold Kiss** *by Steven Savile*

IN THE DARK *and gothic Warhammer world, the foul magic of Chaos is everywhere, its corrupting and mutating powers twisting man and beast alike. From the south, the dark armies of the undead attack the realms of man, thirsting to drain all life from the civilised lands. From the north, the endless tide of Chaos sweeps down to kill and capture in the name of the Dark Gods. This collection of fantasy stories follows man's fight for survival in these desperate times.*

WARHAMMER FANTASY STORIES

THE COLD HAND OF BETRAYAL

Edited by Marc Gascoigne & Christian Dunn

A Black Library Publication

First published in Great Britain in 2006 by
BL Publishing,
Games Workshop Ltd.,
Willow Road, Nottingham,
NG7 2WS, UK

10 9 8 7 6 5 4 3 2 1

Cover illustration by Jeff Johnson.
Map by Nuala Kinrade.

A CIP record for this book is available from the British Library.

ISBN 13: 978 1 84416 288 8
ISBN 10: 1 84416 288 5

Distributed in the US by Simon & Schuster
1230 Avenue of the Americas, New York, NY 10020.

Printed and bound in Great Britain by
Bookmarque, Surrey, UK.

See the Black Library on the Internet at
www.blacklibrary.com

Find out more about Games Workshop
and the world of Warhammer at
www.games-workshop.com

THIS IS A DARK age, a bloody age, an age of daemons and of sorcery. It is an age of battle and death, and of the world's ending. Amidst all of the fire, flame and fury it is a time, too, of mighty heroes, of bold deeds and great courage.

AT THE HEART of the Old World sprawls the Empire, the largest and most powerful of the human realms. Known for its engineers, sorcerers, traders and soldiers, it is a land of great mountains, mighty rivers, dark forests and vast cities. And from his throne in Altdorf reigns the Emperor Karl-Franz, sacred descendent of the founder of these lands, Sigmar, and wielder of his magical warhammer.

BUT THESE ARE far from civilised times. Across the length and breadth of the Old World, from the knightly palaces of Bretonnia to ice-bound Kislev in the far north, come rumblings of war. In the towering World's Edge Mountains, the orc tribes are gathering for another assault. Bandits and renegades harry the wild southern lands of the Border Princes. There are rumours of rat-things, the skaven, emerging from the sewers and swamps across the land. And from the northern wildernesses there is the ever-present threat of Chaos, of daemons and beastmen corrupted by the foul powers of the Dark Gods. As the time of battle draws ever near, the Empire needs heroes like never before.

Norsca

Sea of

Sea
of
Chaos...

The
Wasteland.

Laurelorn
forest.

Mid

L'Anguille.

Couronne.

Masienburg.

Arden
forest.

Gisoreux.

Bordeleaux.

Grey Moun

Bretonnia

Loren
forest

Brionne.

Quenelles.

North of Here Lie The
Dreaded Chaos Wastes.

of Claus

Erengrad.

Here Be Trolls...

Praag.

middle mountains.

Kislev

Kislev.

denheim.

Wolfenburg.

Talabheim

The Empire

Alldorf.

Karak Kad

Nuln.

The
Moot.

Sylvania.
Dracken
-hof.

Zhufbar

Averheim.

Black
Water.

Black fire Pass.

Karak
Norn.

CONTENTS

KINSTRIFE
by Graham McNeill

I
NAGGAROTH

THE SLEEK, EAGLE-PROWED vessel travelled along the river without a sound, slicing the dark water as the high elf crew rowed with smooth, rhythmic sweeps of their oars. The silver hull barely reflected on the slate-coloured water and an acrid sulphurous stench was carried on the yellow fog that hugged its black surface.

The vessel's sails were folded away and the mast lowered to avoid the dark, clawing branches of the trees that pressed in on either side of the river, and even though the orb of the sun had yet to reach its zenith, the weak light it cast over the Land of Chill barely penetrated the thick, jagged canopy.

Standing at the prow of the vessel, a tall, long-limbed elf with silver-gold hair bound by a bronze circlet watched the route ahead as the river turned in a lazy bend. In one hand he carried a long, gracefully curved bow inlaid with gold and looped with silver wire, while his other gripped the hilt of a slender, leaf-bladed sword. He wore a sky blue tunic embroidered with a golden horse, beneath which was a glimmering shirt of ithilmar mail. His features were smooth and his face oval, his eyes dark and hooded – almost without whites.

The elf leaned over the side of the boat, trying to see the riverbed through the swirling black water, but he quickly gave up.

'What depth do we have?' he asked, without turning.

'Perhaps three fathoms, Lord Eldain, maybe less,' replied one of the vessel's crew, who knelt a respectful distance behind the tall elf, a weighted sounding line playing out into the water. 'I do not believe we will reach much further up the river than this. I would humbly suggest that we tie up at the bank soon.'

Eldain nodded, turning and marching back down the deck of the shallow-bottomed ship, before nodding to the steersman at the stern to make for the shore. He heard the rush of water as the ship altered course and stared into the ghostly, dark trees that loomed over the river, wondering what catastrophe had befallen this realm to transform it into this bleak, dead landscape.

The ship drew near the bank, and Eldain switched his gaze from the haunted forest to the obsidian surface of the water and the rippling wake that spread in a 'V' from the ship's stern. A dozen more vessels, high prowed and graceful as swans, with hulls of silver and white followed his own, arcing gracefully towards the northern riverbank. Riding high on the prow of the following boat was the imposing figure of Caelir, clad in an exquisitely tailored tunic of scarlet and vermillion, the subtleties of the different colours almost indistinguishable. Trust his brother to wear something best suited to the court of Lothern while hundreds of miles from home on a desperately dangerous raid into the realm of the druchii.

Sensing his brother's scrutiny, Caelir drew his sword and held it above his head, but Eldain did not return the gesture, instead turning to face the approaching bank. Thick bracken and tangled roots reached into the water, and as the ship drew near he leapt gracefully onto the black soil of Naggaroth.

Even through his fine, hand-made boots, Eldain could feel the icy cold of this land, a chill that was not simply of the climate, but of the soul. The evil that had been plotted on this dark land arose from the earth, as though the land sought to expel it... or spread its taint yet further.

Eldain shivered and nocked an arrow to his bow as his vessel's crew swiftly began disembarking and tying up the ship. He scanned the darkened undergrowth and the dead forest for enemies, but there was nothing, no shred of movement nor breath of life.

Dank mist coiled at the base of wretched, black trees that crowded his vision in all directions, and the ashen ground was strewn with jagged rocks and thorny brush that gathered in vile clumps across this blasted forest landscape. Truly this place was a vision of utter desolation. To an elf of Ellyrion, one of the Inner Kingdoms of Ulthuan blessed with bountiful forests brimming with life and magical fecundity, this dismal place was anathema.

Elven shadow warriors, grey-clad scouts who moved like ghosts, slipped past him, fanning out into the black forest with swords or bows at the ready. He relaxed his own bowstring and slipped the arrow back in his quiver, satisfied that nothing could now approach their landing place without the scouts knowing about it.

'It is a grand adventure we are on, is it not, brother?' asked a young and energised voice behind him, and he turned to face Caelir. His younger brother was roguishly handsome, with boyish good looks and a mischievous, infectious grin that had seen him out of more scrapes than his considerable skill with a blade.

'The land of the druchii is not one of adventure, brother,' cautioned Eldain, though he knew it would do nothing to dampen Caelir's spirits. 'Not since Eltharion have high elves raided Naggaroth and returned alive. It is a land of death, torment and suffering.'

Caelir smiled and said, 'It is that, but soon it will be so for our enemies, yes?'

'If all goes to plan and we don't end up like Eltharion; tortured, blinded and driven to madness in the dungeons of the Witch King.'

'Ah, but it is *your* plan, brother,' laughed Caelir, 'and I have faith in you. You were always better at planning things than I.'

Eldain bit back an angry retort and moved further down the riverbank where the ships' masters were efficiently and, more importantly, quietly disembarking their passengers. High elf Ellyrion reavers, resplendent in light mail shirts and cream tunics, swiftly formed a perimeter around the ships as the crews led their magnificent elven steeds onto dry land. The steeds could also sense the darkness in this place, and their high whinnies spoke to him of their unease at being here.

He felt his brother join him, and his irritation rose as Caelir ran forward to vault onto the back of Aedaris, a grey mare he had raised from a foal. The steed reared and kicked the air, glad to have its companion upon its back after the long sea journey from Ulthuan.

Despite himself, Eldain smiled as he saw an elven crewman lead Lotharin down the carved gangplank, patting the black stallion's muscled flanks as the animal tossed its mane in displeasure.

'I know, I know,' whispered Eldain. 'I too wish nothing more than to be away from this dark place, but we are here and we have a mission to fulfil.'

Like Caelir, Eldain had nurtured his steed from a new-born and raised it as his faithful companion. Where the barbarous humans would beat a horse and break its spirit in order to ride it, the elves of the kingdom of Ellyrion devoted their lives to building a bond of trust between rider and steed. To do any less was unthinkable.

Of all the Inner Kingdoms of Ulthuan, Ellyrion was the most beautiful. Of course Eldain knew that an elf from Caledor or Avelorn would say the same thing, but they had not lived their lives in balmy eternal summers, nor ridden a fine Ellyrion steed the length and breadth of the land with the cool wind in their hair. They had not climbed the high, marble peaks of the Annulii, nor galloped along the spine of mountains while chasing a shining storm of raw magic.

The smile faded from Eldain's lips as he glanced over at his brother – who laughed and joked with the other warriors – and tried to recall the last time he had done such things. He pushed the thought from his mind as he checked his steed for any signs of ill effects from the journey, but the ship's crew had taken great care to ensure that the horses arrived in Naggaroth able to do all that would be asked of them.

Eldain swung onto the back of Lotharin, relishing being on horseback after so long at sea. To ride a creature such as this was an honour, and though black steeds were often seen as beasts of ill-omen amongst the high elves, Eldain would sooner cut off his arm than choose another mount.

Caelir rode alongside him as the remainder of their force mounted up, a hundred warriors in all, lightly armoured for speed, and armed with bows and light throwing spears.

'Well, brother are we ready?' asked Caelir, and Eldain could hear the anticipation in his brother's voice.

'We will know soon enough,' said Eldain as one of the shadow warriors slid from the mists enveloping the dark trunks of the black forest.

Eldain considered himself an agile figure, having attended some of the most elaborate masquerades and balls Tor Elyr and Lothern had to offer, performing graceful dances beyond the ability of elves a century younger than he, but this warrior moved as though his feet did not so much touch the ground as float above it. His grey cloak was the colour of woven mist, its fabric shimmering in the pale light and the hood drawn up over his face to shroud his features in darkness.

'The way ahead is clear, Lord Eldain,' said the scout.

'Good,' nodded Eldain. 'Three of your warriors will guide us towards Clar Karond while the rest will remain here to guard our ships.'

'Very good, my lord.'

'The warriors who will accompany us,' said Eldain, 'can they keep up with us on foot or will they require mounts?'

The scout nodded slowly and said, 'they can keep up with you on foot, my lord.' Eldain thought he detected a hint of amusement in the scout's tone. The warrior turned away, and at some unseen signal, the remainder of the scouts emerged soundlessly from the cover of the trees.

'It has been too long since you rode to battle, brother,' said Caelir, leaning close and whispering so that none but Eldain could hear his words.

'What do you mean?' asked Eldain.

'The shadow warriors,' said Caelir. 'I'd wager they could reach Clar Karond and be back at our ships before we were even halfway there.'

'Yes, you are probably right,' agreed Eldain, thinking how foolish a question it had been. 'Still it does no harm to check these things. One must never assume anything, especially in war, doubly so when the battle is against the druchii.'

'You forget, brother, you and father are not the only warriors of our family to have fought the druchii,' said Caelir, holding up his burned hand. 'I too have spilled their blood, remember?'

Eldain remembered all too well. The memory, and the sight of Rhianna's silver pledge ring on Caelir's scarred finger, brought a sour taste to his throat.

II
ULTHUAN – *One year ago*

'SIT HIGH IN the saddle,' said Caelir. 'Let her enjoy the ride too. You're not trying to master her, you're trying to share the experience with her.'

'I'm trying, but she wants to run too fast,' said Rhianna. 'I am afraid I'll fall.'

Caelir smiled as Aedaris cantered in a circle around him, knowing the horse was just playing with the elf-maid who rode upon her back.

'She would never allow you to fall,' said Caelir as Aedaris picked up the pace, and Rhianna let out a squeal of delicious fear and excitement. The mare ran with her head held proudly, and Caelir knew she was showing off to Rhianna's own steed, a fine, silver gelding from Saphery, named Orsien. The gelding's dappled flanks glittered and he had a haughty gleam of intelligence in his pale green eyes, but Aedaris was easily the more powerful animal.

'Are you sure?' asked Rhianna, and Caelir laughed as he saw her relax into the horse's motion, moving in time with her rhythm and getting the measure of her temperament.

'Very sure,' nodded Caelir. 'She likes you, I can tell.'

'Then I truly know I am welcome in the kingdom of Ellyrion if their horses accept me.'

Caelir smiled, but said nothing, content to watch Rhianna circling him on the back of Aedaris and enjoying the sight of two beautiful creatures revelling in the bright afternoon sunshine. Rhianna's long golden hair fanned out behind her as she rode, a stream of honey in the air, and her white gown rippled like the tall banners of the silver helms.

Her features were delicate, but had great strength in them, her almond shaped eyes like dark pools with a hint of gold. She was beautiful, and Caelir longed to touch her, to feel the softness of her hair and the marble smoothness of her skin against his own. He kept such thoughts to himself, for Rhianna was not his woman to have such desires about.

The households of Caelir and Rhianna had been close allies for centuries, and both their fathers had fought alongside the Phoenix King in his wars with the druchii, the dark kin of the elves. Rhianna's father was a mage of great power who lived in a floating citadel in Saphery, a wondrous palace bedecked in luscious flora from all across the Old World. Caelir's own sire was one of the mightiest horselords of Ellyrion, riders and warriors without compare, but a year ago, a druchii assassin's envenomed blade had put paid to his lordship's rule over his domain, leaving him paralysed and in constant pain. While the poison ravaged him, Caelir's brother, Eldain, had taken up the mantle of protecting their lands.

Rhianna laughed as the steed slowed its gallop and began to thread a nimble-footed path through the rocks, once more showing off its skill. Caelir walked towards them, enjoying the sound of her laugher. It had been too long since the halls of his family's villa in Tor Elyr had echoed to such a sound. The summer sunshine did not fill the wide, terrazzo halls for the discomfort it would cause his father, and the happy sound of song and dance no longer drew revellers from nearby villas for feasts and merrymaking.

'Is something wrong?' asked Rhianna.

'No,' said Caelir. 'Why do you ask?'

'A shadow passed across your face.'

Caelir shook his head and let Aedaris nuzzle him. Reaching up to rub behind the horse's ears, he whispered, 'you are a princess amongst steeds, my friend, but you don't need to show off for my benefit.'

The steed whinnied and tossed her mane, pleased to have made her friend proud, and Rhianna dismounted and ran her hands through her golden hair. Caelir patted his horse's neck, watching as the magnificent steed cantered towards Rhianna's gelding. Truly it was a good day to be alive, thought Caelir, tilting his head back and letting the morning sunshine bathe him in warmth.

The heat reflected from the white rocks of the Annulii Mountains, powdered fragments of quartz glittering and making the high peaks shine with a dazzling light. Whipping vortices of magical light were tantalisingly visible through the passes, and this high in the mountains, Caelir could feel the power of that magic as a pounding heat in his veins.

Rhianna reached up and placed her palm against his cheek, and he blushed at the feelings it stirred within him.

'Are you sure nothing troubles you?' she asked.

'Yes,' nodded Caelir, turning away. 'I'm fine. Don't worry.'

'You looked very serious there,' said Rhianna, 'like your brother.'

Caelir felt his jaw clench, uncomfortable with the mention of Eldain. Though his brother had made no betrothal pledge to Rhianna, and her father had offered no dowry, it was widely accepted by the nobles of Ulthuan that Eldain would wed her within the decade.

In an attempt to change the subject, he said, 'I was just thinking of my father and the revenge I will take on the druchii.'

'I see,' said Rhianna. 'He is no better? I had hoped my father's magic would have helped clear his veins of the venom.'

'No, and he grows weaker every day. The assassins of the dark ones brew potent poisons,' said Caelir, moving away from her to sit on the edge of the rocks and stare out over the expanse of Ulthuan laid before him.

From this vantage point, high in the mountains, the rolling grasslands of Ellyrion were a vast, unbroken sward of green far below, and the sight of his homeland calmed Caelir's volatile spirits, as always. Home to the horselords of Ulthuan, great herds of elven steeds roamed the sweeping plains of Ellyrion, and the silver ribbon of the River Elyr snaked across the landscape towards the beautiful city of Tor Elyr before emptying into the bay of the Sea of Dusk.

Built atop a series of verdant islands and sculpted from the living rock, Tor Elyr was a magnificent sight. There were a multitude of sweeping thoroughfares, and the villas and palaces were capped with tall towers of silver and gold. Colourful banners snapped in the breeze, and streamers of magic sparkled and foamed from the garrets of the city's wizards.

Connecting the islands of these magnificent structures was a web of curving bridges that spanned the expanse of emerald green waters with great beauty and an easy grace.

To look upon the realm of Ellyrion was to behold beauty, and Caelir felt his angry heart quelled. Rhianna moved to sit beside him and placed her hand on his arm. His blood quickened at her touch, and when she smiled at him, it filled him with yearning to see such beauty and know that it was not his to have.

'If the physicians cannot cure him, can they at least make him more comfortable?' asked Rhianna.

Caelir shook his head. 'They fuss and mutter and speak of new poultices or magical brews, but they are powerless to stop the poison eating him away from inside.'

'My father will do what he can, but…'

'I know he will,' nodded Caelir, taking her hand. 'He is a good and true friend. As are you.'

'I remember when my father first brought us to Tor Elyr, smiled Rhianna. 'You were but a youth, full of fire and passion. I watched you showing off on your horse and thought that you looked very fine.'

'I remember that day still,' nodded Caelir. 'You wore a gown of azure silk, blue, like the summer sky. And I remember thinking that you were the most beautiful woman I had ever seen.'

Rhianna laughed and said, 'Now you are making fun of me.'

'No,' said Caelir. 'I think I have loved you since first we met.'

'Hush!' whispered Rhianna, though there was no one to hear their words, and Caelir saw the beginnings of a smile crease the corners of her mouth. 'It is not seemly for you to speak of such things while we are without a chaperone.'

'I am your chaperone,' said Caelir. 'Was it not my brother himself who asked me to take you riding and show you the ways of an Ellyrion horseman?'

'Your brother trusts your honour.'

Caelir laughed. 'And he of all people should know better than to trust *me* with such a beauty as you. Anyway, if he was so concerned, why does he not take you riding himself?'

'Your brother bears a heavy burden, maintaining your family lands,' said Rhianna. 'It is a noble thing he does, and takes much of his energies. He has not the time to spend with me in more… frivolous pursuits.'

Caelir's eyes narrowed, hearing the sadness in Rhianna's voice. And though he knew it was wrong, he felt the stirrings of opportunity. With their father incapacitated, Eldain had become dour and uncommunicative, spending all his time seeing to the myriad tasks that the master of a household must deal with every day.

Caelir had not been asked to help nor had he offered aid to his brother, preferring the thrill of venturing into the Annulii Mountains to the drudgery of work. To hunt the fabled white lions, fearsome predators whose snowy pelts were worn by the guards of the Phoenix King himself, was the life for Caelir!

Where was the joy to be had in the running of a household? What honour or glory was there in dull lists and suchlike? No, far better that he roam the mountains as the hunter, or ride the plains as a bold adventurer.

Seeing Caelir's expression, Rhianna said, 'Eldain has a good heart,' but Caelir could see that she was defending his brother because it was the right thing to do, not because she truly believed what she said.

'He does,' agreed Caelir, 'but he is foolish indeed to let a flower as beautiful as you go unplucked. I would never allow myself to be distracted from your happiness.'

Rhianna slipped her hand from his and looked out over the wondrous expanse of Ellyrion, her brows knit in consternation. Behind them, Orsien gave a high whinny of alarm, and both elves turned in surprise.

Caelir could see nothing that might cause the horse to sound a warning, but it was a steed of Saphery and had senses beyond his. He leapt to his feet and offered his hand to Rhianna.

'What is it?' she asked, taking his hand and rising to stand next to him. 'What's the matter?'

'I don't know yet,' he answered, turning and running for his horse. Orsien reared and kicked the air, his neighs of alarm growing more strident. Caelir reached Aedaris and drew his sword, scanning the horizon for any sign of mountain predators.

Rhianna ran to her horse and unsheathed her bow, a fine longbow inset with mother-of-pearl, that exuded the taste of Vaul's magic.

'I don't see anything,' said Rhianna, nocking an arrow to her bowstring.

'Nor I,' said Caelir, 'but this may be no ordinary predator. This close to the magical vortex that circles the Anullii, there's every chance that whatever Orsien has sensed may be something drawn here by the magic. Perhaps a chimera or a hydra. Or worse.'

'Then we should go,' said Rhianna. 'Now.'

Caelir shook his head. 'No, not yet. I want to see what it is. Imagine the creatures brought here by the magic! Don't you want to see what such power can create?'

'No, I do not,' said Rhianna. 'If they are as dangerous as you say, then I very much wish to avoid encountering such a beast. And so should you.'

Caelir scanned the rocks above, catching sight of a slipping shadow where none ought to be.

Something was moving up there... something that did not want to be seen.

He felt the hairs on the back of his neck prickle, and a hot sensation of fear settled in his belly as he realised that this was neither mountain predator nor monster conjured from the mountain's magic. This was something far worse.

'Rhianna,' he said urgently, 'get on your horse and ride for Tor Elyr.'

'What is it?'

'Do it!' he hissed. 'Now. It is the druchii.'

No sooner had the words left his throat than a trio of iron crossbow bolts slashed through the air from the rocks above. Caelir twisted his body, bringing his sword up in a desperate arc to cleave the first pair of bolts in two. He heard Rhianna cry out and risked a glance behind him to see that the third quarrel was lodged in her shoulder. Blood soaked her dress, and Caelir cried out in anger as three dark cloaked warriors emerged from their hiding places in the rocks above.

'Rhianna!' he shouted as she slumped against the flanks of her steed.

'Is that her name?' called out the lead druchii warrior. 'It will make torturing her all the sweeter when I whisper her name as she begs for mercy.'

Caelir turned to face the warrior, a sharp-featured elf with pallid, ivory skin and a hawk-like nose. Like his companions, his head was shaven, with a single, dark topknot dangling from the back of his skull. The druchii wore light tunics of dark cloth that seemed to swallow the day's light, and held their deadly repeater crossbows aimed unwaveringly at Caelir's heart. Each weapon bore an ebony store of bolts on its upper surface, allowing it to fire a hail of bolts rather than a single shot. The range of such weapons was much reduced, as was their stopping power, but Caelir knew that at this range and without any armour, he would be just as dead if pierced by them.

'You will not touch her,' swore Caelir, moving to stand between the druchii and Rhianna.

'And you think you can stop us?' laughed the warrior. 'I am Koradris and I have taken many heads in battle. Yours will simply be one more.'

'I will die before I let you take her.'

'So be it,' said Koradris and pulled the trigger.

But before the firing mechanisms could loose the bolts, the weapons burst into flame. Sparkling magical fire leapt from weapon to weapon, and the druchii cried out in surprise and pain as they dropped them. Caelir felt the surge of magic from behind him and heard Rhianna fall to the ground, this magical gift to him draining the last of her strength.

Without giving the druchii warriors time to recover from their surprise, Caelir leapt forwards, his sword cleaving through the nearest enemy's chest with the speed of a striking snake. The warrior collapsed, choking on his own blood, and Caelir gave an ululating yell as he attacked the others.

Koradris easily parried his blow, sending a lightning riposte to his belly. Caelir only just managed to block the cut, rolling his sword around his opponent's weapon and slashing for his head. The druchii ducked and batted aside Caelir's return stroke, as the second warrior circled to his left.

Koradris lunged and the second druchii warrior attacked at the same moment. Caelir deflected the attack, and, like quicksilver, turned to parry a downward cut from the side, launching an attack of his own.

The druchii parried another strike and launched a deadly thrust to Caelir's chest, but his blow was deflected, and Caelir spun on his heel, slashing his sword at the warrior's head.

His opponent swayed aside, but the tip of Caelir's blade sliced the skin just above his temple and blood flowed from the cut. Koradris moved to encircle his prey. Caelir knew that unless he evened the odds, a duel like this could have only one outcome. Koradris and the other druchii circled him from either side, leering anticipation writ large upon their features.

'You will pay for killing Vranek,' hissed Koradris. 'He was kin to me.'

'I thought the druchii paid no mind to kith and kin,' answered Caelir.

'True enough,' agreed Koradris, charging in once more, 'but he owed me money.'

The blades met with an almighty clang, but Caelir had anticipated this. He leapt back from Koradris and spun, thrusting his sword at the other druchii who sought to slay him from behind. The blade plunged deep into his neck and the druchii's eyes bulged as he toppled to the ground, blood jetting from his torn throat.

Caelir felt the burning kiss of steel across his back as the short blade of Koradris slashed through his jerkin and bit a finger's breadth into his flesh. He cried out in pain, dropping his sword and falling to his knees as Koradris closed in for the kill. Caelir threw himself flat on his belly and rolled as the druchii's blade slashed and stabbed for him.

He needed a weapon, and cried out in agony as he rolled over something hot.

Koradris stood above him, his sword dripping blood and his mouth curled in a sneer of contempt.

'The lords of Naggaroth fill our heads with the might of the Phoenix King's warriors, but you are a pitiful specimen indeed. Tell me, youngling, do you hear the wail of Morai-Heg? She will be coming for you soon.'

Caelir fumbled beneath him and felt the burning touch of seared wood and metal. He gripped a smooth wooden stock, gritting his teeth against the pain.

'If you hear the banshee's wail, it is you she is coming for!' shouted Caelir, swinging round one of the scorched repeater crossbows and pulling the trigger. For the only time in his life, Caelir was grateful for the craftsmanship of the druchii, as the scorched weapon loosed a flurry of iron bolts.

He kept pulling the trigger until the ebony store on the weapon's top was exhausted, heedless of the stench of blistered flesh where the residue of the magical fire still burned him. Koradris looked down at the four bolts embedded in his chest and stomach, and seemed more surprised than in pain.

The sword slid from his fingers and he fell to the ground as blood began to seep into his dark tunic. Even as his lifeblood poured from him, he sneered at Caelir.

'You think you have won?' he gasped.

'You will die before me,' said Caelir, struggling to his feet.

'You have slain me, youngling, but the dark riders are but moments behind me,' hissed Koradris with his last breath. 'You are still going to die…'

Caelir turned from the dead druchii, retrieved his sword, and limped towards Rhianna. She lay beside her horse, the steed nuzzling her in fear and concern. The druchii bolt had pierced her shoulder, but had ricocheted upwards on her collarbone and the barbed tip protruded from the skin. He could feel the shaft of the bolt just beneath her skin.

'I have never seen the like… you were magnificent…' she whispered, her eyelids fluttering and her skin ashen. 'Like the sword masters of Hoeth.'

'Hold still,' said Caelir, 'this is going to hurt.'

Rhianna nodded and closed her eyes as Caelir sliced the blade of his sword along the line of the bolt and slid it from her body. She screamed, and Caelir held her tight, wishing he could take away her pain.

Caelir and Rhianna struggled to their feet, and Caelir fashioned makeshift bandages from the cloaks of the dead druchii to bind their wounds with.

'We don't have much time,' he said once he was finished. 'There will be more of them and they won't be far behind.'

'We must warn Tor Elyr that the druchii are here in force.'

Caelir nodded and cupped his hands to help Rhianna onto her horse. Before mounting, she leaned in close and put her palm against his cheek.

'You saved my life, Caelir, and I will never forget this,' she said, and kissed him on the lips.

'Anything for you, my lady,' he replied, the pain of his wound quite forgotten.

III
NAGGAROTH

ELDAIN REINED IN his steed as he saw the shadow warrior emerge from behind the thick bole of a black barked tree, and raised his hand in a fist to halt his troop of Ellyrion reavers.

The hooded scout bowed before Eldain and said, 'Clar Karond is beyond the rise, my lord. Where the trees thin out, the land drops away and the towers of the druchii can be clearly seen.'

Eldain sensed the scout's loathing for the druchii in every word and felt a similar stirring in his breast at the thought of taking the fight to those who had slain his father. He stared over the scout's shoulder, seeing the light from beyond the trees.

'Well done,' he told the scout. 'Where are the rest of your warriors?'

The scout waved his hand and the other two warriors emerged from the shadows. Eldain had not noticed either of the scouts, and though it was their forte to avoid being seen, it still irked him that he had not sensed so much as a hint of them.

'Why do we stop?' asked Caelir, riding alongside.

'The trees thin out ahead,' explained Eldain. 'We are close to Clar Karond.'

'At last,' said Caelir. 'I grow weary of this forest. It weighs heavily on the soul.'

'Indeed,' said Eldain, turning away. 'Stay here, I will scout ahead with the shadow warriors.'

Without waiting for Caelir to complain about being left behind, Eldain dismounted and lifted his bow from the oiled, leather case slung from Lotharin's saddle. He nodded to the scout and followed him as he slipped into the forest ahead.

The scout moved effortlessly ahead of him, and Eldain felt as clumsy as a human as he attempted to match his stealth. But it seemed that every brittle branch and leaf deliberately wormed its way beneath the soles of his boots.

Slowly, they crept forwards, and though the light of the afternoon was a welcome sight after five days of travelling through the dense, dark forests of Naggaroth, it was scant comfort to an elf raised on Ulthuan.

Each day had been more grim than the previous, though the warriors made no complaint – as was only proper. Each of them was well used to spending many weeks, or longer, in the wilds as part of their training, but the bleak forests of the Land of Chill were something else altogether.

Though days and nights came and went, the sun neither warmed the skin nor refreshed the soul, instead leeching the life from the world and casting a pall of fear and doubt over their band. As dreary as the days were, the nights were a thousand times worse, with the darkness of Naggaroth unbroken by torch or moonlight. The blackness shrouded them in silence such that each warrior feared to break it with so much as a single word.

Night was a time to fear, doubly so in Naggaroth, as strange sounds echoed in the depths of the forest around them and in the sky above them. Rustling branches, crackling leaves and the drifting echoes of what sounded like the screaming laughter of lunatic children.

Each night as they made cold camp, Eldain would picture Rhianna and his fears would ease a little, though each time a shard of ice would enter his heart when his treacherous memories would unfold to include Caelir.

Eldain shook off such thoughts as the ground began to rise and he felt a pressure on his shoulder. He looked up into the hooded face of the shadow warrior. The scout nodded slowly and gestured to a thorny patch of briars that clung to the edge of the rise like barbed tangleweed.

The scout dropped to his belly and began crawling towards the briars, and Eldain followed him, conscious that he would need to dispose of this tunic after the mission. A saying of the reavers was that survival never took second place to dignity in the field, but that was all very well when you hadn't had the finest tailors and seamstresses in Lothern fashion your garments.

At last he reached the briar patch and parted the thorny brush to see the vast city of Clar Karond in all its hateful glory.

Three black towers the colour of bloody iron rose from the centre of the city, with tall jagged-roofed temples jockeying for position around them. A high wall, topped with blades and spikes, surrounded the centre of the city, and even from here, Eldain could see the sunlight glinting from the speartips of the city's guards. Beyond this high wall sprawled the peripherals of a city such as could be seen around many other cities: markets, temples, dwellings of the common folk and barracks of the city's soldiery.

But for all the trappings of civilisation, a vile darkness hung over its cobbled streets and black roofs – a sense of violence about to be unleashed, of blood about to be spilled. It chilled Eldain's soul to see such a place, a place of evil that festered beneath a brooding sun, and a place whose inhabitants plotted the destruction of his homeland.

Scattered around the city were tracts of elaborate vineyards, choked with grapes of deepest crimson, and Eldain's lip curled as he realised that these were harvested for the druchii's blood wine. Wretched human slaves tended to the vines, guarded by cruel warriors on horseback who emphasised their commands with blade and whip.

Between the vineyards, and stretching all the way up to their vantage point, the land was scarred by devastation. Shorn tree stumps bore grim testimony to the massive logging operations of the druchii that provided timber for the new war vessels of their raiding fleets. Thousands of trees must have been felled here, and the day echoed still with the distant sound of chopping axe blades and the rasp of saws. More slaves toiled in huge work gangs to the east, felling trees by the dozen and dragging them back towards the desolate city.

'Look to the north-east, my lord,' whispered the scout.

Eldain's eyes travelled to where the scout had indicated and saw their prize, the docks and shipyards for which Clar Karond was justly infamous. Ships filled the dark waters of the rocky bay that slowly widened until it emptied into the Sea of Malice. A warren of interlinked jetties and quays spread out into the water from the shoreline, each with great reaper bolt throwers on the seaward side, mighty war-machines capable of launching huge iron bolts that could pierce the hull of even the mightiest ship.

'What do you see?' asked the scout.

'Reavers mostly,' said Eldain, 'some sloops of war, a few reaper-ships and... and there's something beyond that mountain spur, but I can't quite see it.'

'Look again, my lord,' said the scout. 'That's no mountain.'

Eldain looked closer and the breath caught in his throat as he saw that what he had at first mistaken for a mountain spur of the bay was something else entirely.

'Asuryan's mercy!' he hissed as he saw that the scout spoke true.

This was no mountain... this colossus was one of the dreaded black arks.

A mountainous castle set adrift on the sea and held together by the most powerful enchantments, the black ark was a sinister floating fortress, tower upon tower, spire upon spire of living rock sundered from the isle of Ulthuan over five thousand years ago.

Crewed by an entire army, and dismal home to thousands of slaves, the black arks were the most feared and mightiest sea-going vessels in the world. Some said that the bulk they displayed above the surface of the water was but a fraction of their true size, with great vaulted caverns below the waterline that were home to terrible monsters, slaves and all manner of foul witchcraft. The truth of such things was beyond Eldain; all he knew was that the arks brought with them terror and death on a scale undreamt of.

Great chains, each link thicker than the trunk of a tree, looped from a cluster of towers at the prow of the black ark, curving down towards the impossibly huge draconic head of some monstrous and terrible sea beast that lay, half-submerged in the dark waters of the harbour. Even from here, Eldain could sense the powerful magic keeping the colossal beast docile while the black ark was berthed at Clar Karond.

Eldain heard someone behind him and turned to see Caelir low-crawling towards the lip of the ridge. His brother had almost reached Eldain before he had become aware of his presence, and he masked his jealousy of Caelir's talents with anger at his disobeying orders.

'Blood of Khaine!' swore Caelir. 'Is that a black ark?'

'What are you doing here, Caelir?' asked Eldain, ignoring his brother's question. 'I told you to wait with the rest of the warriors.'

Caelir waved his scarred hand dismissively. 'Our warriors do not need me to tell them how to prepare for battle. I wish to see the enemy for myself.'

'You will see them soon enough,' replied Eldain. 'And be careful what you wish for.'

'It will be good to avenge father,' said Caelir, staring fixedly at the spires of Clar Karond and the black ark. 'I have great vengeance to wreak upon them.'

'We both do,' said Eldain.

'Nothing is forgotten. Nothing is forgiven,' whispered Caelir, and Eldain recognised the words as those of Alith Anar, the Shadow King of the shattered kingdom of Nagarythe, a brutal ruler who had led the shadow warriors in the years following the Sundering.

'How will we come at them?' asked Caelir.

'From the north-east,' replied Eldain, pointing to the logging works. 'The shadow warriors will lead us around to the forested hills above where those slaves are working, and under cover of darkness we shall ride into the harbour, fire as many ships as we can and cause bloody mayhem before pulling back.'

'The druchii will pay in blood for what they have taken from me,' said Caelir, and Eldain saw that his brother unconsciously rubbed his scarred hand as he spoke.

Looking at the burned flesh of his brother's hand, Eldain remembered the day Caelir and Rhianna had ridden breathlessly through the portal of the family villa on the eastern slopes of the Annullii. Both had been badly hurt, but Caelir had seen them to safety, and delivered his warning of the druchii raiders, before collapsing.

The tale of how he had heroically defended Rhianna from the dark kin had spread quickly through the courts of Tor Elyr, and Caelir's reputation as a dashing hero was established.

No one thought to mention that it had been foolish of him to take Rhianna so high into the mountains and so close to the Eagle Gate. No, thought Eldain bitterly, to do so would have been to tarnish the heroic tale of Caelir the Protector. In the weeks that followed, he had watched as Caelir and Rhianna grew closer, powerless to prevent his brother from bewitching the woman he loved with his wayward charms.

'Come, brother,' snapped Eldain, turning and preparing to rejoin the rest of the warriors. 'We should get back. If we are to reach the northeastern slopes before nightfall, we must be away soon.'

Caelir simply nodded and crawled back with him, vaulting to his feet when they were safely out of sight below the ridge. Back with the rest of the high elven warriors, Eldain felt his spirits lift once more as he saw, by their proud and elegant features, that they were ready for battle. To have penetrated so far into the realm of the druchii was accomplishment enough, but they would achieve something that would show the dark kin what it was to live in fear of raiders from across the sea.

He issued his orders quickly and efficiently, and within minutes the band of warriors was on the move once more, stealthily riding around the eastern fringes of Clar Karond.

As the day wore on and the sun sank lower in the sky, Eldain thought of the coming raid and his brother's caution that it had been too long since he had fought in battle. True, it had been many years since he had wielded a blade, but the finest tutors had taught him, and he knew that when the blood was flowing and the thrill of battle was upon him, he would be as deadly as he had ever been.

A bruised dusk was drawing in as the scouts once again halted their progress and informed him that they were in position. He dismounted and drew his sword, dropping to his knees and reciting the vow of the sword masters.

'From the darkness I cry for you.
The tears you shed for us
are the blood of the elven kind.
O Isha,
here I stand
on the last shore,
a sword in my hand.
Ulthuan shall never fall.'

Though he was not one of the legendary warriors of the White Tower of Hoeth, mystic guardians of knowledge and wisdom who were masters of the martial arts, the words gave him comfort and focused his concentration on the death yet to be dealt.

The sun continued to fall until the fearful darkness of Naggaroth began to encroach upon the world, and Eldain knew that it was time. The warriors around him began their preparations for battle, weaving iron cords into their long hair – symbolic of strength, power and nobility, the mark of a true warrior – to ensure that an enemy's blade would not cut it in the heat of battle.

Eldain prayed to the Emperor of the Heavens to guide his blade and watch over him this night, and though he knew there was soon to be blood on his hands, he asked forgiveness from the elven gods. His prayers went unanswered in the darkness, but he felt at peace and knew that his soul was ready for battle. His senses spread out and he could feel the breathing of his men, the harsh whinnies of their steeds and the tense anticipation that gripped them all.

No... not all. Around Caelir was nothing but a thirst for vengeance that burned brightly in the night. Eldain was not gifted with wizard sight, but even he could feel Caelir's aggressive soul. The spirit of Kurnous burned in his brother's breast, the elven god of the wild hunt, of untamed forests, wild animals and the trackless wilderness. Many in Ellyrion venerated Kurnous, as did their rustic kin across the ocean who dwelt beneath the boughs of Athel Loren, but the fire of the hunt was stronger in his brother than he could ever remember sensing in anyone before.

But beyond even his brother's desire for vengeance, he sensed something else. Something crude to be sure, but something with a spirit burning brightly with fear and desperation.

And it was coming straight towards them.

From the primal vulgarity of the spirit, Eldain knew it must be of the race of man. He leapt to his feet, his spirit sight fading as the shadow warriors slid from their vantage points to intercept the threat.

Eldain sprinted towards his men and ordered them, with a gesture, to silently scatter. The Ellyrion reavers vanished into the forest, as Eldain crouched beside a tall, claw-branched tree and risked a glance through the dark forest. His elf-sight easily pierced the gloom and he saw a group of six naked and skeletally thin men running towards the forest, their flesh bruised and scarred from months in captivity.

Behind them, Eldain saw a host of armoured druchii riders on dark steeds, in pursuit of the escaped slaves. One loosed a flurry of bolts from a repeater crossbow and slew one of the escapees. The slaves were almost at the trees, but Eldain knew they would never reach them before the dark riders overtook them.

He saw the leader of the shadow warriors raise his bow and aim at the druchii who had fired his crossbow.

'No,' he whispered. 'Stay your hand. If we are discovered now, then all we have achieved so far is for nothing.'

The shadow warrior nodded and relaxed his bowstring, commanding his scouts to do the same with some unseen and unheard signal.

Eldain watched dispassionately as the druchii quickly surrounded the escaped slaves and, rather than herd them back to their work gangs, slaughtered them where they stood. Cruel laughter drifted from the scene of butchery as the druchii killed their prey and took their heads to mount upon their saddle horns.

Within moments it was over, and the druchii warriors were riding back towards their dark city with their bloody trophies. Eldain let out his breath, relieved the druchii had been too intent on bloodshed to notice the raiders not a hundred yards from them.

As the druchii departed, Caelir approached him and said, 'that was too close.'

'Indeed,' replied Eldain.

'We should have helped them.'

'Helped them?' asked Eldain. 'To what end? Would you take them back to Tor Elyr and have them for your servants? No, to die like that was probably easier for them than to go on living.'

'Perhaps,' said Caelir, 'but it sits ill with me that we just let them die.'

'They were only humans, Caelir,' said Eldain. 'Do not trouble yourself with them. Now get some rest, we move out within the hour.'

Caelir nodded and returned to his steed, and Eldain lay back against the tree, watching him go. Emotions warred within him and to calm himself before going into battle, he closed his eyes and thought of the last time he had spoken with Rhianna.

* * *

IV
ULTHUAN – *Two Months Ago*

LOTHERN. MOST MAGNIFICENT city of all Ulthuan.

Situated in the midst of the Straits of Lothern, it guarded the approaches to the Inner Sea of Ulthuan. Men who saw the city described it to their companions back home as one of the wonders of the world, and such a title was richly deserved. Principal city of the Kingdom of Eataine, Lothern was a sprawling city-state, the lands around it dotted with vineyards, villas and summer estates to which the noble families of the city retired. The centre of power of Eataine, it was rightly said that no one who ever laid eyes upon it would ever forget it.

Set around a glittering lagoon, the tall spires of Lothern ringed the coastline, sublime palaces and elegant villas fanning upwards from the coast, their white towers climbing gracefully into the foothills of the distant mountains.

But Lothern was not simply built around the lagoon; hundreds of artificial islands had been raised within its waters and on these isles rested great palaces, temples and storehouses, forming an intricate network of canals. Statues of the great elven gods ringed the lagoon: Asuryan, Lileath, Kurnous, Isha and many others, but all these creations were dwarfed by the colossi that towered above the city and faced one another across the mouth of the bay. Statues of the Phoenix King and the Everqueen – twin rulers of Ulthuan – two-hundred feet high and carved from the marble of the mountainside by the power of the elven mages, dominated the southern skyline before the Sapphire Gate. Sailors from around the world spoke of their size, and were each story to be believed, then the statues must surely have climbed all the way to heaven.

Thousands of vessels filled the harbour, bobbing gently in the swell. Trading ships of the elven merchants, pleasure barges, and the sleek and deadly eagle-prowed warships of Lord Aislinn's battlefleet.

Dotted amongst the elven ships were vessels from all across the Old World. Since Finubar the Seafarer had persuaded Bel-Hathor to raise the interdict that forbade humans from setting foot on Ulthuan, almost four hundred years ago, trade had flowed into Lothern like never before. Dhows from Araby were tied up next to groaning merchantmen and galleons from Marienburg, who shared berths with clippers from Magritta and longships from the Norse, who, after the defeat of Erik Redaxe's fleet, realised that there was more to be gained by trading with the elves of Ulthuan than by trying to raid them.

A thriving city of culture, arts, poetry and trade, Lothern was the cosmopolitan heart of Ulthuan, and home to those elves who considered themselves part of the world rather than those who would see Ulthuan remain in splendid isolation.

Eldain and Caelir walked along the Boulevard of the Phoenix, so named for the current Phoenix King of Ulthuan who hailed from Eataine. They had set sail from Tor Elyr a week ago and passed through the gate of ruby and gold that separated the Inner Sea from Lothern only three days ago. Although both had visited the city before, its glory never failed to stir their hearts.

The boulevard ran the length of the mercantile district of the city and bustled with the activity of traders and shopkeepers, busy haggling with customers in the spirit of good natured banter. Swarthy skinned merchants in elaborate, brightly coloured robes and feathered headdresses waved their arms expansively as they held out bolts of fine silk, and incense sellers wafted their wares into the faces of passers-by.

Food sellers and wine merchants offered delicacies from all across the Old World, promising epicurean delights to satisfy even the most demanding palate.

Caelir stopped to purchase some wine and joked with the merchant that it was the finest wine he had tasted that afternoon. Eldain scowled at his brother when he had done with the merchant and said, 'It is serious business we are on, brother. We have not time to dally.'

'There's always time to enjoy a fine wine, Eldain.'

'And was that fine wine?' asked Eldain.

'No,' admitted Caelir. 'It was Tilean vinegar, but it never hurts to try new things. They say that the wines from the New World are exquisite. I met a trader, recently arrived from the Citadel of Dusk, who promised me a bottle of Lustrian venom wine.'

'Venom wine?' asked Eldain, appalled. 'That sounds utterly vile.'

'I know, but he swears it has a flavour to make the finest Avelorn vintage taste like swill.'

'And you believe him?'

'Of course not, but with a boast like that I simply have to taste it,' laughed Caelir.

Eldain shook his head and said, 'Caelir, I swear you would make a warrior of Tiranoc forget his chariot with your inane babble. Have you forgotten why we are here?'

Caelir shrugged. 'No, I haven't, brother, but we do not set sail for Naggaroth for another three weeks. We have time to enjoy the city a little, do we not?'

'Perhaps,' allowed Eldain, 'but I wish to ensure our expedition has all the supplies it needs before then. There is much that still needs to be done. Food and water to be provisioned, and weapons, armour and arrows need to be bought and stowed aboard our ships. I also need to take father's will to the counting house of Cerion to release the funds we will need. All this takes time and who is going to take responsibility, you?'

Caelir raised his hands before him in mock surrender and said, 'Very well, we'll do it your way, brother. Might we be better splitting up, then, and seeing to separate tasks?'

Eldain knew that Caelir was simply looking to get away from him and he found himself not averse to the idea. His brother was already irritating him and they had only been in Lothern for a few days.

'So be it,' he said. 'Take these promissory notes against father's estate and secure us feed for the horses; enough to see us to Naggaroth and back, with two weeks' worth for when we are on land.'

'Feed for the horses,' sighed Caelir. 'Such a glorious task.'

'A necessary one,' reminded Eldain. 'Now be off with you, and I do not want to see you until you have the feed. And get a good price, our funds are not limitless.'

'I know, I know,' said Caelir. 'I'm not a fool, Eldain.'

Eldain struggled to hold his temper at his brother's petulance and simply said, 'Then I will see you back at our lodgings at sunset, yes?'

Caelir did not answer, stalking off through the crowds of traders, and Eldain let out a long, calming breath. He knew all too well that at least one of the promissory notes he had given Caelir would be spent in a wine shop or tailor's boutique, but was too glad of the peace that Caelir's departure brought him to care overmuch.

He closed his eyes and let the bustle of Lothern soothe his spirit, though he knew he must be attracting his fair share of odd looks – standing with his eyes closed in the middle of a busy thoroughfare.

'Eldain?' asked a sweet, female voice. 'Eldain is that you?'

He opened his eyes and his heart lurched to see Rhianna standing before him, a linen covered basket held in the crook of her arm. She wore a simple, high-necked dress of emerald green with golden thread woven in curling patterns at the hem and cuffs, and was as beautiful as he remembered. Unconsciously, his eyes darted to her shoulder where she had been wounded, but the skin was hidden below the fabric of her dress.

Caelir had told Eldain that the fashion this season in Lothern was for risqué dresses that exposed the shoulders and a sizeable amount of decolletage, but Rhianna's dress exposed not one inch of skin more than was necessary.

Sensing his scrutiny of her old wound, Rhianna said, 'It still pains me now and then.'

'I'm sorry, Rhianna,' said Eldain, 'I did not mean to –'

'Don't worry,' she said smoothly. 'Caelir removed the bolt swiftly, but the druchii left me an ugly scar and I do not like to display it.'

Taking a moment to recover his composure, Eldain said, 'It is good to see you again, my lady. It has been too long since you visited us in Tor Elyr.'

'I know,' she said. 'I wanted to come for your father's funeral, but, well…'

'I understand,' said Eldain. 'Your father brought us your condolences. They were most welcome.'

An awkward silence descended upon the pair until Rhianna asked, 'Have you eaten yet?'

'Eaten? No, I have not,' said Eldain. 'I have had much to do today and have not had the time.'

'Nor have I. Will you join me in some food and wine? You are right, it has been too long since we talked.'

Eldain was about to refuse when he thought back to Caelir's advice that there was always time for a fine wine – especially with a beautiful woman – and said, 'I would be honoured to join you, my lady.'

Smiling, she accepted his offered support and the two of them strolled down the Boulevard of the Phoenix arm in arm, looking for all the world like two lovers out for an afternoon constitutional. Just being near Rhianna made Eldain feel more at peace than he had done in a long time, and as they walked, he cast sly glances at her face, remembering touching her skin and whispering promises of love in her gently tapered ear... what seemed like an age ago.

They walked in a companionable silence, turning into a narrow side street with many brightly coloured awnings providing cool shade for the patrons of the eating-houses and wineries that filled the street. Rhianna led him towards a shop with a glittering front, fashioned from coloured chips of polished glass to depict a pastoral land-scape of great beauty.

'I know the owner of this establishment,' explained Rhianna. 'He sells only the finest honeycakes and fresh-est sweetmeats. And he has a friend that brings him bottles of Avelorn dreamwine...'

'Dreamwine,' said Eldain. 'I have not tasted it before, but am told it is fine indeed.'

'Then we shall each have a glass,' stated Rhianna. 'Take a seat and I will see to our order.'

As a proud male, Eldain knew he should see to their food and drink, but as an elf obviously not from Lothern, he knew that he would seem like a bumpkin to the ven-dors of the city. He found an unoccupied table near the wall and examined the mosaic on the shopfront in more detail. It truly was magnificent and it struck him as unnecessarily ostentatious for something so mundane as a shop, but then what did he know of city ways?

Rhianna soon returned, bearing a silver tray laden with succulent cakes that smelled of sweet honey and roasted cinnamon, and two tall, slender necked flutes filled with shimmering wine.

'Dreamwine?' he asked.

'Dreamwine,' agreed Rhianna. 'Fermented from the waking dreams of the handmaidens of Avelorn and sung into liquid form by the magic of Everqueen. Be careful though, be sure to only take a small amount at a time.'

Eldain nodded and lifted the flute from the tray, taking a delicate sniff of the ethereal wine. It seemed to run like liquid smoke in his glass and its bouquet was that of a wild forest of ancient glamours where creatures of legend still roamed free. Rhianna smiled and they both took a small sip of the wine.

It was sweet, almost unbearably so, and Eldain replaced the flute on the table as he saw visions of fabulous gardens of oak and suntree tended by the ancient treemen of the forest, sun-dappled glades of unicorn and great eagles nesting in the enchanted forest's rolling hills. The image of the shopfront blurred and swam, the green of its landscape becoming incredibly rich in detail, and Eldain had the sensation that he could reach into it. Indeed, he could smell the scent of honeysuckle and jasmine, taste the salt of sea spray and feel the soft wind blowing across the hills on his face.

Rhianna said, 'It's good, yes?'

He smiled in contentment and said, 'Yes… it's very good. I can see why you are only supposed to take small sips at a time.'

The wine also had the effect of reminding him of his hunger and he devoured two honeycakes in quick succession before taking another sip of wine. More prepared for what wonders it might bring, he was nevertheless intoxicated by their splendour.

He saw beautiful elves with golden skin dancing in leafy bowers, silken pavilions of myriad colours like a great carnival, and darting faeries that lit everything with their silver laughter and sparkling light. Amidst the gaiety, Eldain saw a woman of heartbreaking beauty, with the grace and wisdom of Isha in her eyes, and knew her to be Alarielle, the Everqueen of Avelorn and consort of the Phoenix King. Her flowing hair was like a golden cloud, and graceful birds of purest white attended her as she moved effortlessly through her adoring subjects.

Tears gathered in his eyes as the face of the Everqueen faded, only to be replaced by that of Rhianna, and he pushed the flute with the rest of his dreamwine away, spilling it across the table where it instantly evaporated like mist.

'Eldain? What's the matter?' asked Rhianna, reaching out to touch his hand.

'Nothing,' he said, pulling his arm back. 'This was a mistake.'

'A mistake?' asked Rhianna. 'What was a mistake?'

'Coming here,' said Eldain, pushing his chair back. 'It has reopened old wounds that would be better left alone.'

'No, Eldain, stay. Please,' urged Rhianna. 'We should talk. We *have* to talk.'

'Why?'

Startled by the boldness of the question, Rhianna hesitated before saying, 'because there are things that must be said between us before you set sail for Naggaroth.'

'You know of our journey?'

Rhianna nodded and said, 'Caelir sent word to my home of the blood oath you swore against the druchii upon your father's coffin. He told me you would be travelling to Lothern and asked me to come.'

'Caelir asked you to come to Lothern, why? He said nothing to me.'

'I met with him yesterday morning and…' began Rhianna, extending her hand across the table towards him. He swallowed hard as he saw a silver ring engraved with two entwined hearts shining upon her middle finger. He couldn't believe that he had not noticed it earlier.

'A pledge ring,' he said. 'Caelir gave you that?'

'He did,' confirmed Rhianna. 'We have exchanged pledge rings, and upon his return from Naggaroth he will plight his troth to me. I will make the pilgrimage to the Gaean Vale, and we shall be wed in Tor Elyr the following year.'

'Wed? You will be wed to Caelir?' laughed Eldain, though there was no humour to it.

'Yes, I love him. I am sorry that I hurt you, but I cannot change what I feel.'

'You don't love Caelir!' snapped Eldain. 'You are infatuated with him. He saved your life and you feel you ought to fall in love with him. Your heart has been clouded by his charms and his brashness. Listen to your head instead.'

'Perhaps you are right,' said Rhianna archly, 'but it does not matter now what my head tells me, my heart speaks with a louder voice.'

Eldain sat back in his chair and felt the bitterness that had festered within him since his father's poisoning, well up within him. He wanted to lash out, to hurt her, to make her feel something of the pain he now felt, but his iron control reasserted itself before he said something he knew he would later regret. He had sacrificed everything, his own happiness and the woman he loved, to protect his domain and his kin, and this was his reward?

But he could not hurt her... to do so would demean him.

'I loved you, Rhianna,' he said at last.

'I know you did, and I will always love you too, Eldain, but I am to be Caelir's upon his return from the land of the druchii,' said Rhianna. 'If things had been different I know you would have been a good husband to me and I a good wife to you, but life often takes turns we do not expect. I am sorry, but please... for my sake, do not hate Caelir for this.'

Eldain nodded and stood, scattering a handful of coins upon the table.

He bowed stiffly to Rhianna and said, 'I love you, and while I live I will love no other.'

As he walked away, Rhianna said, 'Eldain, wait…'

But he did not turn around.

V
NAGGAROTH

THE NIGHT PRESSED in around them, and though the horses picked a silent path through the tall vines, Eldain felt sure they would be unmasked any second. Sounds of weeping men and women drifted on the cold night air, and slaves left to lie where they had fallen in exhaustion curled in terror as they passed, too brutalised by their captors to tell the difference between high elf and druchii.

They were elves, and that was enough to send those slaves who could still move crawling into the undergrowth in terror. The stench of the blood grapes was almost intolerable, and Eldain pulled his scarf tighter about his face to block out the acrid aroma.

As they drew nearer to their goal, Eldain saw occasional druchii corpses lying amid the vines, throats slit by the shadow warriors who ranged ahead of the hundred riders making their way to the docks of Clar Karond. The ride from the trees had been fraught with danger, each passing second bringing them closer to their goal, but also closer to being discovered. But now they were within the concealing vineyards, and Eldain could see through the vines that the entrance to the shipyards was less than a hundred yards away.

The ground was ravaged, but relatively flat, ground into channels by the passage of countless logs dragged from the hills above Clar Karond and brought within the docks for sawing and shaping. Hundreds of slaves –

humans and dwarfs mostly – slept in huddled groups, no fire to warm them or blankets to cover them, and Eldain knew that these pitiful creatures were the key to them getting into the shipyards. Beyond the slaves, an open gateway was set within a timber palisade of sharpened logs with tall, spiked towers to either side.

Eldain twisted in the saddle to ensure his warriors were ready, that arrows were nocked and swords were bared. He had personally handed each warrior three of the copper coloured arrows, etched with the rune of Saroir, that Rhianna's father had presented them with on the dockside of Lothern the day they had set sail for this accursed land. Vaul's magic was upon them, and he had made sure to impress upon each warrior that these arrows must not be wasted.

'Are we ready?' asked Caelir, his bow held loosely in his left hand. The longbow was inset with mother-of-pearl, and radiated powerful magic. Eldain recognised it as Rhianna's bow and felt his jaw clench at the sight of it.

'Yes, we are,' he said.

'Good luck, brother,' said Caelir and extended his hand.

Eldain looked down at his brother's palm, the skin rough and scarred where the druchii's red-hot crossbow had burned it, and the silver pledge ring bright in the darkness.

'And to you too,' he said, taking Caelir's hand.

Caelir nodded and said, 'Then give the word, brother.'

Eldain drew his own sword and shouted a command at Lotharin, who leapt from the concealment of the vines and bore his rider towards the shivering slaves. The hundred Ellyrion reavers followed him, screaming at the top of their lungs and riding for the heart of the slave encampment.

The ground shook with the thunder of hooves as the high elves rode towards the log palisade. Shaken from their nightmares by the noise, the slaves awoke in panic, screaming in terror at the sight of a hundred horsemen bearing down upon them. Some curled into weeping foetal balls, while others ran towards them with arms outstretched, thinking them rescuers.

But as Eldain had planned, the majority fled in blind terror away from them, towards the gateway of Clar Karond's shipyards. Within moments of their appearance, torch-wielding druchii with whips emerged from behind the walls, demanding to know what in the name of Khaine was going on.

They died without knowing what danger came their way, the arrows of the shadow warriors piercing their throats or slicing through their eye sockets. More druchii emerged from the shipyards, and Eldain saw that these were the feared druchii corsairs, warrior knights with tall helmets, shrouded in scaled cloaks, who bore long spears and cruelly serrated swords. The mad press of slaves desperate to find shelter beyond the palisade prevented them from mustering a cohesive defence, so they stabbed their spear points through the bodies of slaves as they fought to discover the source of the alarm.

Eldain loosed a blue-fletched arrow and felled a corsair as a flurry of arrows slashed from the charging Ellyrion reavers. Another volley cut down yet more of the druchii, and then they were amongst them.

Elven blades rose and fell, killing many druchii in the chaos and panic of the fleeing slaves. Blood and screams filled the night air as confusion spread from the gateway, and the slaves took advantage of their captors' disarray to have their revenge. A rampaging mob of slaves spread rapidly through the shipyards, yelling and toppling whatever they could.

He heard cries of alarm from druchii who recognised them as high elves, but as each shout was raised, an elven arrow quickly silenced it.

An alarm bell began chiming. Eldain shouted, 'With me!' and rode swiftly through the mad, swirling melee. The elven riders obeyed his shouted order with a discipline and speed that made him proud as they rode onwards through the screaming slaves. In a sweeping mass, they charged through wide streets lined with huge piles of lumber, long saws and chained axes. Along each thoroughfare were bloody altars to Khaine, headsmans' blocks, and cauldrons brimming with red fluid. Whether wine or blood, Eldain had no wish to know, but each sat beneath the mutilated body of a slave nailed to a crude cross.

The stench of stagnant, sea air was pungent, and Eldain rode towards the source of the rank odour, guiding Lotharin with his knees while loosing shaft after shaft into any druchii who dared come between him and his goal. Caelir rode alongside him, dropping the warriors of the dark kin with a speed and ease that was astonishing, the magic of the bow he used finding the weakness in every druchii's armour.

Their course carried them past great, vaulted structures stacked high with timber planks, shaped and treated for use in ships' hulls, and Eldain plucked one of the copper Saroir arrows from his doeskin quiver. He loosed the arrow into the midst of the timber, the head thudding into the heart of the stored planks.

No sooner had the arrow struck the wood than it erupted into a mass of searing fire, bright orange flames spreading swiftly from the point of impact. Within moments, the entirety of the timber was ablaze, and flames raced through the chamber as thick pillars of black smoke curled skywards.

'Not a bad wedding present, eh?' shouted Caelir, and Eldain had to admit that the fire enchantment placed upon the magic arrows was powerful indeed.

Within minutes, the sky was lit with a dreadful orange glow as more of the druchii timber stores went up in flames, years' worth of materials destroyed in moments. A wild exultation gripped Eldain as he shot yet more druchii, but the strategist in him saw that they would not be able to keep this momentum going for much longer. Soon, the druchii would organise themselves, and if he and his warriors were trapped within the shipyards, it would only be a matter of time before they were hunted down and killed.

The rank odour of the Sea of Malice grew strong in his nostrils, and the cobbled street opened onto a great granite quay laden with crates, barrels and coils of hemp rope. Hundreds of ships at anchor wallowed in the dark waters, their sleek and deadly hulls festooned with jagged blades, icons of Khaine and the rune of the Witch King, Malekith himself.

Riders galloped out onto the quayside, and Eldain saw that they had not penetrated this far into the shipyards of Clar Karond without loss. A dozen or more steeds were without riders, and many of the warriors who still fought were bloodied. He saw that Caelir was still alive, blood running from a shallow cut on his leg, but otherwise unharmed.

'Spread out!' yelled Eldain, unslinging an Ellyrion hunting horn from his saddle and holding it high. 'Use the Saroir arrows and burn as many ships as you can. When you hear me blow the signal to retreat get out immediately, no hesitation. We will rally at the top of the ridge where we began this glorious work! Now go!'

Whooping and yelling, the Ellyrion reavers spread through the quay, galloping along the warren of jetties and piers that connected the berthed ships. Eldain, Caelir and ten warriors charged along a wide, tar-stained jetty to their left, riding parallel to the bloated, mountainous form of the black ark. Arrows slashed through the night to slay druchii crewmen who peered out over the gunwales, and flames leapt skyward as the high elves made good use of their magic arrows. Eldain knew that, no matter what happened now, their mission to Naggaroth would be seen as a triumph.

He fired a Saroir arrow into a heavy Reaper ship, laughing in released tension as the arrow exploded with flames and the tarred planks instantly caught light. More and more ships burned as the high elves rampaged through the maze of jetties. Burning Corsairs leapt from their blazing vessels into the water, but Eldain felt no pity, only a thirst to kill more of the evil druchii.

Ahead, a group of corsairs charged from their doomed ship, bearing long spears and swords. Behind them, a group of druchii crossbowmen lining the gunwale shot a volley of lethal bolts towards them. Eldain cried out as a bolt sliced through the flesh of his bicep, but the wound was not deep and the bolt passed onwards without lodging.

Six of his warriors were not so lucky and tumbled from their saddles, pierced through by the deadly iron bolts. The druchii shouted something, but Eldain could not hear it over the roar of flames and the thunder of hooves on timber. Another volley slashed out, another three reavers fell, and Eldain felt his fury grow hotter than the flames billowing around him.

Twin streaks of copper flashed from Caelir's bow, and Eldain saw two of the Saroir arrows slam into the vessel. An enormous explosion of fire mushroomed from the deck of the ship as the magical flames exploded outwards, hurling the crossbowmen through the air and breaking the ship in two. The corsairs were hurled to the ground by the force of the blast, and the high elves gave them no chance to recover their wits, charging home and slaying them without mercy.

Eldain and Caelir rode amidst the corsairs, their swords flashing in the firelight as they killed the druchii. Caelir's face was lit with savage joy as he fought, and Eldain had a fleeting vision of his brother atop a great white, wearing the *Ithiltaen* of the Silver Helms.

A druchii Corsair stabbed up at him, and Eldain desperately twisted his steed around, but the spear penetrated his thigh and he screamed in pain as blood streamed down his leg. He fought to turn and bring his sword to bear, but the howling druchii was quicker and the spear lanced towards his heart.

A slashing sword split the spear apart in a shower of splinters, and Caelir's reverse stroke beheaded the Corsair as he rode between Eldain and his attacker.

'Come on, brother!' shouted Caelir, turning his steed and riding further out along the wide jetty. 'This way! Hurry!'

Eldain watched as blood fountained from the druchii's neck and the corpse toppled from the jetty into the water. His breath came in great, sucking lungfuls as he realised how close he had come to death. They had pushed their luck far enough, hundreds of ships were ablaze, and even though his warriors had surely loosed every one of the Saroir arrows, the wind was certain to fan the flames to those vessels that had thus far escaped.

Yes, it was time to go.

Eldain lifted the hunting horn from his saddle and blew three rising notes followed by one low, mournful one, the eerie sound carrying all across the harbour – even over the roar of flames, the crack of splitting timbers and the screams of the dying.

Even now, his warriors would be retreating and making their way back to safety.

'My lord?' shouted the last of his warriors over the din. 'Your brother!'

'I know,' returned Eldain. 'I will get him, you get out of here! Now!'

The warrior hesitated, torn between obeying his lord's order and his duty to protect him. Eldain saw his dilemma and said, 'you do me proud with your devotion, but I would be a poor master indeed if I let my warriors die thanks to my brother's foolishness. Now go!'

The reaver nodded and turned his horse, galloping hard for the quayside. Eldain turned and with a yell, rode after Caelir. He heard iron bolts whipping past him and glanced up to see crossbowmen lining the turrets and crags of the black ark. At such range, it was doubtful they could hit him, but such were their numbers that it would only take one lucky bolt to fell him or his horse. What in the name of Isha had driven Caelir to ride onwards? Had the spirit of Loec seized him with wild abandon?

Through the glow of the firelight, he saw Caelir ahead, battling a knot of druchii warriors in the shadow of one of the giant repeater bolt throwers. Enemy warriors pressed in around him, but Caelir fought like Tyrion himself, his sword stabbing and slashing amongst the druchii like quicksilver. The combat was over before Eldain reached his brother and shouted, 'what are you doing? Didn't you hear the signal to retreat?'

Caelir nodded, too out of breath to reply, and swiftly vaulted from the back of his horse.

'What are you doing?' repeated Eldain as more bolts from the crew of the black ark thudded into the timber of the jetty.

Caelir shouted, 'come on, help me with this!' as he swung the massive bolt thrower around on greased runners to face the black ark. Many times larger than the Eagle's Claw bolt throwers employed by the armies of the Phoenix King, this monstrous weapon was designed for punching holes below the waterline of enemy ships.

'You have got to be joking,' said Eldain. 'That won't even scratch the side of a black ark!'

'I'm not aiming for the black ark!' shouted Caelir as he pulled the firing handle and a thick iron bolt, longer than three bowstaves, flashed through the air. Eldain watched as the bolt flew towards... not the ark, but the head of the great beast tethered by the massive chains to its front!

The bolt hammered into the great dragon's head, burying itself completely in its flesh. Purple flickers of magical light erupted around it as the powerful enchantments keeping it placid fought to contain the monster's agony. The Ark shook with the beast's pain, and its head rose from the water slightly, exposing a fiery red eye and terrifying fangs longer than a knight's lance. Heavy waves rocked the jetty as the massive form of the ark shifted in the water, and giant breakers foamed at its base as the beasts kept chained in its depths were unleashed. Eldain saw spined and sinuous forms slicing through the churning waters towards them and turned to face his brother, who struggled to load another bolt onto the firing runners.

'Come on!' shouted Caelir. 'Help me!'

Despite his better judgement, Eldain leapt from the saddle, crying out in pain as he landed on his wounded leg, and limped towards Caelir. Together they heaved the bolt into position and began furiously cranking the windlass mechanism.

'This is madness!' yelled Eldain.

'You're probably right!' answered Caelir. 'Do you have any Saroir arrows left?'

'Just one.'

'Tie it to the shaft of the bolt.'

'What?'

'Do it! Hurry!' shouted Caelir, as the firing mechanism clicked home and the weapon was ready to fire. Swiftly, Eldain pulled out his last magical arrow and snapped the bowstring from his longbow. He clambered onto the giant bolt thrower's curving front section and lashed the copper arrow to the jagged iron head of the bolt.

'Ready?' shouted Caelir.

'Done!' answered Eldain, leaping to the jetty as his brother fired the machine once more.

'Now let's get out of here.' cried Caelir, vaulting onto the back of his horse. Eldain followed suit, watching as the bolt streaked straight and true into the eye of the mighty sea dragon. The baleful red light was snuffed out and an explosion of purple light flared in the fire-lit darkness as the beast's agonies overcame the placating magic. Flames sheeted upwards from the dragon's head as the Saroir arrow ignited and seared a burning path through the beast's skull and into its brain.

The two brothers rode like the wind as the ark rocked in the water and huge swells broke across the bay. Splintering wood erupted behind them as the beasts unleashed from the ark smashed into the jetty, hungry for blood.

Eldain glanced behind him to see a monstrous sea creature with jaws the size of an eagle's wingspan tearing up the jetty towards them. Tarred planks flew in all directions, splintered and snapped by its weight and bulk. The great sea dragon's bellows of pain were deafening, and Eldain heard a tremendous groaning as its convulsions tore the black ark free of its moorings. Bolts hammered down around them as those druchii who still remained in the harbour sought to exact some last revenge against their attackers.

Caelir whooped and shrieked ahead of him, the adrenalin rush of what they had just done inuring him to the fear of what might yet befall them. The monster behind them drew ever closer, huge waves of water drenching them as the sea dragon's death throes rocked the waters of the bay with the force of an earthquake.

Ahead, Eldain saw Caelir reach the granite of the quayside. He heard the crack of wood from behind him and felt the rank breath of the monster from the deep on his neck.

'Jump!' shouted Caelir, and Eldain dug his heels hard into Lotharin's flanks.

The black stallion leapt towards the quayside as the sea monster's jaws slammed shut on the last of the jetty, smashing it to shards. Lotharin landed on the solid quay as the great beast slammed into it beneath the water, and Eldain let out a great, shuddering breath as his steed skidded to a halt.

A massive, groaning crack of splitting stone made both brothers look up in time to see the incredible sight of the black ark toppling into the bay, its mighty towers brought low, and hundreds of druchii falling to their deaths as the dying sea dragon thrashed in its chains. The monstrous floating fortress broke apart as it hit the water and a great tidal wave of black foam surged towards the shore of the bay.

The brothers turned their steeds and galloped back the way they had come, fighting their way through the shocked druchii towards their escape. Past blazing timber stores and ruined piles of blackened lumber, spears stabbed for them and repeater crossbow bolts slashed through the air, but their speed carried them past most of their attackers without a fight.

Eldain slashed his sword through the arm of a Corsair guarding the gateway and hacked down another before riding clear. He stole a glance over his shoulder to see his brother slay a pair of druchii who sought to hamstring his horse. Caelir killed them both, but he had been slowed enough for other druchii to take aim with their crossbows, and a hail of bolts slashed towards him.

One pierced his hip and pitched him from his horse, while others hammered into his steed's chest and flanks. The horse collapsed, blood frothing from its mouth and its legs thrashing in agony.

Caelir picked himself up and ran as fast as he could towards the gateway. More bolts flashed through the air, another burying itself in his shoulder. He stumbled, but kept running.

'Brother!' he yelled, holding out his hand towards Eldain.

Eldain watched Caelir run, silhouetted in the firelight from the blazing wreckage of Clar Karond, and his vision narrowed as he focussed on Caelir's outstretched hand.

He saw the callused burns of his brother's wounded hand, Rhianna's silver pledge ring shining brightly in the flames.

Eldain said, 'Goodbye, Caelir.' He turned his horse towards the hills and rode away.

He did not look back, but pushed his steed hard through the vineyards towards the survivors of the attack. He heard shouts and screams and the clash of blades behind him, but paid them no heed as he galloped onwards.

As he crested the rise and entered the dark forest, he rode for some minutes before reaching his warriors. Bloody and exhausted, they were nevertheless magnificent, and he felt a strange freedom in his soul as he thought of all that had been achieved this night.

'My lord?' asked the leader of the shadow warriors. 'Where is Caelir?'

'He is dead,' replied Eldain sadly.

'Dead? Isha's mercy, no!'

'The druchii killed him,' said Eldain. 'He fought bravely, but there was nothing I could do to save him.'

'Our swords are yours!' promised the shadow warrior. 'We will avenge him!'

Eldain could see the same resolve in the face of every one of his warriors and said, 'We have won a great victory here, but we must return to our homeland now. The druchii will not remain in disarray for long and we have many days travel ahead of us before we may count ourselves safe. My brother *will* be avenged, but not this day.'

He turned his horse towards home and shouted, 'We ride for Ulthuan!'

VI

ULTHUAN – *One Month Ago*

THE OMENS WERE good, thought Eldain as the ships pulled smoothly away from the Lothern quayside towards the Sapphire Gate. The morning sun was bright and a fair wind ruffled the white sails of the Eagle ships. Caelir stood at the vessel's stern, waving to Rhianna, who stood on the dockside beside her father, a tall, powerful elf in the swirling robes of an archmage.

The holds of each ship were laden with horses and supplies – food, grain, water and weapons, all that was necessary for an expedition to Naggaroth. Wrapped in oiled leather was a crate sealed with mystical wards, that had come from Rhianna's father, in which there were three hundred magical arrows. A sheepish Caelir had told him that they were an early wedding gift from Rhianna's father, and though it left the bitter taste of ashes in his throat to have such a reminder of her affection for his brother, Eldain knew that they would be invaluable.

The ships passed through the shadow of the mighty statues of the Phoenix King and the Everqueen as the Sapphire Gate at the mouth of the lagoon began to open. A gate of shining silver, set with sapphires the size of a man's head, a glittering edifice that smoothly drew wider to allow their small fleet to pass through.

Beyond the Sapphire gate, an elven pilot vessel waited to guide their ships through the magically shifting sandbanks that protected the Straits of Lothern from attackers.

Eldain made his way to the vessel's prow and felt a shiver of anticipation as the gate behind them closed and they found themselves in a wide channel between sheer cliffs of white. Castles equipped with repeater bolt throwers, ramparts and seaward defences manned by ithilmar armoured warriors of the sea guard protected the Straits of Lothern, and Eldain knew almost nothing could penetrate these defences.

Eventually, the channel narrowed until they reached the great fortified arch that was the Emerald Gate, foremost of the great sea gates that guarded Lothern. Two vast valves of carved bronze studded with great emeralds were set into the cliffs and, as the pilot guided them towards the gate, it swung open on mighty hinges to grant them passage to the open ocean.

The ships passed onwards, the great gate shutting soundlessly behind them as Eldain had his first sight of the Glittering Tower.

Rearing up from the sea atop a rocky isle in the mouth of the bay, the Glittering Tower was a great lighthouse filled with thousands of lamps that could never be extinguished. Mighty fortifications clustered at its base, each bastion equipped with scores of bolt throwers and hundreds of sea guard warriors.

Caelir joined him at the prow and said, 'It is magnificent.'

'Yes,' agreed Eldain. 'It truly is.'

'Eldain...' said Caelir hesitantly. 'I just wanted to say, well, that I am sorry I didn't tell you about Rhianna. I meant to say something to you sooner, I really did.'

'It doesn't matter anymore, little brother.'

'It doesn't?' asked Caelir, the relief plain in his voice.

Eldain shook his head. 'No. It doesn't.'

Caelir let out a nervous laugh and leaned out over the vessel's side as the Glittering Tower receded into the distance and the wind filled the sails of the ship. The two brothers watched in silence as it vanished over the horizon and Caelir eventually said, 'I wonder if I will ever see Ulthuan again?'

'What do you mean?'

Caelir didn't answer for a moment, as though weighing up whether or not he should speak, but eventually he said, 'I have been having evil dreams of late, brother.'

'What kind of dreams?' asked Eldain.

'When I wake I do not remember the substance of them, but in each of them I hear the wail of Morai-heg.'

'The Keeper of Souls,' said Eldain.

Caelir nodded. 'I hear her banshees wailing in my dreams and I fear she holds my fate in her withered palm. I am afraid she has decided that it is my time to die.'

'They are just dreams, Caelir.'

'Maybe so, Eldain, but I fear them. I fear what they might mean for me in Naggaroth.'

Eldain was about to reply, but Caelir was not yet finished. 'I want you to promise me something, Eldain.'

'What would you have me promise?' he asked.

'If... if I do not return from Naggaroth, promise me that you will take care of Rhianna.'

'Rhianna?' asked Eldain, genuinely surprised.

'Yes,' said Caelir, 'I know she still cares for you, so if I die, promise me you will take care of her.'

Eldain smiled and said, 'Of course I will, brother. You can count on me.'

SMALL MERCY
by Richard Ford

THE AROMA OF sour ale hung thick in the oppressive confines of the border inn. The door was closed against the chill autumn wind and a sputtering fire struggled for life in one murky corner. A bright midday sun shone through the grime-stained windows, framing the patrons as they nursed their tankards. A ragged urchin played between their legs; the only source of any sound. For the most part he was ignored, though he would receive the occasional scolding glance if his reverie became too high-pitched.

Swinging his crooked, wooden 'sword' wildly the lad sped around the inn, his bare feet clapping against the uneven boards as he pursued his foes, shouting curses and black oaths as they fled.

With an ear-splitting crack that disrupted the room's muted atmosphere, the inn door burst open. All at once the boy's game was over as a battered body was flung into the inn, heralded by a snow-whipped gust of air. The pulped figure hit the wooden floor with a moist thud, like a drum being struck with a damp rag. He lay there unmoving, his face a matted mass of beard and clotting crimson, leaking his juices onto the filth-encrusted floorboards. Rusty chains bound his wrists and their reddened appearance suggested that he had been dragged for many miles.

Two bearded men stepped into the inn behind him, wrapped in wolfskin and leather. One of them grabbed the battered body by the hair and dragged it towards the centre of the inn. The second hirsute figure approached the bar.

'You can't bring that in here,' shouted the innkeeper, Boris. The boy had never seen him sound so panicked before.

'Keep your hair on, barkeep. There are no other Kurgan for a hundred leagues. We caught this one scouting a village further west but they wouldn't pay the bounty. All we want is a meal and a drink and we'll be gone.'

Boris frowned, considered their tale and then gave a reluctant shrug. The bounty hunter turned to his companion and nodded. Quickly he tied a rope to the rusted manacles and flung it over the inn's low rafters, hoisting the body up. There was a harsh creak as the rafters strained against the weight of the sinewy body.

Some of the inn's patrons dared to creep a little closer as the bounty hunter tied the rope off against the footrail of the bar. The urchin could only stand and stare, having never seen a real corpse before.

As the braver patrons crept forward, there was a sudden expulsion of air, like a thin breeze creeping beneath the jamb of a door. One eye flickered open on the corpse's face, a bright blue orb against a red mass of hair and gore. The gathering crowd forgot their bravery and stumbled backwards, cries of alarm echoing through the fusty room. Amidst them all, the boy stood, transfixed by the piercing eye. It locked on him, holding him in its grip.

'He's still alive,' shouted Boris. 'Are you mad?'

'The elector counts pay twice as much for live captives. Who knows what information he has? He
wouldn't tell us a thing,' the bounty hunter glanced over
at the broken figure strung from the rafter, 'but the tor-
turers of Ostermark have methods all their own…'

This brought several sniggers from the patrons, who
were steadily regaining their nerve.

'So how did you manage to bring him down alive?'
asked Boris.

'Well, it certainly wasn't easy…' he began. Eager bodies soon surrounded the bounty hunter. In their
clamour to hear his story they forgot about the
marauder and the waif, who was still held enraptured
by the single eye.

The boy took a step forward, his fear overcome by
curiosity. The captive opened his mouth as if to speak
but only a line of bloody drool oozed out. Looking
around, the urchin spied an abandoned tankard. He
picked it up, pleased that there was still a drop of pungent ale within. There was a harsh scraping sound as he
pulled a chair up in front of the man and climbed onto
it, holding the tankard up to the cracked and swollen
lips. Alerted by the sharp noise, the bounty hunter,
whose companion was still locked in the midst of his
tale, glanced up, a look of horror crossing his face.

No sooner had the tankard touched the captive's lips
than the boy was struck on the side of the head. It was
an opened-palmed blow and the sound echoed across
the inn. The urchin fell, the tankard bouncing off the
hard floor beside him and spilling its contents on his
ragged jerkin.

'Idiot boy,' scolded the bounty hunter. 'Don't you
know what this is?' He turned his attention to the captive, who still stared defiantly. The bounty hunter raised
his hand again, this time balling a fist. Before his blow
could land, the door to the inn burst open for a second

time. The horror that spewed in took the patrons and their bounty-hunting visitors completely by surprise.

A mob of bearded devils rushed in, screaming fell curses the urchin could not comprehend. They charged past the prone boy and fell upon the inn's occupants with unrestrained savagery, swinging their axes, severing heads and slicing limbs with huge swords. Despite the horror before him, the boy could not pull his eyes away as he watched folk he had known all his short life cut asunder by blade and battleaxe. There were grins of ecstasy on the bearded faces, whoops of joy as they dismembered man and woman alike, yet still the boy watched as the carnage raged around him. When it was over he was the only soul left alive amidst a pool of cooling blood and broken bodies.

The savages cut down the captive and sheared his manacles in two, patting him on the shoulder as though they had all just shared some raucous joke. One of the bearded wild-men noticed the lone child, still lying on the floor. He smiled, a friendly, genuine smile, and began to approach, lifting his axe. Before he could move two steps a gore spattered arm grabbed the axe's shaft. The bearded man looked to his side and into the single, deep-blue eye. He uttered harsh words in his strange language, words of obvious protest, but he was forced to stand down, cowed by the gaping blue orb. One by one the barbarians filed past and left the inn.

Slowly the former captive walked up to the urchin, once again locking him in the enchantment of his gaze. 'My brothers wish me to end you,' he said in a thick accent. 'They believe mercy is a sign of weakness, but I think you can be spared.'

With that he was gone from the confines of the inn. The wind blew through the open door, snow drifting in to cover the steaming body parts. It was a long time before the boy found the will to stand.

THE RAIN BEAT HARD against late summer leaves, but its sound was not enough to drown out the screams of the dying. It was a grim afternoon, the sun hidden behind a grey mask of cloud, the uncharacteristic weather having followed Archaon's forces down from the wastes. They called it a 'tactical retreat', luring the invading armies deeper into the Empire, holding them off long enough for Valten, Huss and Karl-Franz to march their forces forward. It had been more like a complete rout.

Captain Bauer struggled through knee-deep puddles, his armour weighing him down and his greatsword now a hindrance, despite the number of times it had saved his life. His men lay dead around him, alongside the corrupted bodies of their foes. The fact that there were more corpses that belonged to the enemy this day was little consolation.

There was a sudden splashing behind him as a figure hastily approached, racing through the boggy woodland. Bauer turned raising his sword, expecting another foe. Instead, he saw the desperate face of an Imperial archer, his bow long forgotten, his empty quiver bashing feverishly against his leg as he ran headlong through the wood.

Bauer lifted his hand in an unspoken order for the man to stop but he was ignored, the man streaking past without pause. Noise from the direction the archer had come from told Bauer why he was in such a hurry. He lowered the visor of his sallet and tried to position himself on a less saturated area. No sooner had he found a dry patch of ground than two of Archaon's warriors burst from the shadows with absurd speed. They seemed to disregard the fact that they wore heavy armour, charging forward like unsaddled geldings.

As they moved in, Bauer dodged to the side, narrowly avoiding their ferocious attacks. His own greatsword swept down, bouncing off the nearest spiked shield, which carried an impaled head, a rictus grin spread across its blank face. The warrior kept his guard up, waiting for Bauer's next attack, whilst his comrade tried to manoeuvre around the flank. Recognising their plan, Bauer staggered backwards, trying to keep both of the fiends in front of him. Seeing that Bauer had spotted their intention they charged forward. Bauer's sword crashed down a second time against the head-bearing shield. The second warrior was quick to counter and Bauer barely ducked in time as the dark iron sword swept towards him. It struck a tree, showering the back of his head with splinters. He just had time to look up to see a second dark sword sweeping towards his head.

There was a dull ring of steel on iron before the blow could land. General Metzger crashed into the Chaos warriors with a fury that even the most berserk Kurgan could not have matched. The first was taken by surprise, unable to raise his shield in time to catch Metzger's blow. It smashed into the horned helm, buckling the front plate and crushing the head within. Blood spewed from the neatly sliced metal and the warrior dropped like a felled oak.

Bauer wasted no time and quickly engaged his remaining opponent. The northern invader parried Bauer's sword with ease but again Metzger charged in, screaming like a wounded dog, his face a mask of vengeful rage. There could be no defence against the general's onslaught as his greatsword swooped down from over his right shoulder. The blow shattered the metal shield and severed the arm beneath. Despite the grievous wound the Chaos knight kept on coming, but Metzger was ready. With seemingly divine strength he thrust his greatsword forward, straight through the warrior's breastplate. Bauer wasted no time, hacking his own greatsword into the blood-spattered shoulder plate. The huge figure dropped to its knees. Metzger wrenched his weapon free and kicked out, knocking the body back into the sodden earth.

Bauer looked to his general, trying to find words of thanks but Metzger did not pause for breath. 'Rally to me!' he bellowed, racing towards the sound of fighting further off through the trees. 'Men of Middenheim! For Todbringer and for Ulric, rally to me!' Bauer instantly heard the sound of men's voices carrying through the wood. He quickly followed, adding his own voice to the general's, urging any survivors to gather to their call.

One by one their men began to appear through the trees, heartened by the sound of their leaders. Within minutes there was a group of thirty Middenheimers tearing through the wood, swordsmen, handgunners and archers alike. Archaon's troops were not far behind and Bauer knew they would not stop until they had slaughtered every last one of the Imperials. He had already seen them cut down wounded men, hacking them to pieces just for the thrill of seeing their muti-lated parts.

Metzger stopped a little way ahead, turning to face the oncoming horde. 'Keep moving,' he shouted to his flee-ing troops. 'We will take them on open ground. Remember, you have the fire of Ulric in your bellies. What we do today we do for Middenheim and the glory of Karl-Franz.' His eyes were twisted in rage and his wild hair and beard made him look more like a Norscan than an Imperial general.

Soon the fleeing troops broke the tree line and ran across an open field. They could hear their heavily armoured pursuers crashing through the undergrowth, every second bringing them nearer. As Bauer raced to join the thin ranks that remained, he suddenly saw something at the top of a nearby hillock. Through the rising dark he could just make out the silhouette of a building.

'Look,' Bauer pointed. Metzger turned, his mask of fury suddenly lifting.

'A keep,' he suddenly cried. 'Ranald smiles on us this day!' With a wave of his huge greatsword the general led the way up the rise towards the looming construction. Bauer waited until all his men were on the move and then took up the rearguard. He glanced over his shoulder towards the edge of the wood, expecting the Northmen to burst onto the field and run them down any second.

It was a struggle to make it up the rise, the way was muddy and damp and several men slipped, sprawling in the filth. More than once Bauer had to pick up a panicked bowman or a pistolier with terror scrawled across his face.

When they eventually made it up the hill and Bauer saw the dereliction of the building, his heart sank. The keep was little more than a shell, long since abandoned to the elements. There was no way this could be made into any kind of defensible stronghold.

Despite the crumbling walls and paltry defences, Metzger began organising his men. By the time Bauer entered within the walls of the keep, the general had ordered his swordsmen into two ranks at the far end of the courtyard. The pistoliers and archers had been ordered to mount the battlements and hide themselves. Bauer instantly saw the sense in Metzger's plan.

Glancing over his shoulder he could see the horde had broken from the woods and was following the muddy trail left by the Imperials.

'They come,' shouted Bauer, rushing forward to join the swordsmen. The walls of the keep would not stop the Chaos warriors, but that was what Metzger was hoping. A large gap in the wall would lead the howling pack straight towards the swordsmen, who were standing as bait on one side. As they charged it was unlikely they would notice the archers and pistoliers crouched on the battlements.

'On my order,' said Metzger, his voice echoing within the ruins.

Iron-shod boots broke the silence of the keep as they drew closer. There were two dozen, maybe more, Bauer could not tell.

'Stand fast men,' whispered Metzger. 'We charge on my order.'

With a diabolical howl, the first Northman leapt over the remains of the keep wall. As he raced forward he was closely followed by other iron-clad figures. Their boots pounded against the cracked flagstones as they drew closer, covering the yards with an unholy speed, but still Metzger did not give his order. Twenty yards away... fifteen... ten...

'Fire!' screamed the general.

Bauer winced as the sound of pistol fire reverberated around the shell of the keep. Smoke billowed from the battlements as lead shot was propelled towards the onrushing juggernaut. With it, white-feathered arrows flew. Those warriors not felled by pistol shot were impaled, their bodies falling with foot-long shafts standing to attention from their twitching bodies. Bauer could feel the swordsmen behind him itching to press forward, keenly anticipating the order to charge, but Metzger still held his tongue.

Three Chaos warriors charged on, despite the arrows and shot holes peppering their armour. The archers quickly re-knocked and loosed their bows, felling them before they could reach the waiting swordsmen.

More of the enemy poured in. Metzger allowed five more warriors to enter the keep then began to race towards them, bellowing his long-awaited order. Bauer was sure the general had shouted 'charge' but it sounded more like a war cry; a feral shriek of rage.

'At them!' Bauer added, as he and the swordsmen raced forward.

Before the general could engage, some of the pistoliers had managed to reload, sending their shot into the approaching warriors. Metzger vaulted the falling bodies of two Chaos knights and smashed into the warriors behind them. Realising they would only hit their own men with further fire into the courtyard, the archers and pistoliers leaned over the makeshift battlements of the keep and began to fire down on the Chaos forces approaching up the field.

Bauer rushed forward, flanked by his swordsmen. Metzger had already dropped one of the warriors and was locked in combat with a second, their swords bouncing together as each tried to grind the other down. More warriors poured into the keep and the swordsmen met them, equalling the ferocity of the savage Northers. Bauer dropped his shoulder and rushed at the first black-armoured warrior he could see, barging into his shield. His opponent was knocked back a step, just long enough for Bauer to press forward, lunging to the side of the shield and bringing his sword around in a wide, horizontal arc. The weapon cut through his opponent's arm at the shoulder and it fell to the ground, still gripping the rusted shield. Bauer hacked once more, this time aiming at the black helmet. A spurt of blood crested upwards as Bauer severed his enemy's head and he quickly glanced around for his next target.

The swordsmen were more than holding their own against the Chaos forces but Metzger was in trouble. Surrounded by three warriors he was tiring, wearing himself down with each frenzied attack. Bauer bolted forward and by the time he reached his general, one of the three Chaos knights had fallen, a wide gash splitting his breastplate. The other warriors pressed in, one of them scoring a hit and denting Metzger's vambrace. The general dropped his sword arm, leaving his body open for an attack. Bauer intercepted, taking the brunt of the blow on his spaulder whilst simultaneously spearing the warrior's abdomen. As he fell back the warrior grasped Bauer by the lip of his sallet and both of them tumbled to the ground. Quickly, Bauer slipped his head out of the helmet, the warrior still grasping it in dead hands. He turned in time to see Metzger cut down his remaining opponent, a twisted smile shining through his dishevelled beard.

Bauer grabbed his helm and pulled himself to his feet, ready to rejoin the fray. As he stood he saw his swordsmen chopping down the last of their enemies. He dashed to the break in the wall of the keep and saw the rest of Archaon's warriors retreating into the woods.

General Metzger howled like a baying wolf. 'For Ulric,' he cried, his face racked with elation.

Bauer looked from the general to his men. They were bewildered, elated from their victory but physically exhausted. For their sake he hoped the coming night would be brief.

THE SCREAMS OF tormented men rose from the woods. For hours the sound of tortured captives assailed the keep's terrified defenders.

As his men cowered beneath the weathered buttresses, Bauer stared out across the fields. There was little illumination; a thick layer of cloud covered the gibbous moon. Despite this, Bauer knew the enemy was waiting, could hear their reverie in anticipation of the morning's slaughter.

'Tomorrow we will face them.'

The voice made Bauer's skin tighten. He looked over his shoulder to see Metzger leaning in closer. 'Fear not, captain. You will have your day.'

Bauer gave no reply, unsure of what answer to give his general, who even now seemed only too eager to face their relentless foe.

'But we have a defensible position, general. Why leave it?'

'The enemy we face cares little for the manner of our death, or how long it takes. We have no supplies and the longer we stay, the weaker we will become. Our foe will simply wait. I fear more daemon-serving scum will arrive to aid their brethren long before any allies of our own. Tomorrow we will make our escape or we will die.'

Bauer made no protest; despite the hopelessness of the plan there seemed no alternative.

'Are you scared Bauer?' Metzger asked, as though it were a reasonable question.

'I fear for my men,' lied Bauer, wishing he could express just how terrified he was.

'Don't. This is a fight we must all be a part of. The fate of the Empire rests with us. The men fight for their families, for their homes, they will not falter. And when this is all over they can travel home again and hold their wives and their children and be proud of the glory they have brought themselves.' Metzger suddenly looked down, as though his thoughts had drifted elsewhere.

Bauer could only imagine what he was thinking. What must have happened in the old general's past to make him so driven, willing to sacrifice so much to face and defeat the enemy.

The general looked up suddenly, his despondence disappearing as quickly as it had arrived.

'Tomorrow,' he growled, a wild glint in his eye. With that he strode off across the wall of the keep.

Bauer watched him go as another screech of pain echoed from within the woods.

'PISTOLIERS TO THE right flank, archers to the left!'

It was a misty morning and the men were exhausted. Bauer could only feel pity for them. All night they had been kept awake by the screams of their comrades and now they were preparing to charge straight into the maw of the beast. Amongst them strode Metzger like a caged tiger, his eagerness to face his fate all too obvious.

'We will be moving fast so stay close. Sokh is due east of here. We do not stop until we have her in our sights.'

The men mustered together, some fearful, others showing dull-eyed resignation. Bauer's hands tightened on the grip of his sword as he stared down the hill towards the trees. He could not see the enemy beyond but he knew they were there, eagerly awaiting their prey.

'Men of the Empire! Men of Middenheim, on me,' shouted Metzger, lifting his greatsword high and leaping from the protection of the keep.

As one, the ragged group of swordsmen, pistoliers and archers raced down the hill. Bauer could still see no sign of the Chaos horde and all he could hear was the sound of his own men, their panting breath, their feet tramping on the dewy earth.

Metzger was first to storm into the woods, Bauer following close behind. At first there was still no sign of the enemy. Then, one by one, they began to appear, approaching from both flanks. The first few were cut down by arrow and shot, not reaching within ten yards, but then three warriors appeared from the front, barring the way.

'Lead them on Bauer,' cried Metzger as he bowled into the wall of pitch-covered armour.

Bauer ran past, this time not thinking of the general, only of himself and his men. If the general wanted to go down fighting then so be it, Bauer would not stop him.

As he charged on Bauer was relieved that he was still followed by his men, they were obeying their orders and not stopping to engage the enemy. He ducked beneath a low branch and, as his head came up again, he almost stopped dead. Up ahead, tied to the branches and bows of trees were the freshly tortured bodies of his captured men. The soldiers behind him gasped, some crying out in anguish, but Bauer was not about to stop. Without breaking a step he continued through the woodland charnel house.

They ran for a mile or more, Bauer occasionally glancing over his shoulder to make sure he was still being followed, until eventually he found himself leaving the corpse-strewn wood. In front was a thick mist but it was open ground. Sokh could not be far away!

'Gorag, kas'at naza!' The words pealed from the mist ahead. Bauer stopped, holding up an arm to halt his men. An archer stopped at Bauer's shoulder, straining forward, his eyes trying desperately to penetrate the grey wall. With a hiss, a black-shafted arrow shot from the fog, embedding itself in the archer's throat. He fell forward without a sound.

Ahead, the mist suddenly swirled and lifted. From beneath his visor, Bauer could see two ranks of warriors; dark sentinels from his deepest nightmares. At the front was their massive chieftain, one horn missing from his huge helmet. With his armour and the bearskin that adorned his shoulders he was at least seven feet tall and almost as wide.

'Greg'oz karas'nak,' he bellowed and his warriors began to spread themselves wide, blocking Bauer's escape route.

He was suddenly overcome. Everything Metzger had said suddenly made sense. Better to die with sword in hand than cowering in fear.

Bauer ran forward, straight at the massive warrior. His first strike was clumsy but powerful, aimed straight at the chieftain's head. With a lazy swipe of his arm the Northman's own sword swept up to parry. Before Bauer could bring his weapon about, Archaon's captain had countered, easily swinging his sword back and landing a stinging blow against Bauer's head.

The sallet spun off into the mist as Bauer crashed to the ground. He was dazed, his sword lying on the grass several feet away, blood seeping from his ears. The chieftain towered above him, raising his sword. Bauer stared up defiantly, ready to take the final blow.

Slowly, the chieftain lowered his weapon. Bauer could hear his men behind, shuffling, uncertain of what to do.

Reaching up with one massive, mailed fist the chieftain gripped the single horn of his helmet and lifted it from his head. He stared down at Bauer with a single, piercing blue eye.

Bauer recognised it immediately. It was not the same face he had seen in the tavern those long years ago, it was now infinitely more corrupted, but the eye was unmistakable.

Slowly a smile spread across the chieftain's twisted face. He held out his hand to Bauer, mouth opening as though to speak.

The misty air was cut by a bellow of rage as Metzger charged forward, greatsword raised. The chieftain had just enough time to hoist his own sword before the blow fell. Their weapons clashed and became locked together as Imperial general and Chaos chieftain stared at each other over crossed blades.

Metzger suddenly swung his greatsword around, twisting his opponent's weapon from his grip and sending it spinning away. The chieftain swiftly grabbed the blade of the sword with one hand and Metzger's wrist with the other. Metzger in turn grabbed his blade and pushed it forward towards the chieftain's head. They wrestled for several perilous seconds, their men watching spellbound. Slowly the blade drew closer to the chieftain's face as Metzger began to win their contest of strength.

A sudden smile spread on the twisted face, the single blue eye brightening. The chieftain opened his mouth wide and bit down on the blade. As his yellow teeth gnashed against the solid, Middenland steel, the blade began to buckle. Corrosive blood poured from the chieftain's gums, causing the blade to hiss and melt.

Growling like a wounded animal, Metzger wrenched the damaged greatsword aside, pulling the chieftain over. Both fell to the ground and Bauer, still dazed, could only watch as they wrestled like two starving bears, fighting over rotten scraps.

In turn, each seemed to take the edge over the other – pounding, biting and clawing – until eventually Metzger was on top of the huge warrior, one arm and one knee pinned his adversary to the ground. Without hesitating he smashed his armoured fist into the grinning face. Again and again the fist flew down, smashing teeth and bone and pulping the shining blue eye. Metzger was like a smith at the anvil, hammering his enemy's head into mush.

When there was nothing left to hit, Metzger stood, panting from the exertion.

The remaining Chaos warriors, seeing their leader bested, looked at one another uncertainly. Several brandished their weapons threateningly while others took a pace backwards. A pistolier suddenly raised his weapon and fired, his round immediately joined by a volley of arrows and burning shot. Faced by such a sudden onslaught the warriors began to flee, retreating into the dense mist.

Bauer managed to rise to his feet and approach the general who was staring at the body at his feet.

'General?' said Bauer, reaching out a hand towards Metzger's shoulder.

The general turned before Bauer could touch him and took a purposeful step forward. 'Traitor!' he hissed, smashing his gore-encrusted fist into his captain's face.

Bauer was unconscious before he hit the ground.

THE OAK'S THICK branch groaned in protest against the rope tied to it. In turn, the rope seemed to creak in complaint about the body that hung below. Bauer, swinging gently in the breeze, did not complain – his tongue was too swollen in his head and his last gasping breath was long gone.

One of the pistoliers approached warily, glancing about him, unsure of whether the invaders would spring from the trees at any moment.

'General?' he said quietly, 'are we to leave now?'

General Metzger stared upwards, sorrow tainting his wrinkled brow.

'Yes,' he replied. 'We should not tarry here.'

'Was it really necessary to hang the captain?' asked the soldier, instantly regretting his candid question.

Metzger looked down at the handgunner, sorrow still marking his face.

'Should I so obviously show truck with the followers of the Ruinous Powers, I would expect the same mercy.' He clapped the pistolier on the shoulder, the flame returning to his eyes. 'Now come. Sokh is at least a day away and there are still enemies abroad.'

As they set off eastwards the pistolier took one last look towards Bauer's swinging body. Silently, he prayed to Shallya that the northern daemons never showed him any mercy.

PERFECT ASSASSIN
by Nick Kyme

RANNICK WITHDREW HIS rapier from the quivering body of Frenzini Lucrenzza with satisfying ease. As he wiped the long, slender blade upon the merchant's silken shirts, which bulged from his swollen girth, his prey looked on pleadingly with dying eyes.

Within the merchant's inner sanctum, a cluttered but opulent domicile awash with a faint veneer of burnished gold, Rannick allowed himself a smile. He was the finest assassin in all of Luccini, even Tilea, and Frenzini had learnt that to his cost. What were all his trappings and gilt possessions worth now? Nothing. Everything was dust in the end. Prestige, that was what mattered.

'To your health,' Rannick said mockingly, raising a gilded goblet to his lips from which, only moments before, Frenzini had been supping. Taking a careful sip and savouring the wonderful taste, he regarded the merchant's dying befuddlement with cold, unemotional eyes.

'It's not me,' he stated, and brought down his blade.

* * *

SLIPPING THROUGH THE merchant's mansion house like a shadow, Rannick made a silent escape. His alias, the Living Shade, was well founded, for he moved as if he were a part of the murky dark that crept through the windows.

Two bodies lay ahead; Rannick had passed them on the way in. Their thick metal armour bore no crest or insignia; they were mercenaries, well armed, trained killers. Now they grew cold in a dead merchant's trophy corridor, the stark marble stained with blood that welled from their eyes, ears and mouths. The tiny darts protruding from their soft necks bore a deadly and agonizing poison. Fast-acting, they didn't even have time to scream.

The guards were gone, a forgotten memory as Rannick sped on. The corridor was long, designed to impress guests and traders with its opulence. All manner of superb finery from numerous far-flung continents sped past in an blur. It would have been easy to stop, even slow momentarily, and grasp a small trinket to augment the fee. But it went against the code, the doctrine by which all assassins live.

Assassins' Code #32: Always agree your fee beforehand and never waver from it. Unexpected 'difficulties' can arise from padding...

OUT INTO THE GROUNDS and a thick frost crunched underfoot, a white veil overlayed the luxuriant vista of marblesque towers and finely wrought garden fountains. In the chill silence of a Tilean winter night, a gong sounded.

Frenzini had been discovered.

The peal of the bell rang out a resonant warning; the sound clung to Rannick's ear drums as he slipped through the night.

Great arboreal structures depicting griffons, pegasi and other fabulous beasts loomed high and menacing in the midnight gloom. Dusted with white powder they took on an eldritch quality against the pale moon as Rannick darted through them. At the end of a gravel path and secreted within a frost tinged bush Rannick found the rope and grapple he had hidden there for his escape.

Booted feet tramped heavily over stone walkways beyond and above him, and shouts carried loudly through the windless night.

Rannick shut away the noise. Low and stealthy, his lithe, muscled body blended with the night. He glanced back to check on his pursuers.

A band of three had gathered, two with swords, a third with a crossbow. They stood upon a high balcony, lost in confusion, impotent with undisguised fear of the dark. It had come alive and slipped into their master's impregnable fortress with silent menace and left him dead.

The grapple found purchase almost silently. Rannick tested the strength of the hold and scaled the wall to the stone walkway above.

He surprised a guard who patrolled above. The guard fumbled with a half-drawn sword as the dark apparition slipped past him. He tried to choke a warning as the assassin slipped over the wall and into the gloom below, before he realised his throat had been slit.

WITHIN THE LABYRINTHINE streets, alleys and forgotten plazas of Luccini, Rannick made good his escape.

He was pleased. Frenzini's retirement had unfolded as planned. The commotion, when combined with the sheer audacity of the attack would send shivers down the spines of his employer's rivals.

A mercantile war was being waged, more like a state of perpetual conflict given Tilea's fractious nature, and the Living Shade was a ready tool for one of the most powerful merchant houses staking its claim.

Rannick negotiated vast twisting pathways, shrouded in sibilant, crawling shadows.

He came to a dead end, stark in the wan glow of silver moonlight. He stepped forward and shed the darkness. It was here that Rannick found what he was looking for.

A set of crates and fire-baked urns, rich tan turned sickly pink in the light, sat against the alley walls. They cunningly obscured a small door sunk deep into terracotta. A world lay beyond, subterranean and sworn into death-threatened secrecy. A clandestine knock: three raps, a pause, two more and then a sixth and the Living Shade was admitted into the dark where his fee awaited.

A LONG, DANK corridor stretched before him, the entry guard evaporating into the blackness, as Rannick padded quickly down stone steps.

A hundred broad steps and a flame flared at the end of the tunnel. Rannick stepped through the light into a vast and impressive hall, the Assassins' Guild, an organisation more valuable than the very throne of Tilea itself.

'Rannick!' a voice cried from a vast throng of cloaked and mysterious figures, weaponsmiths, poison makers, engineers and more. Here men and dwarfs convened in a hive of subdued and secretive activity that bustled below the few remaining steps to the hall.

Rannick keenly picked out his man and for the first time that night, drew back his hood.

Deep brown eyes flashed bright in the firelight as he pushed back a swathe of dark, luxuriant hair from his tanned and well-defined face. Rannick paused a moment, allowing his man to come to him, privately basking in the imagined glory of his own countenance.

Not only was he the best, he was the most handsome as well.

'Rannick,' the man repeated, slightly out of breath. He was short, a mere dwarf compared to Rannick's own impressive stature, and advanced in years. A balding pate held obvious traces of grey around the temples and above the ears. Remy was his accountant.

'Frenzini has been retired,' Rannick stated coldly with a hint of suave, self-confidence. He strode down the steps, regarding his colleagues imperiously, removing his black gloves and slapping them, without looking, into Remy's outstretched hands.

'Excellent,' Remy acknowledged, skipping a little to keep pace. 'I will have the gold in your treasury by the morning,' he assured him.

'See that it is,' Rannick ordered, striding through the mass. 'You have my next contract.' It was more of a statement than a question.

'We need to talk about something first,' Remy warned tentatively.

'Business first, Remy.'

'Yes but…'

'Business.' Rannick turned and fixed Remy with an icy stare. 'I didn't attain the mantle of best assassin in all of Luccini by being distracted by details.'

'No, sir,' Remy conceded, a little uneasily. A speech was coming.

'I have retired public figures, merchant leaders, politicians, warlords and barons. I have travelled beyond these shores, fought in the mercenary legions of Lorenzo Lupo, slain the orc chieftain Grushult Bonesneer and even had an audience with the arch-poison mistress Lucrezzia Belladonna herself, have I not?'

Assassins' Code #62: Never extol the virtues of your own skill and undertakings. Weakness can be derived from such knowledge, particularly when said plaudits are embellished or false.

'Indeed sir, my humble apologies.'

Satisfied, Rannick continued. There was a large board ahead, set at the very back of the voluminous hall. It was adorned with all manner of contracts, wanted posters and death notices. Each had an artist's impression of the mark or the deceased as well as a scribed report as to the contract's status.

'Busy night,' Rannick remarked sarcastically to a thinning, bespectacled man working from sketches within a wooden partition. He glared daggers before returning to his furious scribblings.

Rannick knew him. He was Callini Faust, known simply as 'The Artist'. He killed his victims with a sharpened quill filled with poison ink before drawing their dead bodies with their own blood off the murder weapon. If business was slow he worked a sideline as a contract artist.

'He's been scribing for the past four nights,' Remy told him.

'Four?' Rannick turned again. 'What of the regular employers?'

Assassins' Code #2: In Tilea, somebody always wants somebody else dead.

'That's what I need to talk to you about sir.' Subconsciously Remy recoiled, awaiting the backlash.

Rannick's eyes narrowed. He bid Remy to go on.

'The regular contracts,' he said, faltering, swallowing back his fear, 'have all been retired.'

'All of them? Even Manlect the Obese, Merchant Prince of Sartosa!'

'Even Manlect.'

'That was my contract,' Rannick muttered. 'I only stole the plans to the manor house last night!'

'The assassin climbed to Manlect's roof, bored two tiny holes through the slats. Through the first he espied Manlect asleep on his back as is necessary for a man of such generous girth,' Remy explained. 'Through the second bore hole he extended a length of fine twine, almost invisible to the naked eye as it was dark. He trickled a potent concoction of poison, black lotus I believe, into Manlect's snoring mouth. He was dead by morning, physicians were baffled.'

'Not without cunning,' Rannick admitted quietly, making a mental note to burn the manor house plans and crush the ashes underfoot. Rannick smiled as he imagined the head of his usurper crushed beneath his boot instead.

Assassins' Code #6: If something goes wrong always destroy all evidence of a transaction. Any monies exchanged are fair trade for compensation.

'What about the tax-collector, Demitri Vallenheim? He's been on my books for weeks,' Rannick asked, turning back to find Demitri's contract on the board.

'Him too.'

A mask of controlled fury swept across Rannick's face.

'It is the work of one man,' Remy told him.

'One man,' he stated with frightening calm.

At least twenty new contracts had been posted over the last month; it was a busy time in the assassination business. Each and every one had been daubed over with red ink, the word 'retired' emblazoned over their portraits.

'Who?' Rannick uttered deeply.

'He's new, been in the city for six months. He's been improving his tally since he arrived.'

'Name.'

'I only know his alias. No one has ever seen him. He sends street urchins with wax-sealed envelopes to collect his contracts.'

'And the alias?'

'The Black Crowe.'

'What is his standing?'

Remy waited nervously, unwilling to answer.

Rannick turned to him with rage in his eyes. 'His standing?' he repeated.

'It rivals your own, sir,' he admitted in a choked whisper.

Rannick swept his gaze across the hall to another wooden board where a rat-faced man on a rope and pulley chiselled a name near the top.

'The Black Crowe,' Rannick read with disbelief, his own name only one place above. It was a large, prestigious record of an assassin's achievements. Rannick had always luxuriated in his own supremacy, his retirements always inexplicably higher than his nearest rival. Now he shared that honour with another.

For a moment Rannick was speechless.

'I tried to warn you sir,' Remy blathered.

Anger turned to self-preservation as the horrified Rannick felt his crown slipping. To be the best meant something. It was not only prestigious, it was financially lucrative. Powerful, wealthy employers always requested the best. Up until now, that had been him.

'What marks are left?' he asked quickly in desperation, scanning the contracts again.

'Only one,' Remy's voice was like prophecy as he wiped sweat from his bald head. 'Count Banquo Degusta.'

Rannick held his breath and looked over at the only unretired notice on the entire board, where it had remained for the last eight months.

Count Banquo Degusta; known within the guild as the impossible mark. Seven separate attempts had been made on the man's life. All seven had failed, and as Rannick contemplated the suicidal nature of such a task, Faust pinned up an eighth with a dagger.

'Sour-fingered Krellen,' Rannick read. 'Retired by his own poison spoon.'

'Ah Krellen,' Remy sighed a wistful lament. 'He was good.'

'He was careless,' Rannick countered coldly. 'Assassins' code, article fifteen,' he quoted confidently. '"Never use another man's cutlery," Krellen and the Duke Bastille learnt that to their mutual demise.' He turned on his heel and began striding back across the hall.

'Rannick?' Remy called after him, taken aback by his master's abruptness.

'I'll be at the Drowned Man inn,' he told him, walking away.

'And the count?'

Rannick paused, careful to block out the faces of the eight dead assassins.

'He's been buying up property and businesses all over Luccini and holds sway in the mercantile war. His rivals would pay handsomely for his retirement. You could name your price!' Remy urged with a wry smile.

Krellen's face flashed before Rannick; ashen pallor of the dead upon his flesh, a withered tongue protruding from his mouth.

'I will consider it,' Rannick sidestepped. 'But first I need information on this "Crowe" character,' he said, exiting hastily back into the gloom of the entrance way.

THE DROWNED MAN was a darkly mysterious taverna upon the very fringe of the market plaza of Luccini. Much like the secret entrance to the Assassins' Guild it was located through a series of clandestine passages and alleyways. Outwardly it had little to distinguish itself: dark wood and sun-bleached stone, gloomy windows with an orange tinge. A sign hung from a solitary length of rope and swung languidly in the winter breeze. It depicted a nondescript body washed up upon a barren shore. It was a fitting epitaph to those that dealt in a business concerned with the faceless dead.

Inside the gloom persisted. A perpetual pall of smoke clung to the interior even when pipes were doused and the fire smothered. Tonight though, the fire roared in an effort to banish away the cold. Suspicious faces huddled around tables and in darkened corners.

A bar rested at the far end of a crowded room, cluttered with innumerable chairs and tables. A vast quantity of bottles and urns resided behind the counter away from prying eyes. Some bore the tell-tale hue of milky jade absinthe, others the corruptive yet agonisingly addictive luminescence of warp dust-infused potions.

Two broad wings were set back from the throng, smouldering pipe weed serving as the only illumination. These areas were reserved for especially illustrious patrons. It was here that Rannick sat in silent contemplation.

He surveyed the filthy clot of thieves, beggars, urchins and mercenaries before him, raising a warming glass of Bretonnian rouge to his lips. Without realising, he had drained it and was about to order another when a name he recognised called his attention.

'That's right, twenty,' the urchin confirmed, his filth-encrusted face glowing with relish.

'All slain by the Black Crowe?' a broad-looking dwarf pirate remarked. He regarded the urchin suspiciously, sucking deep on his pipe, absently scratching beneath his eye patch.

'Yes,' the urchin responded, leaping excitedly upon the table, swinging his gaze around the entire establishment.

The dwarf rested his hand upon a pistol at his belt.

'He is the greatest assassin in all of Tilea!'

He was a wretch, Rannick decided, inwardly seething at this proclamation. Bedecked in tattered rags, a second skin of dirt and street detritus smothering him, the urchin could have been any age. It mattered not; this was the link Rannick had been seeking. Through the urchin he could get to the Crowe.

'He could best even Vespero!' the urchin boasted, wavering drunkenly as he upended a few glasses, one into the mercenary dwarf's lap.

'A bold statement,' the ale-drenched dwarf said, reaching for his pistol, enraged at the urchin's undisguised amusement.

'Bold and inaccurate,' another voice said. A man, pale and severe, black beard neat and trim, moved out of one of the wings, the darkness peeling away at his approach. Clad in black, he drew a duelling sword from beneath a deep crimson cloak.

The urchin's amusement turned to sober concern as he staggered down from the table.

Rannick watched with interest.

'Enough!' a loud voice bellowed from the back of the room. A thickly muscled barkeep, tanned and weatherbeaten, held a stout looking blunderbuss across the bar.

'Back to your seats,' he urged with menacing politeness. The blunderbuss shot could shred everything before him. Several of the patrons with minds on their own business looked nervously, pleadingly between the mouth of the gun and the trio of man, dwarf and urchin.

The dwarf raised his hand and returned to his seat with a muttered oath. The duellist disappeared silently, back into the gloom.

'And as for you,' the barkeep said, 'out!'

As if suddenly scalded, and with a last glance at the gaping maw of the blunderbuss, the urchin was gone, lost in the dark.

THE NIGHT DREW in around him, cold and silent as the urchin tramped dazedly through the streets. Snow was falling and it covered the approaching plaza with a whitening veil.

He looked up into the night and watched the flakes drift down languidly, disintegrating quickly on his alcohol warmed skin. When he looked back there was a shadow figure before him and the prick of a dagger at his neck.

'Wha...' the urchin began but was silenced when the blade was pressed harder, nearly piercing the skin.

'You work for the Black Crowe,' a voice like hardening ice told him.

'The Black Crowe? No, I–'

'This,' the voice said, a second dagger urging a filthy hand into the moonlight, 'tells me different.' A gold ring shone, its emblem picked out in sharp relief, that of a bird in flight, a crow. The urchin's skinny hand quivered with fear.

'You have only this chance to save yourself,' the voice warned. 'Where is he and what are his plans?'

Tears ploughed watery furrows through the grime on the urchin's face revealing pale, white skin beneath.

'I don't know,' he rasped, constricted by fear and the dagger at his neck. The shadow pressed harder and a ruby of blood peeled away down the blade.

'Wait!' the urchin begged, 'I have only met him once in the shadows. He said he needed eyes and ears in the city, that it was dangerous for him in the open. I was promised a generous pay and that a bird would bring instructions,' he explained with blathering speed. 'I take the note to the guild house and I send the contracts back with the bird.'

'When?' the shadow asked, increasing the blade pressure.

'All hours, he contacts me when he needs me, I swear by Taal!' he said with difficulty.

'His plans?'

'A murder,' was the urchin's choked retort, 'tonight.'

'Who?'

'Count Banquo.'

The shadow assailing him appeared to flinch, if only slightly, but then composed itself.

'He will kill me for this,' the urchin sobbed, the blade released at last. He fell to his knees as if in penance, exhausted, shining with dappled sweat.

'Pray that he does,' the shadow figure replied. The night enveloped him as he retreated. In moments he was a merely a dark memory, one with the shadow.

THE WINTER WIND whipped a bleak and chilling chorus as Rannick crouched upon the barren rooftop of a lofty tenement. Through a powerful lens he espied the austere and well-fortified bastion of Count Banquo. The lens had been gifted to him by an Empire explorer for the retirement of a persistent necromancer. An esoteric payment, it had nonetheless proved invaluable on many occasions.

Six guards patrolled the outer wall upon a circumventing walkway. They were mercenaries, possibly marksmen; a tattoo common to the principality of Miragliano upon one cheek. They held low-slung crossbows with practiced ease and watched the night with keen eyes. Two watchtowers surged high into the dark, jutting from the ochre walls like spikes. Staves that gleamed like silver blades in the moonlight were set around them. Each held a garrison of two men similarly armed. There was a single gate, wooden with iron studs bored into the timber. It was barred and set solid with a heavy lock. The guard patrol was thickest here.

The count's first mistake.

Assassins' Code #46: The strongest resistance will always stand at the obvious entrance. Attack obliquely and catch your enemy where he expects you the least.

At such a high vantage point Rannick could see right over the forbidding wall and into the grounds. It smacked of the usual flamboyant opulence enjoyed by those with privilege, but more interestingly was bereft of any guards. There were three hounds left free to wander, sleek and brutish, heavily muscled and doubtlessly vicious if no guard was willing to be amongst them. The entrance to the count's inner sanctum lay across their stalking ground up stone steps and through two marble pillars. It was decorative and held little threat of determined resistance. Rannick had found his opening.

If he was to believe the filthy urchin, and the panic in his eyes told Rannick he was honest, then he had little time to act. The lackey would no doubt try to get a warning to his master. He had been left alive and undamaged precisely for this purpose. How sweet it would be to sweep in and retire the count and then watch from the shadows, the Black Crowe enraged at Rannick's audacious bid to turn the tables. And besides, the urchin's death would have gone against the code.

Assassins' Code #3: Unless it's personal, never kill someone without first agreeing a fee.

Speed now paramount, Rannick slid down the tenement with controlled urgency, landing athletically into the sheltered street below. Tall and arching domiciles, businesses and taverns cloaked his advance superbly. Rannick clung to the shadows cast by the overhead moonlight. He scampered through the winding streets until he was poised at the very threshold of the count's dominion.

The guard was re-doubled at the gate so Rannick slipped around the south-facing wall where the shadows were the deepest. Within their dark embrace he watched as the guard patrols overlapped. There was a moment when the wall was left unprotected. Rannick scaled up in a second, soundless and deadly. Upon the walkway he scurried across to the flat wall of the first watchtower. The angle would make it impossible to be seen by the marksmen above. A few more seconds and the patrolling mercenary would return. A moment to ensure his path was clear and Rannick traversed the width of the walkway and plunged into the leafy void below.

Within a thick, evergreen bush Rannick drew forth a small thin pipe from one of the voluminous pockets that bedecked his blackened garb. From another pouch came three darts, made in such a way that they would not reflect any light. His keen senses told him the dogs were closing on him. His scent had alerted them that an intruder was present.

In the noiseless dark, Rannick waited.

It only took a few patient moments and a long, muscled canine loped into view. Rannick waited until he caught sight of the other two. They were advancing toward him, long pink tongues lapping the air for scent clues, eyes pricked up alertly, bodies poised with the threat of violence.

Rannick fired. Three times, three hits, each an expert shot into the jugular, immediately getting into the bloodstream. The dogs fell, slumbering almost instantly, the wolfish features made tame by sleep.

Rannick could have used a deadly poison, this way his time in the mansion would be curtailed, but he took the assassins' code very seriously.

Assassins' Code #18: Killing a man by mistake is fine, but a dog… Many difficulties can arise from killing a dog…

Certain that the guards could not see him, Rannick sneaked through the foliage that reminded him of Frenzini's Mansion.

Perhaps all such habitations adhered to a floor plan, he wondered briefly before speeding silently up the stone steps and beyond the marble pillars of the entrance.

As he had suspected, the door was not locked nor barred and swung open freely. Rannick allowed a wedge of moonlight to spill into the hall beyond and slipped through, closing the door behind him with an almost undetectable click.

The hallway confronting him was dark, thrown into greyish half-light by a glass-domed ceiling of the vast lobby beyond. The immense room was pockmarked with marble and bronze statuettes, amongst them Borgio, the mercenary captain known as the Besieger, slain in his own bathtub, and the scientist Leonardo de Miragliano, holding aloft an alchemist's globe. There were others too: merchant princes, entrepreneurs and even a conceited likeness of the count himself, every inch the statesman. There were tapestries also, depicting ancient battles, treaties and coronations. The count was indeed a controlling factor in the mercantile war if the trappings of his domicile were any gauge.

Rannick smiled. This contract would be both prestigious and lucrative. As he advanced slowly, heading for a large and ornately fashioned marble staircase up which he assumed would be the count's bedrooms and study, a thought occurred to him.

Where are the guards?

No dogs, no men, not even a decent alarm. This Count Banquo was arrogant indeed if he thought he only needed protection outside his little empire. Rannick imagined him as vainglorious, full of his own self-importance, unwilling perhaps to even share his vast quarters with the hired riffraff that patrolled the cold stone at his border.

'That arrogance shall prove your undoing, dear count,' Rannick whispered as he trod softly up the staircase, his padded shoes making no sound upon the chilled stone.

The mansion was immense. There had to be a hundred or so rooms, but as Rannick reached the very top of the staircase he was rewarded for his intuition. A faint wash of yellowing light was visible down a passage directly before him. A thick oaken banister ran around the platform, upon which he was standing, and several passages and portals lay along its circumference. Here was the route Rannick sought.

Tentatively Rannick edged forward down the corridor. The silence persisted, filled with the threat of discovery. Rannick ignored it, and eventually reached a closed door at the end of the corridor, a hazy blade of yellow light issuing from the crack.

Rannick pressed his ear against the door and listened hard. There was movement and muttering from beyond. It sounded distant, likely from within another corridor behind it, possibly leading to the count's private chambers. The door was off its latch and carefully Rannick eased it open a fraction so that he could peer at what was beyond.

He was right, another corridor lay before him. Shorter this time, a junction peeling off to the east and west at its terminus. A shadow was cast over the western passage, thrown by the wan lamplight set at intervals, arranged in gilt wall-mounted candelabras. Rannick slid within, hugging the right hand wall, stepping quickly up the corridor until he reached the junction.

Without breath he peered around the corner, low and cloaked by shadows. And there he was – mythical, untouchable, death warrant of assassins from across the length and breadth of Tilea, the impossible mark: the Count Banquo Degusta.

Now that he saw him, Rannick could not help but feel let down. He was a youthful man, indeed, but held no presence, no ardour and was at least a full half-head shorter than he; a man, that was all, and soon to be a dead one. Rannick wondered briefly how he could ever have lasted this long. His contemporaries had been sloppy, allowing their judgement to be clouded. Now they were dead, lives thrown away in vain to perpetuate a myth of mere flesh and blood. He would give no such quarter.

The count bumbled down the corridor towards an open door. From what Rannick could see, it appeared to be a study, a bookcase and the hint of a decanter and wine beyond. He wore a long crimson cloak with fur trim, night robes, and in his left hand held a glass of red wine. He had his back to him but Rannick was unconcerned about this. There was no honour in this act. He would not be another portrait on Faust's wall. He pulled the blowpipe from his pocket once more and this time produced a black dart with a red band at the tip.

Black venom.

His death would be slow and painful. The poison would first paralyse his vocal chords, silencing his screams, then it would attack his lungs, making it feel as if he were swallowing his own blood. After the visions and the blinding pain it would stop his heart. He would be able to feel it slow even through his agony and know the moment at which Morr had come for him.

Rannick balanced the pipe carefully between two fingers and picked out a spot on the back of the count's neck and fired. Then something happened for which Rannick had not prepared.

He missed.

Doubtlessly addled from the liquor in his bloodstream the count stumbled at the very last second, the deadly dart missing by the scantest possible distance. Instead it hit a low hung tapestry, embedding soundlessly.

Rannick shrunk back, watching as the count upended most of the wine onto a plush ivory carpet, oblivious to the fact that he had just escaped certain death but for a lucky chance!

He shuffled off, careful to avoid the spill, and slipped into the open doorway of the study. Once his back was to him again, Rannick peeled away from the darkness and trod, silently and purposefully, after the count. He wouldn't miss again.

The count busied himself with a glass and decanter within a plush looking study that held a strong aroma of lavender. It was filled with vast volumes of history, geography, art and even warfare – an impressive collection. It was almost a pity he would never read them again. Just as the count had finished filling a second glass of red wine, he felt cold steel at his neck.

Rannick had tired of waiting. Time was slipping away. The sleeping draught he had given to the hounds would soon expire. He had to retire the count and be gone before the Black Crowe could mount a counter move.

'Turn,' Rannick's voice was ice as the count faced him, shocked at the intrusion.

'I am the Living Shade, greatest assassin in all of Luccini and Tilea and I have come to kill you,' he announced.

The count's shock turned quickly to defeat as his shoulders slumped and his face fell.

'There is no escape for you,' Rannick told him, the lavender stench pricking at his nostrils. 'I'm barring the only door, it is shut tight and no guard or hound will hear you.'

'Then it ends at last,' the count sighed with resignation. 'I have survived eight assassination attempts. You are the first to breach my inner sanctum and live,' he told him and then added, 'Can I ask whom it was who ordered my execution?'

'I know not,' Rannick answered truthfully, slightly wrong-footed by the count's demeanour. He was used to crying, begging, offers of gold and jewels, even his victims soiling themselves. Not this cold-hearted pragmatism.

He had to make haste. He suspected the Black Crowe would have heard by now and would be on his way. He tensed his rapier arm and shaped for a death lunge into the count's throat.

'Wait!' the count urged.

This was more like it. Every mark was the same. They always beg.

'A final request,' the count added, 'to honour your achievement.'

That was vexing. This count was full of surprises. Rannick flicked up his rapier point slightly and nodded the count to go on.

'To join me in a final glass of wine,' he asked calmly. 'I have heard of your exploits, that you toast your victims before the final death strike. I would be honoured if you would grant me such an indulgence.'

Rannick scrutinised the count for a moment. He was a plain-looking man, not nearly as regal as his statuette in the ground floor lobby. It made him look honest. And after all he was beaten. He would have toasted him anyway. It was flattering to know that such an esteemed member of the community followed his work and held such a regard. Perhaps the count had tired of life and all its strains. That or he was mad.

'One glass,' Rannick told him, 'that one.' He pointed to that held in the count's hand.

Obligingly the count handed Rannick the glass and quickly poured another for himself.

'To your victory,' the count said.

'Indeed, and your health,' Rannick mocked, the glass almost touching his lips as a strange aroma assaulted his nostrils, faint amongst the cloying lavender.

Rannick threw the glass to the floor where it shattered violently.

'A trick,' Rannick whispered his eyes full of imperious hate. 'You hesitated. You wanted me to drink first. It is poison.'

'No, I...'

'You have failed, count!' Rannick proclaimed exultant. 'Little wonder you have ensnared so many of my trade, for you are indeed canny.' Secretly Rannick applauded him. He had got close. 'Now you drink,' he ordered at rapier point. It was a fitting end, poison the poisoner.

Reluctantly the count swilled back the wine, swallowing hard.

'At least you were slain by the best,' Rannick scoffed, waiting for his prey to keel over and foam at the mouth.

It didn't happen. Instead Rannick's head began to swim. He went to lunge but the rapier fell from useless fingers as he slumped unwillingly to his knees. His throat constricted, making it difficult to breathe.

'Would you like a hand?' the count offered innocuously.

Rannick saw a gold ring upon his finger, an emblem upon it, that of a bird in flight – a crow. One of the fingernails was badly chipped but now held firm like rock.

'You!' Rannick rasped. 'But how?'

'The air you breathe,' the Black Crowe explained. 'It is a slow acting poison to which this potion is the only antidote.' He indicated the wine glass. 'You triggered its container after you closed the door to the study. It's perfectly harmless after a few more minutes,' he explained. 'Alas, it is already in your blood stream.

'The Count Banquo is dead. I killed him months ago, an exterior contract,' he added. 'I assumed his identity so that I might watch your movements better and learn of your ways as well as reap the benefits as a major power in the mercantile war.'

Rannick looked on incredulously, powerless and enraged.

'You see, I had to draw you out and this was the bait,' he gestured to his garb and disguise. 'That and the amateur dramatics at the Drowned Man. All designed to bring you here, to bring you to me.'

The Black Crowe drew closer, mere infuriating inches from Rannick's face.

'I have your title now, through arrogance and self-inflated flattery you have let it slip,' he told him darkly, watching as the last moments of Rannick's life drained away. 'Be wary of another man's cutlery indeed. But what of his glass?' the Black Crowe smiled, standing.

'It's not personal,' he said impassively. 'Never make it personal. You were merely an obstacle.' His tone was condescending and accusatory.

Rannick clenched his teeth, tears pouring down his face as he screwed up all of his willpower to speak for one last time.

'I am still the greatest assassin!' he spat through his agony.

'No, you're not,' the Black Crowe corrected. 'But very soon it won't matter what you think,' he added. 'In a few moments you'll be dead.'

The Black Crowe walked away, opening the door to the study. 'Still,' he said, turning, just visible in the corner of Rannick's eye, 'my thanks for not killing the dogs.'

SICKHOUSE
by C L Werner

THE ATMOSPHERE IN the dingy little cellar room was, if anything, even more stifling than the sweltering Miragliano streets overhead. Strings of wet linen had been set between the thick wooden posts that supported the tannery above the cellar, yet far from cooling the dank chamber they had served only to increase the humidity. Coupled with the rich stink of rotten vegetables and the other refuse that lay heaped in piles all around the chamber, the effect was not unlike entering one of the blighted swamps that crouched beyond the city walls. Certainly the cellar's lone denizen should not have looked out of place in such an environment.

The feeble creature that sprawled upon the rickety cot rolled onto his side, stretching a thin, wasted limb toward the small oil lamp that rested on the floor beside him. Thick, wormy digits that were more tentacles than fingers raised the flame, increasing the illumination within the miserable rat-hole. The mutant scowled as his visitor sank into the chair facing him without invitation. The creature muttered under his breath.

Manners were often lacking in those who still deigned to visit Tessari the information broker.

'What you want to know will cost you two pieces of silver,' the mutant croaked. The man sitting in the chair smiled thinly at the crippled monster.

'And how do you know that, Snake-Fingers?' the visitor's harsh voice sneered. 'I haven't said anything yet.' There was a note of suspicion and challenge to the man's voice, an unspoken threat behind his words. Tessari leaned back, his eyes narrowing.

'There is no mystery to my price, bounty killer,' Tessari replied, putting as much distaste in the title as his visitor had in describing the mutant's affliction. 'I need two pieces of silver to secure a new supply of blankets before winter sets in. Therefore, whatever it is you wish to know, the price is two pieces of silver.'

For a moment, the bounty hunter was silent, as though pondering Tessari's price. At length, he nodded his head in agreement. 'Very well, cellar-rat, I am looking for the thief Riano. So far, I haven't been able to find him. Rats have ears, tell me what you have heard.'

'Have you tried searching the back rooms of the Maid of Albion?' Tessari inquired. 'Riano has done favours for the owner of that drinking hole in the past.'

'I've already looked there,' the bounty hunter snarled. 'Riano's nowhere in Miragliano.'

'How can you be certain?' Tessari pressed, his tones bubbling with interest. The wormy fingers of his hand twitched in a loathsomely boneless fashion.

'Because if he was in Miragliano, I'd have found him already,' the bounty hunter retorted, his temper rising. 'It seems clear to me that you do not know anything, Maggot-Hand.' The killer began to rise from the chair.

'Don't be hasty!' Tessari cried out, surging forward, reaching toward the bounty hunter. 'Sit, and talk with me.'

'I've better ways to spend my time than wasting it down in this rat's den of yours,' the bounty hunter snapped. 'If you can't help me, I'll find someone who can.'

'The man you are looking for has left Miragliano,' Tessari called out to the killer's back, frightened by the prospect of being left alone once more within the dank cellar. 'If so, then he has gone somewhere he can lie low until the price on his head diminishes. Someplace he will feel safe.'

The bounty hunter hesitated, turning slowly, one hand gripping the weapon hanging from his belt. 'And where would that be?' he demanded. Tessari held out the less deformed of his hands, waiting until his visitor walked back and placed a silver coin in his palm. The bounty killer held the other one poised between his thumb and forefinger.

'I'll give you this one if your information is useful,' he informed the mutant. Tessari shrank back into his bedding.

'Riano grew up in the small village of Decimas,' the mutant stated. 'If he has fled Miragliano, he can only have gone back to Decimas, where he has many friends. Friends who might make things rather hard for men of your profession.'

'I doubt it,' the bounty hunter told Tessari, tossing the other coin to the mutant. The bounty hunter turned away once more.

'Wait!' Tessari cried. 'There is more, something else that would be of interest to a man like you.' The visitor turned back, glaring down at the deformed man.

'I grow tired of these games, lice-breeder,' the warrior hissed. 'What else do you have to say?'

Tessari's twisted face spread into an avaricious smile. 'It will cost you another silver piece.' The bounty hunter drew another coin from a pouch fixed to his belt, holding it once more between his fingers.

'There is another man looking for Riano, a bounty killer like yourself.' Tessari leaned forward, voice dropping into a conspiratorial whisper. 'Would it interest you to know that two days ago another man was standing where you are now, asking me the same questions you've been asking?'

'Out with it, dung-eater! Who else is on Riano's trail?'

'Brunner,' Tessari told his visitor, enjoying the sudden unease that manifested upon the other man's features. The mutant grimaced as the bounty hunter returned the silver coin to its pouch. 'That was mine!' Tessari growled.

'And how much did Brunner pay for his information?' his guest demanded. Tessari glared at the other man, wormy fingers coiling like angry pythons. The bounty hunter smiled back. 'Since he has a head start on me, I'd be a fool to pay more than he did.' The man withdrew through the gloom of the cellar. Behind him, the twisted Tessari hurled obscenities at his back.

THE SUN HUNG high in the sky, glaring down from the azure plain, causing tiny ripples of heat to shimmer upwards from the scraggly brown grass below. The barren dirt and rock of the narrow road that crawled between the underbrush and the sickly trees had been baked to the solidity of granite, for in this season there would be no kindly rains to counterbalance the sun's tyrannical attentions. No birds flew upon the hot breeze, hiding within whatever shade they could find. The only sign of life was a large grey lizard, its long-taloned fingers clutching the sides of a large stone resting upon the road. The reptile's eyes were closed, its body bobbing up and down in repetitious motion as its cold flesh soaked up the blazing rays. Suddenly, the lizard's scaly lids snapped open and it cocked its head, listening to the vibrations that had disturbed it. With almost blinding speed, the reptile lunged from its perch, streaking across the road to skitter into the sanctuary afforded by a patch of yellowing brambles.

The rider whose approach had disturbed the creature paid its departure little notice, his steely eyes dismissing the lizard as soon as they had reacted to the sudden motion, then returning to their study of the road itself. Behind the rider, a ragged grey packhorse plodded, its back laden down with numerous packs and bags, and several things that were clearly sheathed weapons. The rider's mount, a massive bay warhorse, turned its head, seeming to glance sympathetically at its doughty companion. The rider gave a gentle tug on the reins, recalling his steed to its course. The sooner he found what he was looking for, the sooner all of them would be able to find rest.

The rider was a tall man, panther-like in his build. His features were solid, harsh and weathered, cold blue eyes squinting from the leathery face beneath his close-cropped brown hair. A suit of brigandine armour hung about his frame, a breastplate of dark metal encasing his chest. Weapons dripped from the belts that crossed his torso and circled his waist – the steel fangs of knives, the gaping maw of a pistol, the cruel edge of a hatchet. Upon one hip rested a huge knife with jagged teeth, a savage instrument which its owner had named 'the Headsman' in a moment of sadistic humour. From the other, its golden hilt fashioned in the shape of a dragon with outspread wings, was sheathed the warrior's longsword, the fabled blade named Drakesmalice. From the horn of his saddle, swinging from the leather straps that bound it in place, the rounded steel frame of the bounty hunter's sallet helm cooked beneath the sun's merciless attentions.

Brunner lifted his eyes from the road, glancing at the sign that stood beside the deserted path, its three fingers pointing in every direction save that dominated by the woods at its back. The killer smiled grimly as he noted the topmost sign. Scrawled upon it in charcoal letters was the word 'Decimas'. Brunner shook his head, looking away from the sign. As he did so, he noticed a sorry figure sprawled beneath the sign, almost hidden by the rock pile that formed the signpost's support. Brunner eyed the shape warily, watching for any sign of movement or breath. Without removing his eyes from the prone form, the bounty hunter drew his pistol and carefully dropped down from Fiend's saddle. With cautious glances to either side of the path, the bounty hunter slowly walked toward the shape.

It was a man, dressed in the tattered homespun common to the peasants that populated the Tilean countryside. Brunner nudged the man's side with his steel-toed cavalry boot, watching the body for any sign of reaction. It simply rocked in its position. Putting more effort behind his thrust, Brunner pitched the body onto its back. The bounty hunter stepped away from the sight that greeted him, a gloved hand reaching to his face to keep the smell from his nose.

The man was dead, but neither beast nor man had claimed him. The swollen tongue that protruded from the corpse's contorted face had nearly been bitten clean through during the agonies that had gripped the man. Upon his skin were livid red boils, some nearly the size of Brunner's thumb, each weeping a filmy, scarlet pus. The bounty hunter continued to back away. He had seen too many bodies like this recently. The red pox had returned to Tilea, rampaging across the countryside, striking down all who tempted its pestilent attentions.

Brunner turned away from the corpse, eyes considering the bleak expanse toward the south. His destination lay in that direction, but if the sorry corpse at his feet had come from there, if the red pox was rampant in the south, then in all likelihood he would be making a wasted journey. The dead did not last long when the red pox was abroad, so long as there were still healthy men to burn the diseased corpses. It would be difficult to turn in a pile of ash and blackened bones if Riano had already been claimed by the plague.

The sound of a twig snapping spun the bounty hunter around, lifting him from his thoughts. Brunner cursed under his breath. Worrying about the red pox had made him careless, sloppy. His natural caution had been subordinated to concern about the plague that hovered about the land. The bounty hunter chastised himself. He'd been around long enough to know that a moment of distraction could often last for all eternity.

The creature that had caused the sound rose from where it had been crawling, realising that its stealth had been compromised. It was a miserable, twisted shape, a rotten mockery of the human form. Ragged linen hung about its lean, wasted frame, tied about its waist with a length of rope. Its pallid skin was blotched with ugly red welts and crater-like scars, its face a broken shambles, crazed eyes swollen within their sockets, nose rotten away into a scabrous stump of cartilage. Upon its forehead, the miserable creature had carved a brand, three bloated circles, linked at their centres, each sporting a jagged arrow. The brand was the only vivid thing about the creature's face, weeping a vibrant green pus each time the thing drew a breath. But it was the object clutched in the creature's withered hand that arrested Brunner's attention – a fat-bladed shortsword.

The bounty hunter did not give the twisted abomination a chance to close upon him. With a single deft motion, he ripped his pistol from the holster resting across his belly and fired into the diseased abomination's rotten skull. Watery brain tissue erupted from the back of the creature's head as the bullet tore its way through. The plague-ridden thing did not cry out as its head exploded, but simply crumpled into the road with all the grace of a wilting flower.

The shot's echoes had yet to fade before the bounty hunter discovered that the diseased attacker had not been alone. Other twisted shapes scrambled into view, descending upon the road like a pack of jackals upon a fresh carcass. Some were similar to the one Brunner had put down, ragged, tattered figures that might have been men before their flesh was consumed by the unholy foulness which now claimed them. Several though had never borne the mantle of humanity, their feet ending in cloven hooves, their shapes clothed in mangy fur, their heads cast in the manner of goats and kine. Upon these monstrosities, too, was that pestilent brand, filthy pus drooling from the mark and caking the fur of the beast-men with reeking filth.

Brunner tore his sword from its sheath, cursing anew as the diseased abominations sprung their ambush. There were at least a dozen of them, far too many to face with sword and axe. As the bounty hunter considered this fact, his cold eyes stared longingly at the repeating crossbow lashed to the saddle of his warhorse. He was a master with the weapon, and with it in his hands four of his attackers would have found death. But already there were beasts and once-men between him and his animals, converging on the horses in a frenzied mob. Brunner watched as Fiend reared back, the massive warhorse's iron-shod hooves lashing out and splitting the skull of a degenerate plague-mutant as though it were an egg shell. Whether intent on plunder or horseflesh, the mutants would not claim the horses without a fight.

The bounty hunter braced himself to meet his own attackers. Three of the mutants and a pair of goat-headed pestigors had split from the main pack, their lust for slaughter and bloodshed overwhelming their desire for plunder and meat. The creatures glared at Brunner with rheumy eyes, strings of spittle dripping from slackened mouths. Brunner was not deceived by the apparent simple-mindedness of his attackers, he had seen goblins beneath the haunted caverns of the Vaults given over to similar fits. And though their attacks might have been crude and lacking in co-ordination, their befuddled brains had seemed incapable of understanding pain, even as limbs were hacked from their bodies.

The first of the attackers charged with a wet, gurgling war cry, his mutated face resembling nothing so much as a grinning skull. Brunner prepared to meet the monster's assault, ready to cut the rotten head from its decaying body. But the killing stroke proved unnecessary. With a loud crunch, a five-inch spike of steel smashed into the mutant's face, spilling it to the ground and tripping up the lice-ridden pestigor that followed behind it. The bounty hunter did not waste time considering his good fortune. Even as the mutant dropped he was in motion, his sword lashing out to meet the axe of the mutant closing upon his right. The keen edge of Drakesmalice smashed into the rotten wooden haft of the axe, just beneath its rust-pitted head, shearing through the weapon and severing the reed-thin arm behind it.

The mutant recoiled from the stroke, its stump dripping a filth that was far too dark to be proper blood. The creature seemed to regard the mutilating wound as little more than an inconvenience, reaching down with its remaining arm to retrieve the blade of its axe. The bounty hunter's gut churned at the unnatural sight, stabbing downward between the mutant's shoulders as it bent down. Spitted on the tip of the longsword, the mutant's body trembled for a moment, then grew slack. Brunner tore the weapon free from the corroded body, spinning about to meet his next attacker.

It was the hulking beastman that had fallen over the mutant felled by the mysterious steel spike. The other beastman was down, another of the strange steel spikes sprouting from its heart. It was just as well, Brunner considered as he sized up his adversary. One such foe was more than sufficient.

The pestigor gnashed its fanged jaws, its clawed hands tightening about the grip of its spike-headed mace. The monster's eyes were weeping a filthy yellow ooze, gnats and flies buzzing about its goat-like head. Upon its chest, livid where it had been burned into the mangy fur, the pestilent brand stood out. Brunner felt disgust welling up within him as he beheld the hideous rune, fighting down his revulsion just in time to push aside the monster's brutal attack. The pestigor reared back, snarling some obscenity in its own harsh tongue, then lashed out once more, the bounty hunter managing to turn aside the powerful blow only by putting the weight of his entire body behind his own blade's retort.

From the corner of his eye, Brunner could see the other mutant working his way toward the bounty hunter's back, a short boar-spear gripped in its malformed hands. Unable to free himself from his duel with the pestigor, Brunner knew there was little he could do to protect himself from a stab in the back. The bounty hunter tried to manoeuvre his massive foe around, to place the pestigor between himself and the spear-bearing mutant. But the beastman would have none of it, accepting a slash to its forearm in return for holding its ground. It too had seen the mutant moving toward Brunner's back and was not about to surrender such an advantage.

The sound of steel crunching through bone rumbled through Brunner's ears, followed by the impact of a body falling somewhere behind him. The pestigor's goat-like face contorted into a mask of feral rage and the bounty hunter could guess the source of its fury – the spear-bearing mutant had just been shot down. Brunner did not give the pestigor time to turn its rage into strength. Slipping past the monster's guard, he slashed his sword along its gut, spilling its entrails into the dust. The beastman stumbled backward, the mace falling from its claws as it reached down for the ropy mess hanging from its belly. Brunner slashed at the monster again, this time nearly severing its forearm. The pestigor lifted its horned head, roaring its rage into the barren sky, bloody froth spilling from its jaws. As Brunner moved in for the kill, the pestigor lowered its head, spitting a stream of filth into his face.

It was the bounty hunter's turn to stumble back from his foe, one gloved hand wiping away at the gory muck that now covered his features, finding with disgust that the pestigor's bloody spittle was alive with writhing, wormy shapes. Brunner cleared his eyes just in time to see the pestigor bearing down on him, its remaining claw crunching down about his shoulder, its powerful grip seeking to pull the bounty hunter into the massive horns that curled against the monster's skull. Brunner stabbed into the beastman's side with his blade, punching the length of his sword into the monster's corrupt flesh, transfixing its blackened heart. The pestigor fell to its knees, its eyes glaring into Brunner's own as its unclean life slowly drained from its twisted form. The grip on his shoulder loosened and Brunner watched dispassionately as the pestigor fell backwards and crashed into the dust.

The bounty hunter looked away from his fallen foes, looking back toward his animals. Three mutants lay

sprawled about them, and two others looked to have
fallen victim to the mysterious sharpshooter who had
so fortuitously come to his aid. The others were fleeing
back down the road, forsaking the promise of loot and
provisions in their haste to save their own hides.
Brunner strode toward his horses, keen to inspect the
animals for any sign of injury and to recover his crossbow from Fiend's saddle, lest the twisted ambushers
regain their courage. As he approached, Fiend and the
packhorse, Paychest, retreated from him and it was only
with slow steps and soothing words that he was able to
keep the horses from bolting. Patting Fiend's neck with
a gloved hand, Brunner quickly removed his crossbow
from its holster, slapping the box-like magazine into
place. He turned his head in the direction from which
he judged the mysterious steel shafts to have originated.
He was not surprised to find a lone rider descending the
jagged slope of a low hill. Leaning against the side of his
horse, keeping his crossbow at the ready, Brunner
awaited the approach of his unknown benefactor.

His wait was not a long one, and soon Brunner found
himself confronted by a tall, slender man mounted on
a white steed of similar build, a mount built for speed
rather than war. The man himself was garbed in black,
from the leather boots that encased his feet to the
leather hat on his head. A leather belt crossed the man's
chest, long steel spikes fitted into the loops that rose
along its surface. A number of box-like pouches were fitted to the belt that circled the warrior's waist, along with
a longsword and poinard, both of the simple, utilitarian
style favoured by Tilea's professional duellists. Resting
upon the saddle before the rider was a strange device, a
thing of steel and bronze that looked as though it could
not decide if it were musket or crossbow.

Brunner looked up into the face hiding within the
shadow of the rider's hat. It was a gaunt, hungry face,

with cruel eyes that gleamed with an almost feral cunning. The man's sharp nose stabbed downward above a thin, almost lipless mouth and a slender black moustache. It was the kind of face Brunner knew only too well. The face of a predator. The face of a man like himself.

'I hope you don't mind the intrusion,' the rider said when he brought his horse to a stop a few yards from Brunner, 'but it looked like you had bitten off more than you could handle.' The weasel-eyed man chuckled with grim humour. 'Even the infamous Brunner isn't the equal of a dozen beastmen.'

'Perhaps they didn't know who I was,' Brunner returned, 'or they would have brought twice as many.' The jest brought another sardonic chuckle from the rider. Brunner fixed the other man with his cold stare, the leather of his gloves creaking as he firmed his hold on the crossbow. 'Tell me, Sabarra, how is it that you happen to be in the right place at the right time? I've never been one to place much trust in providence.'

Sabarra grinned back at the other bounty hunter. 'If you are thinking I was expecting you, then you'd be right. There are things we should discuss, you and I.' The rider leaned back in his saddle, gesturing at the dead mutants strewn about the road. 'But it can wait until we put a little distance between ourselves and the road. Just in case their friends stop running and decide to come back this way.'

THE TWO BOUNTY killers took the southern stretch of road, a move that took them away from the village of Decimas. Sabarra's eyes narrowed, studying his rival with undisguised interest and suspicion. For his part, Brunner seemed to be paying little attention to the Tilean, rubbing at his face with a cloth he'd dampened from his waterskin. Sabarra was not fooled by the display, he knew that the Reiklander was even now turning any number of schemes to rid himself of Sabarra over in his mind.

'You know of course that I'm after the same mark as you,' Sabarra declared. It was better to get the matter out in the open sooner rather than later. 'It's a handsome price Riano has on his head.' Brunner did not turn to regard Sabarra, instead dousing the cloth in his hand with more water from the skin. 'Enough for two men, if they aren't greedy,' Sabarra elaborated. Brunner turned cold eyes onto the weasel-faced killer.

'And what if the men in question are greedy?' he inquired. A cruel smile split Sabarra's features.

'Then things could get very upsetting,' Sabarra said. 'One of the men might get there before the other. That might not be so good if Riano has some friends with him.' The bounty hunter's gloved hand whipped upward, catching a buzzing fly between its fingers. 'And, of course, he'd also have to worry about his back,' Sabarra warned, crushing the fly in his fist. 'Because even if he won out, he'd still have something the other man wanted.'

'And what if the men decided they weren't greedy?' Brunner asked, lowering his hand. Sabarra's eyes narrowed with concern as he noticed how near to his pistol Brunner's hand was now poised.

'They might decide to share,' the Tilean suggested. 'Split everything down the middle. The dangers and the gold, divided up equally between them. Rather a good idea with the countryside crawling with beastmen and half-mad with plague.'

Brunner nodded thoughtfully, then lifted the cloth back to his face. 'Of course, they would be foolish to stop watching their backs,' he warned. Sabarra didn't bother hiding the cunning look in his eyes. 'But let's say these men did reach an agreement, where would they start?'

'By sharing information,' Sabarra told him. 'For instance, why are we riding away from Decimas rather than toward i?.'

'Because, as we both know, Riano isn't there,' Brunner said. 'Decimas is gone, the red pox has already done its work there.'

'Then why south?' pressed Sabarra. Brunner continued to rub at his face.

'You should spend more time learning about your prey,' Brunner said. 'Don't place all your wager on a single informant. I have my reasons to believe Riano headed south if he had to quit Decimas.'

'And those would be?' Sabarra asked.

'I prefer to keep that information to myself,' Brunner replied. 'That way I won't have to watch my back.' The Reiklander continued to dab at the blistered skin of his face, trying to soothe the raw, irritating itch that had seeped into his skin. Sabarra's smile widened as he noted the ugly rash.

'I'd be worried about that,' he told Brunner. 'Who knows what foulness was in that animal's blood. I'd get myself to the nearest hospice of Shallya if I were you. Let the priestesses bleed the contamination out of you. Maybe let someone else finish this hunt for you, bring you your percentage later.'

Brunner threw the cloth down. 'Either I die or I don't,' he told Sabarra. 'I'll not go crawling to anybody, not even the gods. I'm through with all of that, through playing their games.'

'Have a care,' Sabarra warned his rival. 'You die and I might never find Riano. I'd hate to miss that payday because an impious fool went and caught the plague.'

Brunner's response was spoken in a tone as menacing as the grave. 'Then I suggest you start praying I don't get sick.'

* * *

THE DISEASE-RIDDEN mutant crept into the foul-smelling hovel, bent almost in half, cringing at every step as though it were a whipped cur rather than a man. The room he had entered was a shambles: furniture overturned, walls fouled with blood and mucus, the air filled with buzzing flies. Bodies littered the floor, their skin blackening as necrotic bacteria speedily consumed their diseased flesh, the final trademark of the ghastly red pox. But it was not this reminder of the hideous disease that so unnerved the once-human wretch. It was the five armoured shapes looming against the far wall.

The warriors were huge, hulking monsters, their powerful forms encased within suits of plate armour, the steel pitted with corruption. Upon their breastplates had been stamped the mark of their deity, the daemon god to whom each of the corrupt warriors had pledged his life and soul. Three circles and three arrows – the mark of Nurgle, Grandfather of pestilence and decay. The close-faced helms of the Chaos warriors did not turn to regard the mutant as he slowly crept toward them, intent instead on the miserable figure sprawled upon the filthy floor before them. It was an old man, his body disfigured by the profusion of red boils that peppered his skin. His diseased frame trembled and shook as the agonies of the plague ripped at him, yet the Chaos warriors made no motion to end his suffering. Plague was the handiwork of their god, and to the Chaos warriors, what they were witnessing was a holy sacrament, and they stood as if in the presence of their loathsome deity.

Nervously, the mutant cleared his throat, allowing a dry croak to escape his drawn, placid lips. The sound caused the warriors to turn their steel faces upon him, fixing him with their burning eyes. The mutant fought back the urge to flee, holding his ground as the centremost of the armoured warriors strode toward him.

He was a brute, his steel armour fading into a mass of green corruption, leather straps hanging from spikes set into his shoulder-guards displaying a variety of festering trophies. The warrior's helm was cast in the shape of some mammoth insect and there was no sign of any eyes behind the sieve-like holes that pitted the helm's face. The mark of pestilence branded into the warrior's breastplate glowed with a leprous light, marking the creature as favoured by his daemon master – a champion of Chaos.

'Zhere izz reazon why you dizurb uzz,' the droning, buzzing voice of the champion echoed from within his helm. The mutant cowered before the unnatural voice, falling to his knees before the ghastly creature. Pulstlitz gave the mutant only a moment to answer before growing impatient, his armoured hand falling to the massive sword at his side, a gigantic blade of rusted steel that drooled a murky scum from its pitted edge, the filth falling to the floor in sizzling droplets.

'Mercy dread master!' the mutant cried in a voice that seemed to bubble from the bottom of his stomach. 'Your slave did not mean to disturb your devotions! I came to bring word that Folgore is not coming back.'

A seething growl rasped behind the insect-helm. Pulstlitz took another menacing step toward the mutant. 'That vermin darezz defy my command! I will carve the name of Pulzlizz upon hizz bonezz for zhizz betrayal of Nurgle!' The other Chaos warriors watched their master warily, knowing too well that when their champion was in such a state, death hovered near. The mutant buried his face into the floor, unwilling to gaze upon the favoured of the Plague God.

'Folgore is dead, master!' the mutant whined. 'Slain upon the road by a traveller who wore not the blessings of the Grandfather!'

'You rizked attack when I commanded you here?' Pulstlitz demanded, the droning buzz of his voice seeming to come not from one but a dozen throats. 'When I need every mangy beazman and acolyte? When I prepare to raze the hozpizz of thrice-accurzed Zhallya? It izz at zuch time you zee fit to dizobey?' The enraged plague champion lifted his armoured foot, bringing it smashing downward into the abased mutant. Bones cracked as Pulstlitz brought his weight down upon the mutant's neck, then ground the creature's skull into the floor beneath his foot. When nothing solid remained beneath his boot, Pulstlitz turned to his warriors.

'We wait no longer!' the Chaos champion droned. 'Zhiz night we ride for the hozpizz! I will zee it burn!' The warriors did not pause to question their leader's command, but hastened to follow the monster into the night, leaving the old man to complete his communion with the Plague God in solitude and silence.

SABARRA WATCHED AS the white walls of the structure finally manifested in the distance. The bounty hunter cursed under his breath. It was about time he encountered some manner of luck. Since setting out after the price on Riano's head, he'd been met by obstacle after obstacle. It was as if the gods themselves were hurling every misfortune they could conceive in Sabarra's way, as though he were some mighty hero from some Luccini fable rather than a hired killer just trying to maintain a comfortably hedonistic lifestyle. The bounty hunter spat into the dust of the road. The gods! As though they were paying any manner of attention to him. They certainly were not in the mood for answering prayers.

The bounty hunter looked over his shoulder, back at the train of animals that slowly plodded along behind him. Slumped in the saddle of the rearmost horse was

Sabarra's old rival and recent partner, Brunner. The Tilean cursed again. He'd warned Brunner against mocking the gods, but the miserable Reiklander had remained unrepentant. Now he was sick, contaminated by whatever filth had lived within the loathsome blood of the pestigor he'd killed. For three days now, Brunner had been slipping in an out of consciousness as the disease wracked his body.

Sabarra shook his head, cursing his ill luck. During his lucid moments, which were becoming less and less frequent, Brunner's mind had wandered, crawling through the muck of the bounty hunter's bloody career. But he'd still retained enough coherency that he did not respond to Sabarra's promptings for more information – most especially with regards to Riano and whatever hole the thief had relocated himself to. Some deep-rooted instinct of self-preservation stilled Brunner's lips at such times. The bounty hunter's eyes had cleared for a moment, boring into Sabarra's own. 'Get me to a healer,' Brunner's voice had rasped. 'Then I'll tell you what you want to hear.'

By rights he should have left Brunner behind. Sabarra had seen enough of the red pox in his time to recognise its early stages. But the image of the gold being offered for Riano's head had been too tempting. So, Sabarra had lifted the sickly warrior into the saddle of his horse, tying Brunner's hands about the animal's neck, his legs beneath its belly. With Brunner secured to his animal, Sabarra had set out for the only place he could think of where a man suffering from the red pox might find sanctuary and succour. He only hoped that Brunner would last long enough to reach it.

The white walls grew steadily in size, the narrow cross-shaped windows and massive supporting buttresses breaking up the smooth alabaster façade. Sabarra could make out ragged figures huddled in the shadow of the walls, a great sprawl of wretched humanity. The bounty hunter's spirits fell another notch. Just how widespread was this plague? It looked like half of Tilea was camped outside the walls. He risked another look over his shoulder, striving to see if Brunner had reacted at all to the sight, but the man remained as he had for more hours than Sabarra wanted to count. The Tilean looked back toward the walls, noticing this time the vast pit that had been torn from the earth some distance to the west of the structure. Dour, hooded figures were busy there, throwing naked bodies into the yawning chasm as though tossing seed across a field. It was a minute before Sabarra released the breath he hadn't realised he had been holding. Of all the ends he could imagine, being consigned to a plague pit was probably about as bad as it got. Sabarra looked back once more at his charge and scowled.

So long as he found out what he wanted to know, Sabarra didn't much care where Brunner wound up. All the Reiklander had to do was cling on to life long enough to become lucid one last time.

AN AURA OF misery so intense that it seemed to clutch at Sabarra's face greeted the bounty hunter as he drew nearer the white-walled structure. The Tilean struggled to avoid looking down, tried not to see the dejected, forlorn creatures that sprawled upon the ground all around them. Many looked dead already, only the glazed eyes that rolled within their boil-strewn faces betraying the fact that they yet drew breath. Some of these miserable creatures had managed to build crude tents of rag and fur, but the vast majority just lay upon the ground, exposed to the open air and the chill of night. Sabarra tried not to imagine how many of these lost souls would make the journey past the portal of Morr before the sun again rose. Perhaps it was even a kindness to allow them to expire from exposure rather than the suffering the red pox would wrench from their bodies before it was through with them.

Sabarra slowly moved the horses through the sprawl of diseased refugees, the animals hard-pressed to avoid stomping on the miserable wretches. The bounty hunter allowed a slight sigh of relief to escape his throat as he saw the arched doorway that led into the structure behind the white walls and the shimmering marble dove that loomed above the arch's cornerstone. 'Well, friend,' Sabarra declared, glancing back once more at the still unmoving Brunner, 'this is it. The Shrine of the Seven Mercies. The hospice of Shallya.'

As if in response to his declaration, several men suddenly appeared beneath the arch, emerging from the interior of the hospice. Three of the men wore suits of armour, narrow helmets crushed about their ears. Their eyes were red-rimmed and their faces bore a pained, tired expression. But there was nothing fatigued in the way in which they held their spears. Three other men, dressed in the simple sack-cloth of supplicants of Shallya, laboured under the weight of a scrawny, pale burden. Behind the men carrying the corpse, a pair of white-garbed priestesses followed, one bearing a torch, the other carrying a bundle of rags that Sabarra imagined had once clothed the dead man. It was a common custom in cases of the plague. The body was hastily buried, but the clothes and bedding were burned, lest they pass the contagion on to another.

The priestess bearing the torch stared up at the mounted bounty hunter, her eyes red-rimmed and brimming with fatigue. Sabarra was somewhat surprised to find that the priestess was quite comely beneath the lines of worry and overwork. It had always been his experience that the ranks of the priestesses were commonly filled by daughters deemed unfit for a profitable marriage by their fathers. The bounty hunter's face twisted in the faintest hint of a lewd smile. Instantly the woman's eyes narrowed with disapproval, the shadows cast by her hooded robe seeming to grow thicker about her face.

'What do you want here, mercenary?' the priestess asked, her voice soft, yet demanding. Sabarra noted that it was a voice used to the burden of command and guessed that the priestess must be highly ranked among the sisters of the hospice, perhaps even the Sister Superior in charge of the entire shrine. Taking that into consideration, and remembering why he had come, the smile died on the bounty hunter's face. He was all business now.

'I seek the solace of the shrine,' Sabarra answered. 'I am in need of Shallya's mercy and blessing.'

The priestess took a step forward, the torch banishing the shadows from her face. 'You are ill?' she asked. Sabarra shook his head.

'No,' he replied, then gestured to the horses standing behind his own. 'But my friend is in dire need of healing.' Sabarra's voice dropped into a chill whisper. 'I fear it is the red pox.'

The priestess nodded her hooded head, sighing regretfully. 'Your friend is not alone. Many have fallen victim to the pox, and many more must follow before this evil has run its course. The mercies of Shallya are in much demand these days, our hospice is filled far beyond its capacity and still we cannot provide sanctuary for all who would enter.' She extended her arms to indicate the wretched masses clustered about the walls. 'The red pox is swift, once it has a hold on the flesh it is difficult to exorcise. We cannot forsake those in whom the infection is little, those who might recover, to give false hope to those for whom it is already too late.'

Sabarra gritted his teeth. When he first saw the miserable camp on the hospice's doorstep he should have expected as much. He stabbed a finger at the body being carried away. 'It seems there is at least one bed without an owner.' The priestess shook her head.

'And there are twenty already waiting to fill it,' she said sadly, turning to follow the grim procession.

'Dammit! At least you could look at him!' Sabarra snarled. The priestess turned again, her eyes boring into the bounty hunter's. At length she sighed and strode toward the warhorse standing behind Sabarra's own. The woman's steps slowed as she neared Fiend, as her eyes fell on the man lashed to the animal's back. It was a trembling hand that reached out toward the sick man, that lifted his head and stared at his face. The priestess recoiled as though it were a serpent she held in her hand.

'There is no room,' she repeated, her voice quivering. The man lashed to the saddle tilted his head and spoke in a shallow whisper.

'Even the goddess of mercy picks and chooses her prey,' Brunner's fading voice managed to hiss before his head sagged back down into Fiend's mane. The priestess glared at the sick man, then turned her head back toward Sabarra.

'Bring him inside,' Elisia told Sabarra. 'Sister Marcia will show you where.' Elisia did not wait for a response from the bounty hunter, but went after the funeral party, her steps hurried, fed by the doubt and fear that had closed icy fingers about her heart.

She had hoped never to see that face again, hoped never to hear that harsh, unforgiving voice. It had been almost a year since she had undertaken her mission of mercy for the Bertolucci family, wealthy merchants from Miragliano who had fled to a country villa in order to escape enemies in the city. But those enemies had sent an agent in pursuit of them, a hired killer to root them out from their hiding place. Brunner had 'chanced' upon Elisia as she was making her way to the villa, circumstance causing the grim bounty hunter to become her protector against the beastmen that prowled the countryside. Little did the priestess know that both of them had business at the villa – she to bring a new life into the world, the bounty hunter to remove an old one from it. Guilt and despair had wracked her for months afterward, that she had allowed herself to be the unwitting accomplice of the killer, that her actions had helped bring about a good man's death.

How she had wished death upon Brunner. It was true that he had saved her on the road to the villa, but only so that he could use her. She owed the merciless killer nothing. And now, her wish was coming true, Brunner was in the grip of the red pox, its poison coursing through his body. He would die, slowly and in great agony. Why then had she admitted him into the hospice?

Because it was her sacred oath to combat the forces of pestilence, because Brunner had questioned her integrity, made her consider whether she would violate that sacred duty simply to indulge her own desire for vengeance. Far from a wish fulfilled, the bounty hunter's arrival might prove the most arduous test of her faith she had ever endured.

Elisia hesitated, casting a worried look over her shoulder at the white walls of the hospice. Yes, it was a test, but was she equal to that test?

SABARRA STOOD ASIDE as a pair of burly suppliants lowered Brunner onto a straw pallet in one of the hospice's overcrowded wards. Designed to hold perhaps twenty inmates, every spare inch of space had been scavenged to provide room for nearly fifty. The men moved aside, allowing a dour priestess to inspect their latest charge. The old woman produced a small knife and began to strip away the bounty hunter's clothes and armour, her deft hands nimbly plucking weapons from Brunner's belt. The stricken bounty killer did not stir until the old woman's hand tugged at the dragon-hilt of Drakesmalice. Like a shot, Brunner's hand clutched at the weapon, fingers tightening about the blade until his knuckles turned white. The priestess tugged at the imprisoned weapon, trying to free it from the sick man's grasp.

'He doesn't want you to take his sword,' Sabarra stated. 'I suggest you leave it with him.' The old woman cast a sour look at the Tilean, but released her grip on Drakesmalice, hurrying to remove the rest of Brunner's armour. When she had finished, she gathered up the bounty hunter's gear and without a backward glance, strode from the ward. Sabarra waited until she had gone, then crouched beside Brunner's pallet. The reaction to the priestess trying to take his sword encouraged Sabarra that his rival might have slipped back into a moment of relative coherence.

'We're in the hospice, Brunner,' Sabarra told him. The stricken man turned his head weakly in Sabarra's direction. 'You're in the Seven Mercies.'

Brunner's eyes snapped open as he heard the name. The bounty hunter stared at Sabarra for a moment, then cast his gaze across the rest of the ward. Even knocking on the gates to Morr's realm, he seemed to be studying the faces of the men around him, looking for any sign that might put a name to a face and a price to a name.

'You said if I brought you here, you would tell me where Riano has escaped to,' Sabarra reminded Brunner. Brunner's head rolled back to where he could again face the rival bounty killer. A slight smile pulled weakly at his mouth.

'I... I have... recon... reconsidered... the arrangement,' Brunner's words escaped him in a ragged whisper. Sabarra's features flushed crimson with anger and the killer's hand fell to the poinard sheathed at his hip. 'You... you should... start praying again,' Brunner advised the Tilean, seemingly oblivious to Sabarra's fury. 'Pray now that I... that I recover...'

Brunner's words trailed off into oblivion and his eyes closed. Sabarra watched the bounty hunter's body go lax, a part of him hoping that the disease had finished the Reiklander. But another part of him was relieved to note the steady rise and fall of his chest. While Brunner yet drew breath, there was still a chance that Sabarra could draw the information he wanted from the dying man.

The Tilean rose, casting a disgusted look at the wretched, moaning shapes strewn about the room. Sabarra drew the garlic pomander he wore beneath his tunic, lifting the herb to his nose, inhaling its septic fumes. Garlic was said to be proof against disease, but the bounty hunter had no great desire to test that belief any more than he had to. One way or another, he would be rid of Brunner soon. Turning on his heel, Sabarra marched from the ward, determined to find some cleaner air to breathe.

NEVER TAKE THE life of a human being. Elisia knelt before the simple altar that stood within the tiny chapel. There were three such chapels within the grounds of the shrine, but this was the only one that still retained its intended purpose. The others had been transformed into makeshift infirmaries, as had the small courtyard and many of the cells inhabited by the priestesses themselves. They shared rooms now, sleeping in four-hour shifts.

Elisia lifted her eyes to the small marble statue that stood atop the altar – the image of a beautiful woman crafted in the classical Tilean style, a golden heart held in her hands, as though offering the shimmering organ to the supplicant kneeling before the idol. It was symbolic of the selfless sacrifice of the Goddess of Mercy – offering of her own body that others might find solace and peace, the sick might be healed and the halt made whole. It was an example that the priestesses of her faith were expected to follow, a standard to aspire toward.

Never refuse healing to those in need. Such had been the oaths she had taken when she had cast aside the ruin of her old life and become a servant of Shallya. But never before had she felt their weight. Her oaths bit into her, like heavy chains that coiled about her body and strove to crush the breath from her.

The bounty hunter. Why had he come here, of all places? He was dying, Elisia had seen that much in the brief moment when her eyes had again regarded that cold, calculating face. The red pox had already gained a stronghold within his flesh. There was nothing she could do to save him.

Or was that simply what she wanted to believe? It would be so easy to simply step aside, let the disease run its course. That would be just retribution for how Brunner had used her, just vengeance for all the blood that stained the man's hands.

Never take the life of a human being. Elisia cringed as she muttered the oath under her breath. Would she be any better than Brunner if she allowed him to die? She had been wracked with guilt and anguish over being the unwitting accomplice to one man's death, how could she live with being the instrument of another man's? How could she continue to serve Shallya with blood on her own hands?

If the disease claimed Brunner, she would never be certain that she did not allow it. That doubt would always linger behind her eyes, within the pits of her soul.

Elisia rose, walking toward the altar. There was only one thing to be done. She circled the altar, lifting up one of the flagstones set behind it. From the hole beneath the stone she removed a bottle of dark Bretonnian glass. The holy waters of the Temple in Couronne, the blessed spring from which Shallya's tears dripped into the world of men. They were precious beyond the weight of gold, for within the Tears of Shallya were the divine healing powers of the goddess herself. The Seven Mercies had never had a large supply of the Tears, only enough to guard the priestesses themselves against the diseases they hoped to cure, for what good would a healer be if she were to fall victim to the plague?

Elisia lifted the bottle to her breast, holding it close to her heart. What she was doing might be considered blasphemy by others of her faith, squandering some of the precious holy water on a killer and assassin. But it was the only way she could be sure, the only way she would ever know peace again.

BRUNNER GROANED AS soft hands lifted his head from the straw pallet, as cold glass was pressed against his lips. The bounty hunter's eyes snapped open, staring into the sullen face of Elisia. The priestess glared back at him, hatred burning behind her eyes.

'I've come to finish it,' she told the bounty killer, her voice a low hiss. She pushed the bottle higher, letting its contents trickle into Brunner's mouth. The bounty hunter coughed as the cold waters worked their way down his swollen throat.

'Damn you for ever coming here,' Elisia spat as she withdrew the bottle. Already she could see the miraculous waters beginning their work, the redness in Brunner's eyes beginning to fade. 'I have squandered a precious gift on inhuman vermin when this hospice is overflowing with men and women worth a dozen of your kind.'

'Because I… I saved… your life?' the bounty killer asked. Elisia shook her head and turned away from him.

'Because I am too selfish to let you die.'

PULSTLITZ GLARED UPON the white walls of the hospice, disgust and loathing welling up within his polluted form. The blessing of Nurgle, Lord of Pestilence, was a sacred thing, a divine gift handed down to men by the most powerful of the gods. Yet there were so very few who would accept that blessing, clinging to their tired old lives like rats to a sinking ship. The cult of the goddess Shallya had arisen to feed on that foolishness, to drive the breath of Nurgle from the bodies of man. The Chaos champion gripped the hilt of his decaying sword. This would be more than a simple raid, more than slaughter in the name of the Dark Gods. For Pulstlitz, this would be avenging sacrilege, exterminating an affront to the god whom he served.

The plague champion directed his gaze to the ragged figures encamped outside the walls of the hospice. He could see the sickly green aura that seemed to hover over each one, the mark of the Plague God. These were men in whom the blessing of Nurgle had firmly established itself, beyond the power of the Shallyan priestesses to drive from their bodies. They were already claimed by Nurgle, already walking the road that would lead them to the Plague God's realm. But before that, they would serve Nurgle one last time.

Pulstlitz looked over to the brooding ranks of his warband – black-armoured Chaos warriors, ragged diseased mutants and cultists of the Plague God, and the furred shapes of goat-headed pestigors. The champion allowed their feral anticipation to wash over him, letting their eagerness to avenge this insult to their god fire his own ambition. He drew his rusted sword, filth sizzling upon the grass at his feet.

'Drive the rabble to the wallz!' the droning voice of Pulstlitz bellowed. 'Let them know we have come! Let them know Death iz here!'

SABARRA STOOD WITHIN the old courtyard, sitting upon an upended barrel that had been cast aside by the priestesses when its contents had been distributed among their charges. The bounty hunter tried not to think about the sickly wretches lying all around him, focusing instead on the task at hand. The steel frame of his arquebus rested on his knees as the bounty hunter busied himself with scrubbing the inside of the barrel, removing any residual powder lingering within the weapon. It was a tedious, automatic task for Sabarra, and his mind did not need to concentrate upon his work. Instead, he mulled over his arrangement with Brunner and the price on Riano's head. Every hunt had its dangers, but with the red pox all around him, Sabarra was quickly coming to the conclusion that the wealth being offered for Riano was not equal to the risk.

The sound of screams tore Sabarra from his labour. The bounty hunter turned his head in the direction from which the sound had come. It was repeated, and joined by others, becoming a cacophony of terror rising from outside the walls of the hospice. Sabarra jumped up, racing toward the narrow, cross-shaped windows that opened from the walls. He was swiftly joined by temple guards, priestesses and those supplicants still healthy enough to care about what was going on outside.

The bounty hunter's view was partially blocked by the frightened, ragged bodies of the sick rabble that had been camped outside the hospice, their dirty hands and boil-ridden faces filling much of the window. But there were infrequent views of other figures beyond them, the creatures that had put the fear into the rabble and driven them to claw at the walls, begging for sanctuary. Sabarra grimaced, for he had seen their like not long ago – the same sort of diseased, mutated scum he had helped Brunner fight on the road to Decimas.

The bounty hunter pulled away from the window, removing a small paper tube from one of the pouches on his belt, ripping it open with his teeth and pouring the blackpowder down the gaping mouth of his arquebus. Sabarra's hand rose to the belt of steel garros he wore, removing one of the deadly darts. But he hesitated as he prepared to pound the spike into the barrel of his weapon. He turned his eyes back to the windows, now completely filled by groping hands and desperate faces. He'd never be able to find a target with the rabble crowded so close to the temple. Whatever warlord led the Chaos vermin assaulting this place was crafty, herding the sick toward the walls to foil any archery that might be brought to bear on him.

The sound of frenzied pounding at the massive wooden doors of the hospice rose above the screams and cries for mercy. The sounds of terror grew louder from the direction of the door and were soon punctuated by other sounds Sabarra knew only too well; the sounds of blades cutting into flesh and men choking upon their own blood. Temple guards tore themselves away from the windows, hurrying toward the doors. Several of the men put their shoulders to the portal, prepared to defend it against the coming attack.

The guards leaning against the door withdrew, screaming in mortal agony. Sabarra cringed as he saw the skin sloughing away from their arms where they had been holding the door, the links of their chainmail visibly corroding as rust gnawed at them. Behind them, the door was similarly being assailed, the aged wood beginning to crumble and crack as rot consumed it. Iron fittings fell to the floor, devoured by rust. Wooden panels cracked and warped, as though infested with fungus. Far quicker than the eye could follow, the doors aged and withered, at last crashing inward.

Armoured figures filled the opening beyond the door, grim shapes of steel and corruption, their faces hidden behind gruesome helmets. Beside them, leaning tiredly upon a staff of human bones, a goat-headed monster gestured proudly at its sorcerous handiwork. The armoured warriors paid the shaman little heed, striding forward across the ruined portal, crushing its rotten substance into dust beneath their feet.

One of the warriors lifted his sword, filth dripping from its edge, pointing it at those cowering before his approach. A wrathful voice droned from behind the warrior's insect-shaped helm. 'Make of thizz plaze a zacrement to Nurgle!' the monster's voice roared. 'Leave none alive!'

In response to the plague champion's wrath, three white-clad priestesses stepped forward, their voices lowered in a soft chant. Despite the severity of the situation, and the fact that in all likelihood he was going to die horribly in a matter of moments, Sabarra felt a sense of calm flow into him. The reaction of the Chaos warriors was markedly different. The armoured monsters flinched, taking several steps backward, seemingly repulsed by the soothing chant. The insect-helmed leader looked over toward his bestial shaman. The creature nodded its horned head and began to mutter in its own braying voice.

Almost instantly, the sense of calm began to fade as the beastman's dark invocation fouled the very air. The Chaos warriors strode forward once more. The few temple guards who had not been reduced to screaming husks by the decaying sorcery of the shaman rushed forward, interposing themselves between the five warriors and the priestesses. Pulstlitz waved his warriors forward, content to allow them to slake their fury on the spear-men, just as he had been content to let the mob of mutants and pestigors bloody their blades on the rabble outside the walls of the hospice. The Chaos champion was interested in only one sort of prey, and with the few soldiers occupied there was no one to stand between himself and his prey.

Pulstlitz glared down at the white-clad women. They refused to open their eyes, concentrating entirely upon their sacred prayer. The plague champion snorted deri-sively. Sometimes the most satisfying things in life were also the easiest to acquire. 'Tonight, you zhall cower before my god and beg hizz forgivenezz!' Pulstlitz lifted his blade, pausing to savour the moment, then brought the polluted steel rushing downward.

The plague blade stopped short of striking flesh, the sound of crashing steel ringing out as another blade intercepted it. A dull fire seemed to glow within the keen edge of Drakesmalice as the enchanted blade crashed against the polluted metal of the Chaos sword. Pulstlitz recoiled from the unexpected parry. He turned his insect-eyed helm to face the fool who thought to stand between himself and those who had profaned his god.

The brown sack-cloth of a supplicant hung about Brunner's pale figure, sweat dripping from his frame as he struggled to remain on his feet. The Tears of Shallya were posed of miraculous properties, but they were not able to instantly erase days of inactivity and fatigue. The plague champion chortled within his corroded helm. Here, perhaps, was a man worthy of killing, a soul that warranted being sent screaming to the Plague God. Pulstlitz nodded, then swung his foul blade at the bounty hunter's neck. Brunner intercepted the powerful stroke, turning it aside with a manoeuvre he had learned from a Tobaran duellist. The foolish man was skilled, Pulstlitz conceded, but he could not hope to fend off the plague blade indefinitely and it would take but a single scratch from the infected steel to kill him.

However long their little struggle might last, Pulstlitz was certain of the outcome.

SABARRA LIFTED THE heavy arquebus to his cheek, his narrowed eyes considering the carnage unfolding all around him. The guards were almost all dead, but the plague warriors had been mobbed by a desperate pack of supplicants, their malnourished forms clinging to the butchers, slowing the armoured giants with the weight of their dying bodies. Closer at hand, the leader of the plague warriors had been engaged by Brunner. How Sabarra's rival had been able to rise from his sick bed, much less find the strength to wield a sword, was a problem Sabarra would worry about later. The Tilean was relieved that Brunner had stopped the insect-helmed monster, because he had a feeling that if the plague champion were to reach the priestesses, then no one would be leaving the hospice alive. There was another struggle going on, apart from the crash of swords. Gods were at battle here, striving against one another through their chosen priests.

Sabarra turned the arquebus toward the archway, where the twisted shaman continued to bray and moan in its grisly voice. Sickly green light gleamed from the monster's eyes. Sabarra muttered a prayer to Shallya, then put the smouldering hemp match to the touch pan of his arquebus. The weapon shook as the blackpowder ignited and the roar of the discharge overwhelmed all other sounds. Almost at once, the sense of soothing calm returned to Sabarra. As the echoes of the shot faded, the chanting of the priestesses returned, now strident and loud, as though the tones were a caged river flowing through a broken dam. The smoke began to clear and Sabarra was pleased to see the steel spike of his garro sheathed in the dead beastman's skull.

The plague warriors moaned as they reacted to the fading magic of their sorcerer. The loathsome runes carved upon their armour began to weep blood, and it was with painful, awkward movements that the monsters retreated back toward the archway. Outside, the frightened wail of the other plague creatures sounded, followed by the frenzied retreat of malformed shapes, slinking back into the comforting darkness of the woods.

PULTSLITZ SHUDDERED AS the protective magics of the priestesses surrounded him. Without the baleful power of the shaman to counteract the magic energies, the antagonistic energies wracked the plague champion. He felt the healing powers of the goddess entering him, sapping his strength and coordination. The plague champion lifted his blade to ward off the bounty hunter, but the move was too slow. Brunner's sword bit into Pulstlitz's hand, tearing through the corrupt armour. The steel gauntlet dropped to the flagstones with a crash, the plague blade tumbling from its slack fingers. No hand filled the polluted glove, instead a mass of black-shelled cockroaches scuttled into the light, their hideous shapes crumbling as the hostile energies drove the corruption from their tiny shapes.

Pulstlitz, clutching the stump of his arm to his chest, retreated before Brunner. The monster gave a droning howl of fury, then turned and raced from the courtyard. Brunner watched him go, sagging weakly to the ground. He was not one to leave an enemy alive, but what strength had been restored to him had been all but spent during their brief duel. He had a feeling, however, that their paths would cross again, and that only one of them would walk away from that encounter.

Sabarra walked toward the Reiklander, crouching beside him on the flagstones. The Tilean looked Brunner up and down, a cold smile tugging at his weasel-like face.

'So,' Sabarra said, 'it looks like you're recovered. Suppose we have that little talk now?'

BRUNNER STALKED THROUGH the corridors of the hospice like a wolf on the prowl. He had mended his armour, wearing it now once more, his weapons again hanging from his belt. The last traces of the red boils were slowly fading away, sinking back into his skin. Miraculous was the only word to describe the fantastic elixir Elisia had given him. The bounty hunter saw the priestess crouched beside one of the pallets in the ward he had so recently inhabited. He strode down the narrow path between the sick beds toward her.

Sabarra had been quite hasty in his departure, leaving Brunner to complete his recovery on his own. Brunner hoped that his rival was having a nice time in the little village of Montorri. He hadn't lied to Sabarra, Montorri was indeed where Riano's uncle lived. He had simply failed to mention that he no longer had any reason to believe Riano would be found there.

Elisia looked up as the bounty hunter's shadow fell across her, the hate undimmed in her eyes. Brunner respected that, a woman of principle and standards. It had been out of respect for that quality in her and what she had done for him that he had waited this long. The smart move would have been to act as quickly as possible, to reduce how much time Sabarra had to realise his mistake. Instead, Brunner had bided his time.

'How is he?' the bounty hunter asked. Elisia glared at him, wiping a lock of stray hair from her face.

'What you have been waiting for has happened,' she told him, her voice as hard as the roots of the Grey

Mountains. 'The red pox has won. He is dead.' Elisia smoothed the front of her robe as she rose to her feet. 'You are no better than a vulture, a jackal,' she spat. Brunner did not bother to contradict her, instead he stared down into the dead man's face, the face he had recognised when Sabarra had brought him into this room. The face of Riano. When plague had struck Decimas, the outlaw had fled here. If Brunner still gave any thought to the gods, he might have seen the workings of fate that he and Riano should meet by so strange a turn of circumstance. But the bounty hunter no longer gave much thought to gods, only gold.

'Have some of your people help me drag him outside,' Brunner told Elisia, his gloved hand closed about the massive serrated knife he had named the Headsman. 'That way you won't have far to carry the part I don't need.'

IN THE SERVICE
OF SIGMAR
by Adam Troke

The beginning of the end.

LUKAS LOWERED HIS shoulder and threw his weight against the doorway. The force of his body shattered the rusted lock which held the door closed and bent the hinges apart in an instant, causing Lukas to stumble, drawn on by his own momentum. He fell out of the stinking apothecary and into the alley beyond. The first dim rays of morning shone onto his face, chasing away the darkness and the horror that lay behind him. Gasping for breath, he tugged sharply at the rope that secured his burden, a white-faced and injured man who staggered a few paces behind him. He cast his eyes over the group assembled before him in the morning mist.

A dozen soldiers, clad in black leathers and armed with brightly polished halberds formed a defensive line between Lukas and three other figures all of which the young warrior recognised. The first was Rosabella, cradling her injured arm, her face drawn and her brow beaded with sweat despite the cool of the morning.

Next in the group was Henckler. Kriesmann Henckler, Templar of the Cult of Sigmar, a witch hunter. Short, barely five feet if Lukas's eye was any judge, with the kind of fat that a man has when he eats far too much and exercises far too little. His hair was thin and receded, as if he was losing the battle to remain thatched. He stood hunched behind the warriors, apparently ill at ease, regardless of his halberd-armed protectors and unassailable status. The third figure towered over the rest like a warrior from legend. Tall and strong, with a nose hooked like a hunting hawk, Constantin Brandaur was the very embodiment of a knight, the Grand Master of the Order of the Hammer. Lukas looked at him and his heart soared. Brandaur was here, his work was done.

'Take him into custody,' murmured the witch hunter, pointing a finger at the battered figure that Lukas held bound.

At Henckler's command, half of the halberd-armed warriors pressed forwards, seized him from Lukas and dragged him away by the rope. A thousand pleas and excuses bubbled forth from his cracked and bruised lips. He scrabbled and clawed at the muck and litter coating the alley floor, pulling desperately against the rope, terror widening his eyes and giving him a burst of desperate courage. Indifferent to his pathetic supplications, the soldiers silenced his new-found protests of innocence with a balled fist to the guts. They had heard it all hundreds of times before and they certainly had no interest in the lies of another heretic damned to die, not this early in the morning.

Breaking away from the templar master and Rosabella, Henckler stepped towards Lukas, his beady eyes glinting. With a gesture he waved the young warrior over to him, and Lukas obeyed at once, eager to please his employer and be done with the night's business. They paused in the shelter of a boarded-up doorway, huddling conspiratorially in its lee. With a small cough to clear his throat the witch hunter spoke again.

'Lukas, my boy,' he said, keeping his voice low. 'You managed your errand then?' It was not a question that needed an answer, and Lukas stayed his tongue until comment was required. 'There are things I need to ask you about tonight, Lukas.' The man's voice was quiet and intense, and his eyes glistened eagerly. Licking his fat lips to moisten them, he continued. 'I need to know everything that happened, every detail. What happened to the...' he groped for a word, his mouth working silently for a moment, 'the product, where it ended up? How you were able to slay the enemy. Any wounds you suffered. Tell me boy, tell me everything.'

Lukas swallowed hard, and nodded, running a gloved hand through his hair before clearing his throat and beginning, omitting no detail.

Be honest in all your dealings, though it may cost you
your life.

IT WAS FREEZING cold, and dangerously dark in the alleyway, as Lukas Atzwig slowly picked his way through the altquarter towards his target. Tall and strong, with smartly cropped blond hair and a handsome face that bore only a few scars and no pockmarks, Lukas was an imposing figure. Clad in black and brown leathers, with a sword at his side and a knife in his boot he was well protected for the night's work. The small box was in his left hand, leaving his right free to protect himself if the need arose. The crunch and squelch of detritus beneath his feet and the scuttling of small, creeping things were the only sounds. Even the shrieks and cries that punctuated any normal Altdorf night seemed curiously absent as Lukas picked his way from one alleyway to the next.

The instructions were simple enough, he reasoned, stepping over a deep pool of stinking liquid. Gain entry by making use of their abhorrent secret sign. Traverse their foul underground domain, and locate Garramond Kerr. Capture him and slay his accomplices. Bring the 'product' back to the witch hunter, and leave everything within as it was found, to facilitate his investigations.

Lukas Atzwig was a squire in the Order of the Hammer and danger held little fear for him now – he had seen far too much. For seven years he had served Gotthard Jaeger with enthusiasm and dedication, but the old knight had fallen in battle at Middenheim, hewn down by a servant of Chaos, leaving Lukas masterless and totally at the mercy of the order. And merciful though it was, the order could not merely elevate someone of low birth such as Lukas to a full knight, merely because his master had died – such an act would be at odds with the noble lineage of the order and make mockery of its heritage. Constantin Brandaur had explained this to him in hushed tones the day that Gotthard had fallen. If there was anything he could have done, he would have. The grand master assured him of that.

Since then Lukas had excelled himself, fighting at the side of the other squires in the great battles in the north fought by the order, slaying warriors of Chaos with a skill and zeal that all could see. Now, weeks later, as Lukas crept towards his goal, he could see that Brandaur had been true to his word, and this task would see him right. He would become a full knight of the order. He could feel it.

Constantin Brandaur and Kriesmann Henckler had met with him that morning in a strangely clandestine meeting held in the private chambers of the grand master himself. The presence of the witch hunter had put him ill at ease for a moment, for Lukas had heard of squires and even knights succumbing to the madness of

Chaos, especially since the war in the north. As the meeting had progressed, though, the sense of concern had been replaced with elation – this was Lukas's chance. Henckler the witch hunter had outlined his need for Lukas in his plans, explaining how a vile cult was gnawing at the underbelly of Altdorf and a man of subtlety and skill was needed to bring it to its knees. Henckler had planned for another to complete this errand, but an ill fate had befallen him, and with time running short he had turned to his old friend, Constantin. In turn, the grand master recommended Lukas, who was both brave and cunning enough to complete the task, and in exchange for his cooperation, offered him that which he most wanted: a place within the Order of the Hammer, as a full knight. Lukas reasoned that fate had conspired to give him this rare chance to prove himself before Sigmar and earn the right to stand beside his brother knights.

The wall of the shop was pitted and dirty, and paint was peeling from the stone in patches. Checking the worn and faded sign hanging from the old shop front, Lukas made sure he was in the correct place, before raising his hand to beat against the door of the dilapidated apothecary's, just as he had been told to do. Three taps fast, then three slow – the correct way to gain the attention of those within. He waited only a moment, his breath clouding around him in the cold air, before the small peephole in the door slid open. A pair of eyes, the left one milky with blindness, glared at him from within before harshly demanding his business.

'I'm here to see the master,' he answered simply, being sure to keep to the script as he had been told it. The eyes staring at him gave no sign of recognition, and Lukas almost faltered, before continuing. 'I've brought the product,' he said slowly, to avoid mistakes, 'and I have not been followed.'

The figure behind the door still didn't acknowledge him, just stared at him with open hostility. If it was meant to be intimidating to the young warrior though, the door guard was disappointed; Lukas had spent hours on parade under the gaze of men far better and more imposing than the dishevelled miscreant glaring through the peephole. After what felt like an age, the eyes moved away from the doorway to be replaced with a small wooden hammer of Sigmar, apparently worn and well-used.

'What make you of this?' asked a gruff voice. 'What of Sigmar's hammer?'

Lukas felt a small panic rise in his chest as he knew what was required of him. Fighting against the feelings of betrayal and dishonesty that boiled within his breast, he coughed once for effect before spitting directly at the hammer. The spittle splashed across its surface and dribbled down its length to drip onto the ledge of the peephole. Lukas felt his cheeks flush at the sight of what he had done, but steeled himself against it, clenching his fists. With any luck his face was already red from the cold. The hammer was withdrawn and the peephole slid shut with a snap. He could hear the bolts being drawn inside, and moments later the alleyway was flooded with light.

'In,' said the voice that had spoken before.

Lukas obeyed, stepping into the light, blinking as his eyes adjusted from the gloom outside. The small room was clearly once an apothecary's just as the sign outside suggested. Wooden counters were littered with broken vials and bottles of green, brown and clear glass.

As well as the door ward, a scrawny looking fellow of average height with long, greasy black hair, there were three others in the room. Another man, this one of impressive bulk, lurked on the other side of one of the counters, his finger on the trigger of a crossbow, pointed directly at Lukas. The crossbowman had the look of a fighter gone to fat, his muscles sagged and wasted from lack of proper use. The next was a woman, although only a second glance revealed it, her short brown hair was unevenly shaped into a bowl cut and her muscular frame was far from feminine. In her hand was a short sword, and more so than any of the others, she looked fit to use it. Her face was thin and her eyes were sunk deep into her skull, like someone who had gone too long without good sleep. She chewed continually, her eyes never wavering from Lukas as he looked around.

The fourth figure, and the final one to catch his eye, was a good looking woman, made all the more so by her ugly companions. Her plaited hair was the colour of a newly minted coin, and her smooth, clear skin set her above the others at a glance. A few hot meals and Lukas reasoned she might not look too bad at all. Reluctantly he pulled his eyes away from her; he had no time for such distractions now.

'Drop your sword,' said the first of the two women, the unfortunate-looking one, motioning at him with her own weapon. Her voice was harsh and her words were clipped and short. 'Do it now, or else.'

Lukas hesitated only a moment before complying, unbuckling his sword belt and letting it fall gently to the wooden floor with a muffled thud. He stood stock still as they looked him over with unveiled malice.

'Check him out, Bella,' she commanded. The more attractive of the two women came forward and roughly searched him, her hands sifting through pockets without any pause for thought. She made a show of taking a handful of coins from him and pocketed them with a wink that drew chuckles from her accomplices.

'That's all he's got,' said the searcher, motioning to the sword before picking it up and stepping away, back behind one of the counters.

'Come on then, let's not keep him waiting,' said the woman, curling a dirty finger and motioning for Lukas to follow her. And with that she turned on her heel, pulling aside a filthy curtain to reveal a hole roughly smashed into the interior wall that led into a dimly lit passageway. Bella followed her, then the man with the milky eye. The crossbow-armed thug waited till last, motioning for Lukas to walk ahead of him.

'Got to keep you where I can see you,' he said, patting his crossbow knowingly. 'Any time I want to use this, you're dead.' He chuckled to himself, enjoying his little joke.

'I doubt that,' answered Lukas, before pressing on into the gloom behind the others, leaving Crossbow-man to bring up the rear.

Protect the innocent, though it may cost you your life.

THE GROUP DISAPPEARED down a dimly lit corridor where the occasional candle guttered on the walls, impaled on bent and rusty nails rather than proper holders. The grimy corridor, barely tall enough for Lukas to stand upright, led slowly downwards and eventually into an open sewer. The rank odour assailed his nose and drew bile to his throat. If the others noticed the stench they did not show it though, so Lukas pressed on, choking back the urge to vomit.

The group continued in the murky gloom for a hundred paces more, before halting. Lukas could hear metal scraping against stone for a moment, and the sound of someone grunting with effort. Then they pressed forwards again, stooping to duck through a hole in the stonework.

As his eyes adjusted, Lukas realised he was in a large room, the ceiling only just high enough for him to stand upright in. It was barely light enough to see, but despite the darkness, Lukas felt his heart leap to his throat.

The walls of the room were lined with cages made of rusting bars of thick iron. In all, there were thirty cages, perhaps forty and each one of them was occupied. Lukas stumbled forwards unbidden, his eyes wide, trying to take in the details, but scared to do so.

Huddled in the first cage he looked in was a bundle of rags, about the size of a large dog. It twitched occasionally, moaning in a soft, mournful voice. Lukas stooped to get a better look, and wished he hadn't. A small child, perhaps a girl, looked up at him from under the rags that covered her. Her eyes were pools of pain and suffering, her face was plastered with muck and great streaks of snot were gathered under her nose from too much crying. She lay on the cold stone in amongst her own waste, powerless against the iron bars that contained her. In all his life Lukas had never seen such a pitiful sight. He felt fire burning behind his eyes, and blinked hard to extinguish it, moving on to the next cage and the next. One after another they revealed similar horrors. Girls and boys, none older than fifteen or sixteen, in squalid prisons. The sounds of weeping and pleading had got louder since Lukas had begun to pay interest.

'Help us,' one voice piped up, a boy by the sound of it. 'Please sir, for Sigmar's sake, help us.' Lukas turned away, glaring at Kerr's accomplices.

'What is the meaning of this?' he barked, feeling his anger rising within him. It felt good, and he let it loose, his body shaking imperceptibly as his fury filled him. 'What the *hell* is this place?'

The others, who had been watching him with indifference, now gave him their full attention. The crossbow was pointed at his heart once again.

'Is there some problem?' asked the man with the milky eye. 'I thought we were all of the same persuasion.' His hand went to the dagger on his belt, although he tried to keep his voice level.

'What are these children doing here?' Lukas blurted, having to raise his voice to be heard above the pleas for help, which were getting louder and more frequent with each passing moment.

'They're for the trade,' Bella said, her voice calm and clear. 'That's why they're here. The master trades them for the stuff. You know.' She looked at him, her own eyes wide and imploring.

'It's disgusting,' said Lukas, his mind reeling, desperately trying to find a way to free these poor children.

'It's part of the plan. You knew about the plan before you came here, *Lukas*. Don't get on your high horse now.' Beside her the others bristled, obviously considering taking action against Lukas now that he was creating a scene. Lukas was silent though. Bella had said his name.

Henckler had told him that he had an agent on the inside, and that, when the time was right, the agent would make themself known to him. With a sinking feeling, he realised that Bella was that agent. He was endangering her as well as himself and the mission.

'Right,' he said, shrugging and hoping that was an end to it.

With no more than a nod, they made to leave the room, pushing open a heavy wooden door, studded with bolts and reinforced with strips of iron. In the corridor beyond they passed three hunched figures stalking lithely the other way. They were stunted and small, covered in tattered robes with hoods pulled over their heads to mask their faces. Lukas couldn't help but stare. Each held, in gnarled, malformed hands, great lengths of chain. Their odour was so strong that it overpowered the lingering stench of the sewer. Lukas paused for a moment once they were past, and turned back, looking into the cage room. It was dark and ill lit, but he was sure he saw the hooded figures opening the cage doors. The pleas from within the room rose in volume, until Crossbow-man slammed the door shut.

Meet your foe face-on, and slay him in Sigmar's name.

THEY TRAVERSED THE corridors again for perhaps a minute more, Lukas taking the time to gather his thoughts and steel himself against the horrors that he had seen. A deep sense of shame had settled in his guts.

A piercing scream of pain pulled him from his reverie and back into the damp corridor, standing before yet another doorway. There was a dull *whooshing* sound and another scream and then silence.

The woman at the front pushed the door open and stepped inside, followed by Bella and Milky-eye. Lukas followed next, bracing himself against whatever was within. In his wildest imaginings he would never have expected what he saw.

The chamber was neat and tidy. Work desks sat at right-angles with quills and inks and mountains of parchment on each. Carefully stacked tools sat on benches, with tubes, coils and all manner of devices used by the engineers of the Empire. Lukas absorbed all of this in an instant, turning his gaze on the wild-eyed figure holding a handgun.

Or what looked like one. It was longer than any arquebus he had seen, longer even than a Hochland long-rifle and wider too. It had pipes and coils protruding from it at various points along it, several of them leading from it to an enormous metal contraption a few feet away. Like a boiler in a steam baths, or a vast oven in a bakery, it consisted of a series of furnaces and huge copper globes, each with a small dial attached to it. A series of levers was at one end, extending from a large iron box, and the whole thing was a maze of trembling pipes and riveted metal. It was vast and complicated. Whatever else Garramond Kerr was, there was no doubt he was a genius.

Kerr held the gun in shaking hands, elated. He matched the description Henckler had given Lukas perfectly: tall and thin, with grey hair and a bushy moustache. He wore a thick leather apron and sturdy leather gloves to protect him, probably from the weapon he held, the barrel of which hissed and steamed, dripping a thick viscous liquid to bubble and spit on the stone floor.

His target had been a bound figure tied to a stake against the opposite wall. The figure, now dead, steamed and dissolved before Lukas's eyes. Even the bones of his body were eaten away and the rock wall behind him showed signs of disintegration too. Lukas shuddered as he realised that another victim was bound and gagged beside the first. The figure wore plates of steel, looted from the Imperial army by the look of them, more armour than a common footman ever wore. With a sinking feeling, Lukas realised that some of the bubbling liquid pooling at the feet of the first victim had been armour just like it. His mind shuddered at the devastation a weapon like that could wreak on armoured knights.

As Lukas recoiled inwardly, Kerr discussed something animatedly with the hooded figure beside him. Just like the hooded figures from the cage room, this creature was hunched and small. This one, however, was clearly inhuman. A hairy pink tail protruded from beneath the hem of its filthy robes, and a dirty, pox-marked nose extended from it's hood. A *ratman*. Lukas's master had told him of them. Vile servants of Chaos, a cancer on the Empire. Enemies of Sigmar.

The ratman and Kerr gesticulated wildly at the next waiting victim, who shuddered in terror, struggling against his restraints.

'Works, it does,' the rat creature shrieked, pointing at the smouldering mush to make his point. 'Pay now. Pay now, man thing.' Its voice was high-pitched, and sounded strange coming from a creature that was not a human. The sound of it made Lukas feel sick. Kerr seemed to be deflecting whatever payment was demanded, for he offered to demonstrate the weapon again enthusiastically, the strain of the situation evident in his eyes. 'Pay now,' reinforced the ratman one more time.

This time, a shadow detached itself from the corner of the room – another rat man, this one clad in black, its weapon bared and menacing. Its inhuman features were undisguised like the first. It only came to Lukas's chest in height, but it exuded an aura of danger unlike anyone else in the room.

Backed into a corner, Kerr turned to Lukas and the others who had just entered the room.

'Do you have the product?' he asked, his voice shaking and unsure. His eyes scanned the group, before settling on Lukas. 'Do you have the warpstone?'

'Yes,' Lukas answered stepping forward, brandishing the small wooden box. 'Yes, sir.'

'Good, good boy. Bring it here then,' he enthused, apparently greatly relieved.

Lukas stepped forward, flanked by Milky-eyed-man. As he approached, his mind reeled, looking for a way to recover his weapon from Bella.

'Give me box, man thing,' the lead ratman demanded, its gnarled claws outstretched. 'Now.'

Lukas smiled thinly, and unclasped the box for the first time, opened the lid and revealed the dully glowing green stones within. Warpstone. The eyes of the rat, murky black orbs, stared hungrily at the box's contents. With a twitch it stepped forward, grasping for it, but Lukas slammed it shut with a *snap*.

Dropping the small wooden container, Lukas reached down across to Milky-eye and gripped the dagger sheathed at his waist. It was about a foot and a half long and razor sharp, and as Lukas drew it from the sheath he shoved the man hard, causing him to stumble and fall away. Turning back to the ratman, he saw its eyes widen in disbelief as he rammed the knife hard at its throat. Lukas acted so fast that the creature had no time to act and the blade pierced its throat to the hilt. Blood bubbled to the surface instantly, and the ratman gurgled, spitting crimson.

As swiftly as he had struck, he drew the blade out again in a fountain of gore, spinning on his heel to face the other ratman, which in turn was lashing out at him, its own wicked dagger raised high. Its attack was cut short by a burst of intense green light that severed it at the waist and blasted one of the work benches apart. Kerr was screaming and ranting, and had fired in his panic. The second ratman fell smouldering to the floor in two halves. The smell of sulphur and burning flesh filled the room.

Not giving the mad engineer a chance to fire again, Lukas attacked him instead, swinging the dagger upwards. Hatred drove Lukas on and the dagger came up, slashing through two of the coils running from the gun and up into Kerr's hand. The engineer shrieked in pain and horror as three of his fingers were severed. Involuntarily, he dropped the gun and fell in a mewling heap on the floor, cradling his hand as blood pumped steadily from the stumps where his fingers had been.

His main targets dealt with, Lukas turned back to Kerr's enforcers, who were finally beginning to lurch into action. Crossbow-man was first, firing the bolt with trembling fingers. Lukas winced as the shot flew wide, striking something behind him with a wet thud. As the man dropped his crossbow and struggled to unhook a club from his belt, Lukas rushed at him, knife ready. Milky-eye intercepted him, punching him hard on the shoulder and caused him to stumble, then turned to face his attacker. As Lukas fought for his balance he could see Bella and the other woman drawing their own weapons.

Panic galvanised Lukas into action again and he mashed his fist into his assailant's face, smashing his nose with the force of the blow. Milky-eye fell away with a shriek. Crossbow-man had his club out and ready and swung hard at Lukas. The young squire ducked back as he had been trained to do, before stepping in as the weight of the club forced his opponent to over swing. Crossbow-man bellowed in pain as Lukas stabbed the dagger into his guts. Blood flooded out from the wound making the handle slick, and Lukas lost his hold on it as the bulky fighter collapsed, screaming, to the floor.

Panicking, without a weapon in his hand, Lukas spun around to see Bella fighting furiously with the other woman. Both displayed excellent skills with their weapons. Bella was faster, ducking and weaving with her rapier, while the other was stronger and took great swings, any of which could have beheaded her opponent.

A blow to the side of his face sent Lukas reeling, bringing him back to the fight in an explosion of stars. He fell to one knee, his ears ringing from the blow. Milky-eye had picked up a wrench from one of the work stations and was wielding it like a cudgel. Lukas blocked the next blow with his forearm, a flash of pain exploding as the metal object struck him hard. Before his attacker could strike again though, Lukas powered forward into him. The man was far smaller, so Lukas simply tackled him by the waist to the floor and landed heavily on top of him. Both men scrabbled, fists punching and legs kicking as Lukas pulled himself up, sitting astride his foe and pinning his arms down with his knees. Milky-eye howled as Lukas threw his first punch and broke the man's jaw. His second cracked his cheekbone and on the third, Milky-eye lost consciousness. Lukas punched him half a dozen more times for good measure before staggering back to his feet. His body ached from his minor injuries.

Kerr still lay cradling his arm, while behind him his machine was juddering ominously, thick greenish smoke spewing from the pipes that Lukas had severed. Checking Kerr wasn't going anywhere, Lukas turned back to his enemies. Bella stood over the other woman, who was clearly dead, and wiped blood from her rapier with a length of cloth. Crossbow-man had foolishly pulled the knife from his own belly and now vainly tried to stop himself bleeding to death, thick red fluid bubbling from between his fingers. Milky-eye looked dead. Either way though, he was in no state to fight back. Both the ratmen had expired too. The leader had finished twitching some time ago, and lay still.

Turning to Bella, Lukas made a small bow, a friendly guesture, and spoke.

'Lukas Atzwig, at your service,' he said, wiping his sweaty forehead with his sleeve.

'Rosabella Wolfe, at yours,' she replied, taking off his sword from around her waist before passing it back to him. The machine near Kerr was vibrating furiously, the copper pipes chiming as they clanged against one another. All the dials were at red. 'We need to get him out of here,' she added, moving towards Kerr.

Lukas looked down, putting his sword belt back on. He was almost done buckling it when the shot rang out. Lukas looked up, to see Bella stumble away from Kerr, clutching her arm.

'Get away from me!' the engineer shrieked, his face red. 'I'm trying to save the city!' He brandished the pistol at Lukas menacingly, but he could see at a glance it had only one barrel. In two steps he was beside the engineer. Lukas kicked him hard, first in the hand, sending the weapon skittering away, then again in the groin, the chest and the face. Kerr whimpered and lay still, bruised and defeated.

'Are you injured?' Lukas asked, turning to Rosabella, who cradled her arm gingerly.

'I'm fine,' she lied, eyeing the machine behind them. 'But we need to get out of here. Fast.'

'Agreed,' said Atzwig, turning back to the engineer. 'If you can go on ahead and meet up with Henckler, I'll bring him.' Even as he spoke he was pulling off the man's leather glove to reveal the bloody stumps of his fingers. Kerr moaned in pain, but didn't resist.

'All right,' she agreed, after a moment's thought before heading for the door. 'Can you remember the way?' she asked, looking back. Lukas nodded once, and she was gone.

Lukas removed his gloves and got back to work. It took him a minute or two to improvise a bandage and wrap Kerr's bleeding hand in it, and in that time the engineer came around again. He ranted about his precious machine, about his work that had been ruined. He shrieked about the worthlessness of the hammer-god that watched over the Empire, and how only science could save it from Chaos. Lukas cuffed him sharply around the head for his blasphemy, and he fell quiet again.

Next, Lukas scoured the room for the box he had dropped, gathering up the oddly glowing green rocks and carefully placing them back into the wooden case. The machine was spewing thick green vapours now, and Lukas choked as he worked. Once done, he wedged the box into his belt and looked for a rope. In the end he had to settle for the one that bound the second victim to the stake. A bolt protruded from his eye socket and Lukas avoided looking at it as he worked. He fashioned a noose and lassoed Kerr. By now the engineer was pleading with him, urging Lukas to allow him to save his precious machine. Lukas cuffed him again, so Kerr changed tack, insisting that they flee instead. The machine, he warned, would explode unless they did.

Scalding liquid that burned like fire began to spray from the machine as rivets and bolts shook loose. Both Lukas and Kerr were sprayed by a fine green mist that itched and stung as they fled the room. They had barely slammed the door behind them before they were flung from their feet as the giant machine exploded, the booming echo deafening them both for a time.

The End of the End.

HENCKLER SMILED AS Lukas finished explaining his tale, and patted him gingerly on the shoulder with a gloved hand. Lukas couldn't help but feel sullied by his part in the mission, despite its obvious success. At a wave from Henckler, Brandaur approached, his eyes tired.

'Wait here,' Hencker cautioned Lukas, before turning away to speak to the templar master. In whispered tones they conversed. Although Lukas could not hear what was said in detail, he heard his name mentioned and felt a nagging doubt enter his mind.

Eventually Henckler turned back to him, his ruddy jowls shaking from side to side as he shook his head. Behind him Brandaur walked away, disappearing into the morning mist.

Lukas felt a cold knot of fear tighten in his belly.

'Lukas, you did well,' Henckler said, his voice quiet and low, 'but you have allowed yourself to become contaminated with the stuff of Chaos.' He gestured to Lukas's hands, filthy where he had forgotten to put his gloves back on. 'We cannot risk you spreading that taint to others.'

Lukas felt his world spinning as the witch hunter spoke. He felt light-headed and sick. 'What?' he asked, confused. 'I did everything you asked. Everything, witch hunter.'

'I know,' was the reply, cold and hard. 'And Sigmar will love you for it. But I cannot let you contaminate others. There were risks involved, Lukas. We told you there were risks. The threat of contamination is too great.' He shrugged, jamming his hands into the large pockets of his warm coat.

'But you promised me a place in the order. You swore on it.' Lukas was shaking, fear and uncertainty rising in his breast, taking control of him. 'What will happen to me now?'

'Nothing,' replied Henckler, drawing an ornate duelling pistol from within his pocket. 'Nothing at all.'

He fired.

Lukas fell back against the door as the ball took him in the forehead, blasting through his skull and pulping his brain. He slumped to the floor.

Henckler stalked away from Lukas's cooling body, past the guards who moved to gather it up, to where Rosabella Wolfe stood shaking, her hand against her mouth. With eyes as hard as steel he looked at her, measuring her carefully.

'You are quite certain that you weren't contaminated by the warpstone yourself, aren't you?' he asked, no hint of a smile on his face.

Rosabella nodded once. And together they turned, stalked away into the alley and left the soldiers to gather the body for burning.

BLOOD AND SAND
by Matt Ralphs

'The crusades into Araby are a proud leaf in the illustrious history of our Empire. For a hundred years men took up the hammer and sought to bring light and learning into the heathen lands. Many fell, for the path to victory is oft travelled over the bodies of faithful men. And for those who were captured? Well, it was better to die than to become a slave to the men of Araby.'

– From *Armies of the Hammer,*
The Forgotten Crusades

HE KNEW THAT to make a sound was to die.

Echardt Drager winced as sand crunched under his foot. He could hear the deep, rhythmic rasp of the creature's breathing. It remained regular – mercifully undisturbed. Dust motes swirled in a column of light which pierced the gloom, tumbling and turning, kept aloft in the heavy air; illuminated in the light was a patch of scaled skin, the colour of the desert. It reminded Drager of the armour worn by Arabyan warriors: flat, regular-shaped plates of burnished gold that glittered in the sun. But this was no Arabyan soldier, this was a sand dragon.

Despite his fear, he was thrilled. The creatures kept in the emir's bestiary put to shame those of his former lord – the Elector Count of Averland – whom he had served for many years as keeper of the war-beasts before his capture. His Arabyan overseers, recognising his worth, set him to work with the animals, but this was the first time he'd been put in the sand dragon cage.

Drager was within touching distance of the creature. Its body loomed over him, curled sinuously around a boulder. He felt intense heat radiating from its skin; a nerve rippled and scales scratched together, sounding like parchment burning. In the patch of light he spied what he sought: a half-shed scale, about the size of his hand, with a shining new one peeking through beneath.

His fingers closed around the loose scale. It felt like dry leather. He pulled gently and it began to come away. He licked his lips and gave it a tug. His heart missed a beat as the scale tore off. He was felled as the creature's tail whipped out and struck him hard across the chest. The wind was knocked from him as he landed hard on his back. The beast uncurled from around the boulder and hauled itself up onto long hind legs. It turned to face him with fluid grace, its vast, crested head towering up on the end of a lithe neck, black eyes reflecting Drager's terrified face with emotionless curiosity.

Drager saw the dragon's lungs expand and he rolled to one side as its head thrust forward, jaws agape. A blast of burning sand vomited from its throat, rattling against its teeth and blasting the ground where Drager had been a second before. He screamed as scorching particles lacerated his arm and burnt into the flesh. It turned to face him again, head cocked, as if puzzled by something. Drager watched helplessly as it drew in another breath.

Two men, each holding blazing torches, leapt to either side of him, whooping and screaming as they thrust the flames into the dragon's eyes. It bellowed and staggered back, cowering from the light. Drager struggled up and ran for the cage door. His rescuers backed out behind him, keeping their brands held in front as the beast cautiously stalked after them. They stepped into daylight and bolted the cage door shut.

Drager blinked in the bright sun, nursing his blistering arm. He leaned on the heavy cloth draped over the dragon's pen, there to keep out the sun. Drager handed one of the men the scale. He studied it.

'Well done, Empire,' he said in halting Reikspiel. 'This aphrodisiac will replace some of our great emir's lost vitality.' He put the scale in a pouch hanging from his belt. 'You learned valuable lesson today, no? Try not to wake a sleeping sand dragon.'

Drager slumped to the ground as he walked away, chuckling.

IT IS SAID that in Araby, the only people who work in the middle of the day are slaves and slave-drivers. Even sheep, considered by Arabyans to be the lowest of beasts, have the sense to rest in the shade. The sun rode at its zenith, gazing down like a burnished coin, pouring out heat and bleaching all colour from the world.

A line of men – pale except where the heat had burned their skin red – laboured in a line swinging picks along a dusty road. They were tethered together by chains and wore tattered rags. Many had torn strips from their tunics and tied them over their heads. Some still sported the badge of their crusade across their breasts – a knight of the Empire, with the hammer of Sigmar above him, encircled with a ring of flame – as if in defiance of their defeat and capture. These once proud crusaders were now slaves to the people they had sought to subjugate. Around them prowled slave-drivers, armed with whips and cudgels and swathed in long, purple robes and white turbans. They shouted and cursed, and the constant report of the picks was accompanied by the crack of their whips.

Behind them was a city.

It was called Zarekten, and it dominated the valley. A shallow moat – carved through the ochre rock by a river long since dried up – hugged the bottom of a soaring curtain wall. Square towers sprouted along the length of the defences which stretched out from one valley wall and back, like the tip of a spear. The main gate was at its apex, a wide, arched door flanked by two towers. The city gazed blankly through a thousand murder holes. Soldiers patrolled the parapets, long spears over their shoulders, their silver mail coats caught the sunlight and shimmered with many shades of blue. Sloping up behind them as it climbed the rock face was the city itself. Inner walls and bastions were thrown into relief by the sun: flat surfaces dazzled with light, whilst doors, windows, arrow-slits and arches remained black with shadow. As the city climbed ever higher, the defences made way for small, square dwellings with domed roofs. Around these tightly packed buildings was a warren of passages, alleys, bridges, avenues and covered walkways.

Zarekten guarded the entrance to the Great Erg – a blistering, white sand plain visible to the south through the mouth of the valley – and the rich trade routes running through it. It represented the last frontier between the principalities and city-states of the prosperous north, and the nomadic tribes who inhabit the deserts to the south.

Tomas Strauss tore his eyes away from the desert, gulped a breath of hot air and swung his pick into the ground. Every muscle ached and his back felt as if it had been branded with hot coals. He muttered a prayer to Sigmar and made the sign of the hammer with his calloused hands. He spied a slave-driver making his way down the line, dosing out ladles of water to each prisoner. Tomas smiled, it was Huashil. Sigmar had answered him today.

Huashil held the dripping ladle out to Tomas who drank the water, smiled and leaned on his pick. 'Thank you,' he said.

'Slow going, eh, Empire?' Huashil said. He surreptitiously pointed to the ground and dropped two figs at Tomas's feet.

'Aye, but Sigmar lends me strength,' Tomas said, smiling.

Huashil frowned. 'You find your god here, even in the desert? After he abandoned you?'

'Sigmar is everywhere,' Tomas said. 'And he has not abandoned me. I have him always nearby.' He patted the left side of his chest. 'Where do you keep your faith, my friend?'

Huashil was about to speak when searing pain lashed across Tomas's back. He fell to his knees and picked up the figs.

'Work, Empire, work!' a slave-driver screamed in his ear. When Tomas looked up, blinking away tears of pain, Huashil was back to hurriedly ladling water. The slave to Tomas's left leaned over, his freckled face red from the sun. He took the proffered fruit from Tomas and popped it into his mouth before anyone noticed.

'It seems to be working,' he said, chewing delightedly and indicating to Huashil.

'Indeed, Dieter,' Tomas said. 'We may hook the fish yet.'

HUASHIL WALKED TOWARDS the shade cast by Zarekten's walls and sat down. He began to scribe looping, elegant letters into the sand with his finger:

The emir, may the vultures peck out his eyes, has for-
bidden anyone to write. But I must, or I feel I will forget
how.

Again, I cast my mind into the river of my desires. If
I were back home, I would be sat beneath the acacia tree,
copying the chronicles, writing of new births and the
passing away of elders, recording the history of my tribe.
With no one to write the days, my people will lose their
past. But I have no choice. When the Sigmarites came
from across the seas, the emir rounded up the men from
the villages to bolster his army. Now I wring the last
doses of strength from those captured in his wars. I am
a slave, driving slaves.

Why do the Sigmarites come here, with fire and sword
to my land?

I watch the slaves. They are forbidden to practise their
primitive religion, but many has been the time when I
have listened to Tomas as he tells tales of gods like
Sigmar – who was also a man! – who banished evil and
set up a nation united, a nation of learning, light and
scholars, a land of green trees and deep rivers. I look for-
ward to night guard duty, so I can hear again these
wonderful tales.

Already the wind had erased the first sentences. He
watched the desert steal his words, and wondered where
it took them. His thoughts were interrupted by the sound
of swift hoof-beats coming up the road towards the city. A
horse and rider appeared from behind an escarpment of
rock. The rider was standing in the stirrups and riding
hard. Huashil knew no Arabyan would push an animal
like that at this time of day unless he was in desperate
need. A dozen soldiers marched out from the main gate,
spears levelled. The rider dismounted and ran up to them.

Huashil strained to hear their words, but they were
carried away by the breeze. After a minute's

conversation the rider was allowed into the city. The guards beckoned to the slave-drivers who began to hound and whip their charges back towards the gate.

A sonorous blast from the horn in the gatehouse echoed around the valley, bouncing from the sheer walls which only listened impassively.

THE SLAVES WERE herded into the fortress with whips and curses. As the last man passed under the arch, soldiers goaded teams of brightly apparelled camels to heave the iron-studded gates closed. Once more the horn gave forth a mournful cry. The slaves exchanged nervous glances.

As Tomas and Dieter shuffled up the wide thorough-fare, they passed groups of soldiers running to the gate. Townsfolk scurried up alleys, calling to their children and shutting their doors. Tomas grinned.

'I smell trouble,' he said. Another group of Empire slaves jogged up beside them. A muscular man fell into step next to Tomas.

'Greetings, Tomas. Have you heard the rumours?' he said.

'No, Jurgen, but something's stirred up the beehive.'

'Indeed it has,' Jurgen said, laughing. 'I think our opportunity has arrived, my friend. Crusaders are near, and they're heading this way.'

PRINCE FRIEDRICH WEISS, commander of the first grand crusade from Wissenburg, leader of five hundred knights and five thousand men-at-arms, sacker of cities and conqueror of towns, reclined in his chair, grateful for the shade his pavilion afforded from the cursed sun. He had just inspected his siege line, which straggled just beyond bowshot around Zarekten's walls. Bivouacs had been pitched, and his army was settling into the siege with well-practiced skill. But the situation was tenuous:

his engineers judged that the stony ground of the valley made mining the walls impossible; and the besieged had food, water and thick walls to cower behind whereas the crusaders were running low on supplies and could expect attack from the front or the rear at any moment.

From outside the pavilion came the creak of the trebuchets as their beams were ratcheted back, and the *crash* and *swish* as the counterweights were dropped, launching rocks at the city. The siege engines had been toiling like this for a week, to little avail.

The pavilion flap was lifted and a tall man entered. He rested his warhammer against a support pole and ran his hand over his bald scalp. It came away slick with sweat, which he wiped on his robe. He regarded Friedrich through heavy-lidded eyes.

Friedrich returned his gaze and wondered how this warrior priest stayed as pale as a fish's belly in this blasted heat.

'How is my lord today?' the priest said.

'Perfectly fine, Brother Kristoff. Except that I look at the walls and see they are still intact.' He stood up and peered out of the pavilion. 'What I would dearly like to see is that place ablaze. What I dearly want to hear are screams as we put the faithless to the sword.' He looked at Kristoff. 'Sigmar is being cheated of his due.'

'I, too, share your vexation. But Zarekten is a fine fortress.'

'Be careful what you say, brother. It is a citadel of the godless, a cradle of evil. I expect more intolerance from a man of Sigmar.'

'Intolerance has nothing to do with it,' Kristoff said. 'The point is, lord, we still remain outside.'

Friedrich slumped back into his chair. 'It's time we changed tack. We have prisoners?'

'Aye, lord.'

'Pick one. Pick a man with a family, and bring them to the armourer's. Treachery runs in an Arabyans' blood. Let's use that to our advantage.'

Kristoff nodded and left.

UPON DRIVING THE Sultan Jaffar's forces from Estalia, the armies of the Old World had followed them over the sea and into their own land. Prince Friedrich's desire to build a reputation on the field of battle in Araby had given his armourers and weaponsmiths much work to do.

Prince Friedrich's crusade had burnt and slaughtered its way into Araby and was now many miles inland. It had breached the walls of Gobi-Alain on the coast and defeated every hastily mustered army that marched to meet it. Castles, towns and villages were being crushed under the heels of the grand crusades from the Empire and Bretonnia, and Araby was reeling.

The air in the armourer's tent reeked of smoke. Friedrich stirred the white coals in the giant furnace with a brand, as a group of people entered.

'Translate for me, Brother Kristoff,' he said.

'As you wish, lord.'

Four Arabyans were on their knees: a young man and woman, and two young boys. Friedrich felt a twinge of admiration at the defiance in their eyes. He motioned to a guard who stepped forward and grabbed the woman by her hair. She yelped in pain, but kept her eyes on Friedrich. The corner of Friedrich's mouth twitched as he noticed fear flash across the man's face.

'What's his name?' Friedrich asked Kristoff.

'Mashtub, lord.'

'You have a choice to make, Mushtub.' As Friedrich spoke, Kristoff translated in fluent Arabyan. 'If you make the wrong choice, your family will die, but only after my men have had their fun.' Friedrich thrust his face close to Mashtub's, who bowed his head. 'Listen carefully…'

DUSK SETTLED. THE sky, purpled like a bruise, was speckled with stars and formed a benign roof over the shadowed valley walls. The captain of the gate-tower guard leant over the parapet and scrutinised the siege lines. Campfires burned along the crusaders' picket. He heard men's voices drifting on the breeze and wondered what the barbarians were saying.

He was about to go to the guardhouse for a cup of sweet tea when he spied movement in the enemy camp and heard angry shouts. He could see three – no, four – figures running towards his gate. Sigmarite soldiers appeared from bivouacs and chased after them. More shouts were raised as one of the pursued tripped and fell. The soldiers set upon him, beating him with their swords hilts. As the others got closer, the captain could see they were Arabyans.

'Open the gates!' he shouted. Below, the camels lowed hoarsely as they were goaded to stand up.

The escapees had made it halfway when he saw a line of Sigmarites form up in a line. Crossbowmen. They raised their weapons.

'Hurry, get that gate open.'

He heard the staccato rattle as the crossbows fired. One man dropped like a sack of sand with a quarrel through his throat, and another tumbled as a bolt buried itself up to the fletch in the meat of his thigh. He cried out, thrashing on the ground as the Empire soldiers calmly reloaded and took aim.

The last man was nearly at the gates. Another rattle of bolts and the wounded man was silenced forever, just as the survivor squeezed through the door and collapsed. Guards propped him up against a wall.

Mashtub stared at them with wild eyes. His right arm was held against his chest. It ended just above the wrist, the stump seared with a brand shaped with an 'S'.

'Take him to the emir,' the guard captain said.

'YOU'RE A FOOL.'

'And you are a coward.'

Tomas held Drager against the cage wall, his powerful hands gripping his tunic.

'Call me what you want, Tomas, but there is no shame in survival.'

Tomas let him go. 'You call this survival?' he said, waving his hand around the cage. 'This is worse than death.'

'Death is what you will bring us, if you go through with this.'

'We cannot waste the opportunity we now have. Not half-a-mile away are our countrymen. At last we have a chance to escape from these wretches.'

'It's not so bad here…'

'Not so bad for you, you mean,' Tomas shouted.

'Hush, Tomas,' Dieter said. 'You'll have the guards down on us.'

'We toil, feeling the lash on our backs,' Tomas said in an angry whisper. 'They work us like donkeys until we fall down dead. You, meanwhile, work with the beasts in this zoo, shovelling dung and sitting in the shade.'

'It's not like that.'

'Yes it is. I can see the guilt in your eyes.'

'Our lives were no better at home. We worked the fields, and in return we have to fight in the count's wars.'

'This is not just any war. This is a holy crusade.'

'You deceive yourself,' Drager said.

Tomas floored him with a fist and turned to the rest of the prisoners. 'Brothers, we have waited long for this day. Our preparations are not in vain. At last, we now have a place to escape to.' There were mutters of approval and nods of assent. Drager sat down, shaking his head.

'Listen,' Dieter said. 'Someone approaches.'

Arabyan guards marched up to the cage. Huashil opened the door and Mashtub was hurled inside. One of the guards spat on him and slammed the gate closed. Mashtub crawled into a corner, eyes averted, his bandaged arm held close to his chest.

The slaves stared at him. What terrible crime could he have committed to be put in with the lowest of the low?

'He could be a spy,' Dieter whispered.

'Perhaps,' Tomas said. 'Let's get some sleep. We'll have a hard day tomorrow.'

Huashil, hidden in the shadows near the sand dragon cage, crept off, disappointed that there would be no tales of Sigmar or the Empire that night.

'IF ONLY I could see through stone. I would dearly like to know what goes on outside,' Dieter whispered, as he heaved another piece of shattered masonry into the handcart. The slaves had been set to work clearing the roads of debris caused by the constant bombardment from the besiegers' trebuchets.

'I share your thoughts, my friend,' Tomas said. 'But soon we will be marching alongside them, avenging our captivity.'

Drager snorted and spat into the sand. Tomas glared at him. 'You know Dieter,' he said, 'Arabyans rarely spit. They reserve the act as the gravest insult possible. Water is scarce in this land, and they believe that to waste it in such a manner is the act of a bitter or a stupid man.' He picked up another rock and hurled it into the cart. 'Which, I wonder, is Herr Drager?'

After an hour of backbreaking toil, Mashtub sidled up to Tomas. 'You speak Arabyan?' he asked, pronouncing each syllable slowly and loudly.

Tomas continued to work. 'I do. I was appointed leader due to my rank and learning, a go-between 'twixt slave and master. I was taught a smattering of your evil language and have had over a year to ingest its foulness.' Tomas turned to him. 'So there is no need to speak so damned slowly.'

'I am most relieved.' Mashtub leaned closer. 'I am here to help you. I have been sent by your countrymen,' he whispered, pointing towards the curtain wall.

'Why would you help us? We're your enemy.'

'I have no loyalty to the emir. He threw me in a cage. He called me a thief.' He waved his stump at Tomas. 'I told him the Empire dogs did this to me. He said, "No matter, is shame on our people that you were captured".' He bowed his head. 'Besides, they have my family. I have no choice.'

Tomas was not without pity, but, like any opportunity, he grabbed it with both hands. 'What do we need to do?'

'How CAN WE trust him?' Dieter whispered.

'I don't trust him. How can I? He's heathen.' Tomas glanced over his shoulder to make sure Mashtub was asleep. Most of the slaves were slumbering after being herded back to their cage after an exhausting day. 'But I do believe his story. You've seen how these scoundrels behave, they have no loyalty to each other. He'd betray his own people to save his skin.'

'Has he agreed to talk to Huashil?'

'Aye. I just hope he'll see things our way.' He ignored Dieter's sceptical look. 'We'd best get moving,' he said.

Tomas crept over to Mashtub and shook him.

'It's time to go,' Tomas said.

The two men went to the back of the cage where Jurgen pried open a loosened bar. They slid into the narrow gap between the bars and the stone wall and shimmied towards the edge of the cage. They could see the arched gate out of the zoo. As usual it was closed, and two guards stood on the other side. Tomas beckoned Mashtub to follow him.

'We've been working on a way to escape for months,' Tomas whispered. 'We were just waiting for the right opportunity.'

They stopped where the perimeter fence of the bestiary met the cliff wall. Tomas lifted up a curtain of rock-creeper to reveal a gap. They slipped through and began to descend through the city. Tomas led the way, creeping through low walled gardens, over flat rooftops, along deserted alleyways and under window eaves. They often had to wait in shadowed doorways as soldiers or citizens passed by. After an hour of nerve-jangling evasion they reached the city wall, at the sixteenth tower, near the east gate, just as Mashtub had instructed.

They entered the tower. Stone steps spiralled upwards to the parapet, and they made their way up them slowly to the first arrow slit. They could hear sentries' footfalls getting closer, then they faded to silence.

Tomas peered out. The rocky ground sloped away, bathed in the milky glow of the moons. He took a torch from a sconce in the wall and waved it in front of the slit. Nothing moved. The moons were so bright, how could anyone move undetected? Mashtub pointed to the sky. A cloud passed over the moons and the landscape was plunged in darkness.

A figure appeared from behind a boulder and sprinted up to them. Tomas held his breath, expecting the alarm to be raised at any moment, but silence prevailed.

'I'm relieved to see you at last, my friend,' the man said, grasping Tomas's outstretched hand. 'My name is

Brandt, Prince Weiss's chief scout. I'm glad we have help, this fortress is proving a difficult nut to crack.'

'It does this old campaigner's heart good to see a free-man's face again. I am Tomas Strauss, halberdier from the first grand crusade from Averland. My comrades and I are sworn to do whatever you need.'

'Very well. The walls are too strong to break. Tomorrow night, mounted knights will hide themselves near the east gate. We need you to open it, so they can ride in and hold off the heathens until the infantry arrive. A feint attack will be directed at the main gate to distract attention. Can you do this for us?'

Tomas did not hesitate. 'We can, and we will.'

'Sigmar bless you, Tomas.'

'Be careful,' Tomas said, as the scout disappeared amongst the rocks.

Tomas and Mashtub, Arabyan and crusader, made their way back to the bestiary, cooperating to survive, but each one wrestling with his own troubles.

'WE'RE RELYING ON two Arabyans for this to work. Does that not worry you?' Dieter asked.

Tomas heaved another rock into the cart. 'It does, but there is no choice. We need Huashil to cover our escape. We cannot all leave our cage without raising the alarm. Mashtub is going to tell him that Empire men are merciful, and if he takes Sigmar into his heart he will be freed after the city falls.'

'Mashtub will choke on those words,' Dieter chuckled. 'Crusaders cut off his hand and even now hold his family hostage. But is Huashil ready to come over to us?'

'We'll find out soon enough.'

The slaves were clearing rubble from a market square. Tomas spied Huashil sat alone on a low wall, scribing shapes into the sand with his spear butt. Tomas caught Mashtub's eye and motioned to him. Mashtub nodded and edged his way towards Huashil. He began to clear the area around his feet of stones. Tomas and Dieter watched as the two men began to converse. Soon, all the slaves were looking over as well.

Tomas knew the risk he was taking. If Mashtub failed to convince Huashil to help them, their plan would fail before it had even begun. His heart dropped as Mashtub walked towards him, slowly shaking his head. Tomas gripped a rock in his hand. They would not take him without a fight. He waited for Huashil to get up and raise the alarm about the planned escape. But he didn't. He remained seated, eyes downcast as he continued to make swirling lines in the sand.

And Tomas knew he still had one more roll of the dice.

PRINCE WEISS STOOD, arms outstretched, as squires strapped a black steel cuirass around his chest.

'It feels good, does it not?' Weiss said. 'The thought of action at last, after sitting on our arses for so long.'

'For myself, lord, I have been far from idle,' Kristoff said. 'I brought with me many texts to study. And besides, I praise Sigmar in a multitude of ways. Whether it be leading the faithful in rousing prayer, or breaking the faithless with a hammer, it makes no difference to me.'

'Man cannot live on faith alone,' Weiss said irritably. 'If all men of the Empire were like me, we would rule all lands under the sun.'

'If all men were like you, chaste brother, there would be no new men to fill up the ranks of your armies.'

Kristoff's face remained still, but Weiss noticed his hands were balled into fists. He smirked. 'Order the men to launch a fire bail. I want a look at the defences before we set out.' He glanced out of the tent flap at Zarekten. 'Order the feint on the main gate to begin fifteen minutes after my departure.' He turned back to Kristoff, grinning. 'That should distract them, eh?'

TOMAS GAZED UP at the stars. He imagined the Empire knights leading their horses through the rocky defiles towards the east gate, all depending on him. He peered through the bars. He could see two figures behind the zoo gates, and recognised the stooped posture of Huashil. Tomas beckoned to him.

Come on, little fish, he thought.

Huashil opened the gate and made his way towards him. 'I will not help you, Tomas,' he said sadly. 'I cannot betray my people.'

Tomas licked his lips. 'How can it be wrong to turn away from a life without faith, and face the glory of Sigmar?' Tomas said. 'He was a great man, who through learning and wisdom transcended his mortality to become a deity. You are a learned man, I've seen you write. You must understand.'

Huashil looked at the ground and shook his head. 'But I don't believe. My faith is only in what I see and hear.'

Tomas looked despairingly at him, but he caught a flicker of doubt in Huashil's tone.

'I need a sign that Sigmar would recognise my faith and reward it,' Huashil said at last.

'Sigmar will not reward you before you turn to him, for then you are not showing true faith. Only those whose faith is blind will prevail.'

Huashil shook his head, and before Tomas could act he turned and made his way back to the gate.

From behind the distant city walls, a blazing comet of yellow light rose sharply up, smearing the night sky with its radiance. It grew bigger as it arced over the outer buildings of Zarekten, flames roaring like a vengeful dragon. The city was awash in a bright orange glow and the flaming orb seemed to hang in the sky, before plummeting back to the ground on the end of its burning tail. It disintegrated on impact, sending waves of fire and fountains of sparks into the air.

Tomas knew it was a fire bail launched by the crusaders, but he seized this last chance. 'Mercy! See Sigmar's sign.' He rattled the cage, noting with relief that the other guard had disappeared to take a closer look at what had happened. 'Huashil, open the door, Sigmar has sent his comet for you. It's a sign. Do as he says and earn his eternal gratitude.'

Huashil lay face down on the floor, wailing. He picked himself and pulled out his keys, muttering confused prayers. He swung open the cage door. Tomas gestured to Huashil, and Jurgen and another grabbed his arms. Tomas stood in front of him. 'You are marked, Huashil, marked by Sigmar. You must do as I say.'

Huashil nodded. The fish was hooked and landed.

TOMAS LEFT A MAN at the zoo gates, garbed in the sentry's clothes. Huashil chained the slaves together, and led them towards the east gate in a shuffling line. No one took notice of them; the main gate was being assaulted, and all efforts were being made to defend it.

In a deserted courtyard, a street away from the east gate, Huashil unlocked their fetters. The slaves picked up rocks and anything else they could use as weapons. Drager edged to the back of the group, his mind racing. He had no desire to be rescued and made to fight again. A choice had to be made; he slipped away towards the main gate garrison.

Tomas could see the two towers of the east gate rising up behind the buildings on the square. The plan was set, no words were spoken. The men made their way around to the gate from the sides, using the alleys running along the outside of the market square. Tomas hunkered down behind a cart. Clouds scudded across the night sky, and everyone kept to the shadows.

'Where's Drager?' Dieter asked. Tomas shrugged his shoulders.

The crusaders had virtually ignored the east gate during their previous attacks, and the trebuchet crews had concentrated their fire on the front of the great city. Arabyans had bolstered the defences around the main gate, leaving only a small garrison guard to defend this section of the wall. A lone soldier stood in front of the doorway into the tower, leaning on his spear, his eyes fixed in the direction of the main gate where the sounds of combat drifted on the night air.

Tomas signalled to Jurgen, who crouched behind a market stall. He nodded and untied a length of material from around his waist. He picked up a stone and placed it in the improvised sling. He began to spin it around his head. Tomas held his breath. Jurgen stepped out from behind the stall and let loose the missile. It whipped through the air and struck the guard on his cheek with a crunch. He dropped to one knee, clutching his face. Tomas sprinted towards the guard then smashed a rock down on his head, staving in the skull.

He dragged him into a corner, picked up his sword and beckoned to his men. Jurgen procured his spear. He grinned at Tomas and led his men inside the tower to deal with the sentries on the parapet. The rest positioned themselves around the square, hiding in doorways and alcoves.

Tomas followed Jurgen up the stairs. He looked through an arrow slit. Boulders littered the ground and spindly tufts of dry grass twitched in the breeze, but he spied nothing else. He would have to trust that the crusader knights were ready. He crept up the stairs and met Jurgen on his way down. He had blood on his face and was grinning like a maniac.

'Those sentries couldn't guard a virgin's chastity,' he said.

Tomas clapped him on the back. 'Let's open the gates.'

The smiles froze on their faces when they heard the harsh clang of a warning bell and shouts from the courtyard below.

'Sigmar's bones! The game's on, Tomas,' Jurgen said, and pushed past. Tomas raced behind, fearful that the plan might fail, but thrilled by the thought of combat.

TOMAS RAN INTO the square. A phalanx of Arabyan guards had charged into the yard and been set upon by the hidden Sigmarites. The battle was uneven: heavily armoured soldiers against a few undernourished slaves, but they fought with a desperate ferocity that for the moment was giving them an advantage. He saw a group of slaves pull an Arabyan down and bludgeon him with rocks. Dieter struggled with another who was trying to force a dagger into his windpipe, another was skewered on the end of Jurgen's spear, who stood in the middle of the yard like an angry bear, thrusting his weapon at the men who circled him like wary hyenas.

It was a maelstrom of savagely fighting men, and unseen in the shadows Drager stared at the scene, knowing his betrayal had cost these men dear.

Tomas edged around the yard until he stood behind Dieter's assailant. The knife was nearly at his throat. Tomas thrust his sword through the Arabyan's mail coat and into his spine. He shrieked and fell, clutching his back. Tomas stamped hard on his face and he fell silent. Tomas pulled Dieter into a doorway.

'We must open the gate,' he shouted over the din.

Dieter nodded and made for the wooden doors, grabbing a comrade on the way. As they reached the heavy doors and began to unbar them, a dark shadow fell across Tomas. He looked up, and his heart almost stopped.

DRAGER SAW IT too, and he knew his job was done. The uprising was doomed. From a side alley strode the sand dragon, and on its back was the emir himself. Clad in gold mail and holding a long, silver-tipped spear, he urged the creature towards the gate. Men, Arabyan and Empire alike, cried out and ran, but Dieter and his comrade still struggled with the doors, and Tomas was sprinting to help them.

The dragon lunged forward, sand gushing from its mouth, engulfing Dieter's comrade. It ripped into him, stripping skin from flesh, and flesh from bone, spraying blood-red sand into the air. He died without making a sound. Tomas ran at the dragon, his sword jabbing at its throat. The emir turned his mount to face him, his thin face a mask of rage. Tomas leapt to one side as the dragon butted its spine-crowned head at his stomach. It grazed his side and he fell to the ground.

Drager was about to leave when he saw a dark figure make its way to the gate, to where Dieter still struggled with the bar.

TOMAS PICKED HIMSELF up and dived under the dragon's head. The emir drove his spear at him, but the stroke was mistimed and Tomas managed to scramble through its legs. The dragon screeched in frustration and began to turn towards him. Tomas ducked his head, but was too slow as its tail whipped into his arm; his sword flew out of his hand and clattered onto the ground.

He cast around desperately for another weapon.

MASHTUB GRABBED THE end of the heavy bar, which would usually be lifted by a gang of men. He knew he had to do this, for if he failed, his family – the only thing he held dear – would be killed. The courtyard was still heaving with fighting men, too distracted to notice his struggles. He looked at Dieter, who was sweating and cursing. Then he saw another slave come up behind Dieter. Help, at last.

DRAGER SMASHED A rock over Dieter's head. He collapsed, blood streaming from the wound. Drager seized on Mashtub's confusion and leapt at him, swinging the bloody rock at his face.

Mashtub dodged to one side, the rock grazing his cheek, but before he could recover, Drager had grabbed him by the throat with one hand, trying to force him onto the ground. Mashtub struggled to keep balance, but Drager was a soldier and strong; his grip tightened.

Mashtub's vision began to fade.

TOMAS WAS BACKED against a wall. The dragon faced him, the emir held his spear ready to throw. Tomas waited for the end.

'Tomas!'

Jurgen threw a torch to him. Tomas caught it and thrust it into the dragon's face. It recoiled, screeching in panic, wings flailing. The emir dropped his spear, struggling to keep upright, the dragon was sent into further panic as Tomas waved the flames in its eyes. He threw the torch back to Jurgen and ran back to the gates.

MASHTUB'S LIFE SLIPPED from him. The only thing he felt was despair for his family, then the fingers around his throat were gone. He opened his eyes, dragging in huge lungfuls of air. Drager's face was suspended above him, eyes open, pupils wide, dark as night. His mouth sagged, blood spilled over his bottom lip. He swayed and collapsed to one side.

Towering over him was Tomas, a dripping knife in his hand. He dropped it and helped Mashtub to his feet. Together they lifted the bar and opened the gates. A warm desert breeze washed over them, bringing with it the sound of thundering hooves.

THE CHRONICLES RECORD that on that night the city of Zarekten was brought under the merciful dominion of the Empire. In truth, mercy was far from the crusaders' minds. The slaughter lasted for three nights and two days. Prince Weiss ordered that the buildings were to be kept intact, but their inhabitants were to be afforded no such preservation. He knew there was little point in trying to protect the citizens from his soldiers, and he had no compunction to do so anyway. As he said to Brother Kristoff – against the noise of screaming – an army glutted with victory will have its fun, and he'd be damned if he'd lift a finger to stop it. But the savage appetite of his men had, at last, been sated. The sloping streets were stained pink, as the sun burned dry the blood on the ground.

Weiss sat in the emir's high-backed chair at the head of the throne chamber. Suspended from the ceiling, by an ingenious array of ropes, chains and pulleys, was the sand dragon. Its wings were spread across the width of the chamber, and its head was raised proudly. Only its dead eyes and lolling jaw detracted from the overall effect. Weiss savoured the memory of running the beast through as he charged through the east gate. Strapped to the saddle was the emir's naked corpse. His feet and hands had been removed – much to Weiss's amusement – and he was beginning to rot. The startled expression on his ashen face was, as far as Weiss was concerned, fitting humiliation for such a godless son of a whore.

To think the heathen had tried to buy his life with information! Although his talk of a fabled city, Jabal

Sinjar, full of riches across the desert, had planted a kernel of greed in the prince's heart. When the emir had produced maps of its whereabouts, he made up his mind to seek it out. He was a man of considerable vanity and compulsion. He would leave a garrison at Zarekten to protect his rearguard and the valley passage, and venture into the Great Erg. His glorious destiny awaited him.

But there was one more job to do first. He took a swig of wine and waved, beckoning to the guards who waited on the threshold. They marched in, leading Jurgen, Dieter and the rest of the freed Empire slaves up to him. Lastly, in chains, were dragged Mashtub and Huashil.

'Quite an adventure you've had, eh?' Weiss smiled languidly at his countrymen, who bowed their heads in deference. 'Our victory here is, to a great extent, down to your actions. You will not find me ungrateful. You are to join the ranks of my army, charged to bring the light of Sigmar into the dark places of the world.' He was in good humour and of a mood to listen to his own voice. 'I have heard tell, from the great emir himself,' he pointed to the slowly spinning corpse above his head, 'of a great fortress city, brimming with riches and wealth. What better way to honour Sigmar than to bring to his altar the stolen treasures of the heathen?' There was a murmur of excited approval.

'But first we must pass judgement on these specimens,' he said, pointing to the prisoners.

'In Sigmar's name, I pronounce them guilty,' Kristoff said.

'My lords,' Tomas said, shaking off Dieter's restraining hand. 'I must speak up on their behalf.' Both Arabyans looked astounded. Tomas charged on. 'Mashtub was instrumental in our plan. Without him we would never have succeeded. And Huashil has renounced his godless ways, and wishes to be inducted into the Sigmarite faith.'

Kristoff laid a cold stare on Tomas. 'There can be no redemption for these wretches, despite their actions. They are of this land and their blood runs with sin and dishonour. Sigmar shall not be insulted in such a manner.' He nodded to the guards who stepped forward, drawing their swords.

'Wait,' Tomas said. 'To find this city you will need someone to read Arabyan maps, and guide you through the sands.'

'Go on,' Weiss said.

Tomas pointed to Huashil. 'This man is a scholar. He can help you.'

Weiss looked at Huashil. 'Chain him up,' he said at last. 'We will take him with us.' Huashil gave Tomas a grateful look as he was taken from the room.

Mashtub was left alone in the middle of the floor, staring unflinchingly into the prince's eyes.

'I do not forget your part in my victory over your kind, either,' Weiss said smoothly. 'However, your family is not alive to see your imminent sacrifice.' He nodded to a guard. Mashtub roared and leapt at Weiss like a lynx. The prince did not move. With a practiced sweep, the guard clove Mashtub's head neatly from his neck. Tomas closed his eyes, but heard the heavy thump as it hit the floor.

Weiss swept out of the room, with the crusaders in tow. Tomas stayed behind. He knelt over Mashtub's body.

'May Sigmar take you into his keeping,' he whispered, making the sign of the hammer. 'And may he forgive me my sins.'

As he walked out, head bowed, the last drops of blood seeped out of Mashtub's body, to mix red with the golden sand on the floor.

SON OF THE EMPIRE
by Robert Allan

*Sweet Shallya, goddess of mercy, grant me your
protection.*
Fair goddess, I beseech you, protect the innocent.
Deliver them from suffering and harm.
*Noble goddess, Shine the light of your purity into the
eyes of the unholy.*
*Forgiving goddess, lend your strength to mine and your
ears to my plea.*
*Beneficent goddess, mother of clemency, mother of
healing, mother of serenity, I call upon you now.*
Mercy begets purity.

THE LAST ECHOES of the voice floated away on the warm
forest breeze. He blinked, and then gasped.

The Marauder warband filled the edge of the clearing
like a filthy stain, the mere sight of them causing the
bile to rise in his stomach.

The Northmen were huge. Slab-muscled brutes clad
in filthy blood-soaked rags and furs, bronzed armour
plating and studded leather straps, they were a sight to

189

sober the hardest of souls. They stood amongst an ominous thicket of rusting pikes, bloodstained spears and barbed swords. Lurid banners of stained cloth and leathered flesh flapped in the breeze. Banners dedicated to the Ruinous Powers, daubed with symbols that hurt the eyes and sickened the stomachs of the untainted.

Four of the heretics were mounted atop hulking dark equine creatures with frothing mouths and baleful red eyes, while at their side a pack of huge snarling hounds strained at the greased chains holding them at bay. Each creature was much larger than a man and covered in thick, stinking fur, matted and stained with human blood. They howled and roared, straining to be unleashed upon the cowering children, the scent of innocence driving the evil creatures wild.

The children.

He glanced behind him and a row of silent faces met his gaze, innocent and pure. The young children and the priestess stood huddled before the small wooden hospice, its whitewashed walls gleaming beneath the leafy canopy. The children wailed and trembled, hiding their faces in the folds of the woman's discoloured robes. Her piercing eyes glinted as she returned his gaze, speaking of a burning, determined drive that greatly belied her pox-ridden form.

'You would save us, brave warrior?' she called, her broken voice tinged with pain.

He shook his head and turned back to face the warband once more, fingers tightening around the shaft of his spear. The banner tied around the shaft flapped in the warm breeze, the fabled panther of Araby stitched into the fine material seeming to buck and thrash, eager to tear into the enemy.

'Heretics,' he snarled, his eyes burning with rage.

Much to his astonishment the gathered Chaos warriors ignored him, a reaction that served only to further stoke the anger within his noble heart. Some of the fiends laughed and joked amongst themselves, almost as if heedless to the Knight Panther's presence. Others jostled and snarled, ogling the innocents behind him with eager, malicious eyes.

Still, they made no attempt to advance. They were gathered as if waiting for something.

Waiting for him.

'The prayer,' the young woman whispered behind him, almost as if sensing his confusion. He glanced back at the small gathering of innocents, his mind reeling.

'I prayed for you, my lord. It was Shallya who brought you here. I prayed for salvation. I asked the goddess to provide and she answered.'

She lifted her head and threw a nod at the Chaos warriors.

'They do not see you as I do. They are blinded to the presence of one so just.'

Ulgoth drew his head back as he heard this, confusion screaming like a banshee in his mind. He turned his attention towards the gathered heretics once more, his eyes narrowing.

The Marauders continued to communicate raucously between themselves, utterly unconcerned by his presence.

'Shallya is beneficence incarnate, lord,' the priestess continued, sensing his confusion. 'She is able to quell the darkest of souls, if only for a short time.' She bowed her head slowly, almost as if the gesture caused her physical pain. 'I prayed for a light to banish the darkness. You are that light.'

He shook his head, his teeth bared. He found himself relaxing a little in the presence of the Chaos worshippers, his hard muscles loosening a little, though his anger and revulsion remained. The words of the priestess continued to whisper through his psyche.

It was Shallya who brought you here. They do not see you as I do. She is able to quell the darkest of souls.

You are that light.

His felt his face tighten as his senses came flooding back, almost as if triggered by the mention of holy Shallya, Goddess of Mercy.

'I...'

He paused, unable to tear his eyes away from the gathered filth. Thrown, disorientated, his heart continued to beat hard within his chest.

'I am Ulgoth, Knight Panther. Champion of the Empire.' He finally uttered, introducing himself to the lady as any gallant knight would.

The Shallyan priestess smiled weakly as she heard this and she nodded, her red eyes narrowing with pain as she did so. 'Ulgoth, Champion of the Empire,' she echoed with a weak smile, her voice wavering now. The children around her, clearly terrified of the situation, squealed and pressed themselves closer into the folds of her simple sackcloth vestments. Quietly, gently, she whispered reassurances to the infants, her inaudible words seeming to calm them almost instantly.

'I am Reya, lord,' the young woman continued, holding them tight to her breast. 'I am a servant of Shallya, a healer of the sick. I run this simple hospice in order to treat the child victims of the red pox here in the border regions.

'The pox has a hold on these borderlands, sir knight. Shallya has granted me the power to heal the young, though every act of mercy must be made through sacrifice. My own state of health is that sacrifice. I am dying.'

Ulgoth found himself backing away at the very mention of the red pox, recoiling in the presence of the blighted woman. Behind him, the Marauders began to grow agitated, almost impatient.

'Hurry, sire,' he heard Reya wail, her thin voiced strained and broken. 'I fear the effects of the prayer may begin to subside at any time. I fear the darkness may return.'

His face tightened. The particulars of his current predicament no longer mattered. He understood now, the realisation slowly seeping into his mind. Somehow Shallya had guided him to this place of terror and bloodshed, this forest on the northern borders of the Empire. He had a purpose here, this much was clear.

It was enough.

'Fear not, my lady. Shallya's choice was a wise one. This scum will not have their way with you or your charges while ever I draw breath.'

He could feel the righteous fury begin to rise from deep within him like a living thing now, an avatar of wrath and revulsion that bound his soul to the gods. Every last one of the foul filth before him would feel the wrath of Ulgoth.

He could hear the rabble now, laughing and joking amongst themselves, mocking him with their ignorance. He would make them pay.

'What is it? Has your interest in the priestess bitch waned now you've looked upon her pox-ridden form?' He shuddered as he heard this, his head turning slowly to face the gathered enemy.

The warrior responsible was a huge brute, his massive frame wrapped in the pelts of beastmen and the leathered skins of human enemies. His head was a mass of shaggy greying hair, the matted tresses hanging about his scar-laced face in braids and lank knots.

His single remaining eye glistened as he noticed Ulgoth's striding reaction, the cruel smile spread across his lips widening. The others about him roared their approval as they heard this, a cacophony of jeers and whooping laughter rising up across the throng once again, a reaction that served only to goad the barbarian on to express further obscenities.

'Ah, perhaps the female is not to your taste, blighted or otherwise!' the colossus barked, his blackened teeth bared in a malicious grin. 'Perhaps you no longer desire mortal flesh! I sense it now! I sense you truckle to the touch of the daemon, yes?' The rest of the mob erupted once more in cacophonous laughter.

Ulgoth shuddered with rage, his face reddening. To be insulted by a disciple of the Ruinous Powers was an insult no loyal warrior of the Empire could bring himself to bear. He started forward, his fingers tightening around the hilt of the spear once more. A few of those before him seemed to notice this as he neared, their malicious smiles beginning to fade, replaced by expressions of curious uncertainty.

He did not care, for now the Righteous Fury was upon him.

The knight broke into a run and thrust his arm back, a scream of absolute and utter rage shaking his taut, muscled features. He threw his armoured fist forward and flung the spear, driving it into the neck of the profane steed with such unrestrained force that the animal reared back, screaming and baying.

The warrior fell to the floor as the creature smashed down into the Marauders behind, scattering those it did not crush. The shrill of singing metal being drawn cleaved the air as Ulgoth strode over the downed warrior, roaring and bellowing like a madman as he drew his own sword. He fell to one knee and swung his blade around and down into the Marauder's fur-lined chest, both hands tight around the hilt. Shouts and cries of shocked surprise rose up from the rest of the throng as they observed the death of their comrade, followed a heartbeat later by a collective roar of guttural anger.

The debased berserkers began to realise what was happening as if for the first time. A sudden surge of hostile movement passed through the Northmen as they responded to the unexpected threat, shock slowly but surely replacing anger.

Ulgoth rose, his eyes wide and terrible, his sweat-beaded face quivering with righteous rage. He thrust his arm out and began to turn on his heel slowly, his sword held out before him in a clear gesture of threat, his silvered plate armour glistening with the blood of the heretic.

'Hear me, scum! Your rampage is at an end. You will no longer plague the forests of the Empire. I am Ulgoth, Knight Panther, warrior of the Inner Circle. By Sigmar, I swear I will see each and every one of you whoresons wet my blade before the setting of the sun!'

The Marauders howled as they heard this, driven almost to madness by the anger burning within their dark hearts. A sea of rusted pike heads surged forward to meet him, clattering and shaking as they drove forward.

Ulgoth swept his shield out before him and batted the weapons aside, following a heartbeat later with his singing blade. A number of pike heads clattered and fell away, severed by the keen edge. He dug his heels into the ground as he felt a number of the bladed spars slam into the thick plate of his suit, though he did not worry. Such magnificent armour was proof against these corrupt, rusting weapons.

He countered again, driving the pikemen back amid a storm of wide sweeping lunges. Northmen screamed and fell, some bisected cleanly, others clutching opened bellies or bleeding stumps. Heads rolled and throats gurgled and within moments Ulgoth found himself standing at the centre of a small clearing, a scattering of bloodied bodies strewn around him.

A sea of scarred, filth-laden faces stared back, blood-shot eyes wide with shock, throats closed with disbelief. He raised his shield to his chest and thrust his sword out before him, his wild eyes finding each face in turn.

'Sigmar Himself steels my soul! Myrmidia guides my hand! Mighty Ulric stokes the fires of my rage! The gods themselves lend their strength to me, filth! Who will be the next to test my mettle? Who will be the next to throw themselves upon my blade?'

The clattering of hooves began to echo through the forest as the horsemen began to encircle the scene, their coarse cries drifting through the surrounding trees as they overcame their shock. He flinched and grunted as a brace of hissing arrows sailed towards him and raised his shield, halting their progress with a splintering of wood.

Before him the two huge brute handlers snarled unin-telligibly and cast the heavy chains to the floor, staggering back as they loosed the baying hounds.

The great slavering beasts did not advance. They howled and whined, hesitant to attack. Their bestial eyes flashed with wild fear as they regarded the gallant knight. Again and again they started forward, only to turn aside, whimpering and whining in fearful confu-sion.

The pack masters spat obscenities and drew their cruel barbed lashes across the horde of matted fur, incensed by their hesitance.

Ulgoth lunged forward and into them, suffering no such ambivalence. His bright blade flashed from left to right as he hacked his way through bestial flesh, each swing felling another beast. The hounds retaliated albeit hesitantly, vice-like jaws snapping and clawed paws swiping at the warrior, though their efforts were as nothing. The creatures paled before the knight, falling like leaves before the wind.

He turned briefly to see the priestess watching, still rooted to the spot. Her mouth moved swiftly and silently as if in whispered prayer, her efforts no doubt responsible for the confusion of the canine beasts. He promised himself that he would not allow her efforts time to fail.

He spun on his heel and swept his sword before him, taking the heads of the two handlers with one almighty blow. Even as the bodies fell to their knees amid a spray of blood he felt a number of treacherous arrows slam into him, the unexpected assault snatching his breath but for a moment. Hot fingers of pain stabbed into his chest and shoulder where the vicious projectiles had managed to penetrate his armour.

He would not fall. He would not falter. It was the cries and whoops of insane bloodlust rising up around him that steeled his resolve and kept him on his feet.

He looked up to see a wall of screaming, howling malice sprinting towards him, a storm of howling feral hatred. Chaos berserkers, insane with bloodlust, a bloodlust fuelled by the shuddering standard flapping in the breeze behind them.

Ulgoth's eyes left the charging horde for a moment as he looked upon that debased and wicked thing, its roiling leathered surface alive with smouldering malice.

The seven hollering abominations descended upon him in the centre of the glade, a storm of spiked flails and bladed chains, spittle-lined mouths and tattooed bodies. The stink of sweat and blood burned his nostrils as he braced himself, ready to repel the attackers.

Behind him the priestess began to mutter softly beneath her breath, her words lost amid the tumult. It was as if the breeze itself sang to him, the very breath of Shallya passing through his body, and he lifted his eyes as the terrible howling abated almost instantly.

He watched with astonishment as the insane warriors faltered, their mouths closing slowly, their lurching advance grinding to a halt. They came to a standstill as one as a wave of calm swept over them, soil and leaf-mulch dancing around their feet, the fire in their eyes suddenly dimmed.

Chains clanged and blades rattled as they hit the floor, the fingers that had held them loosening. Bare chests still heaved, almost as if the black hearts within had not yet come to realise the sudden arrest of their efforts. The priestess, Reya. This was her doing, it had to be.

He snarled and lunged for the swaying berserkers, lifting his blooded sword high above his head to bring it down into the meaty shoulder of the nearest warrior. The man screamed as the blade bit deep into his flesh, his escaping blood painting Ulgoth's exotic furs red as the blow drove him to his knees.

The death of their comrade seemed to stir the mystified warriors and they started to tense, their glazed eyes blinking.

Ulgoth pulled his blade free and felled another berserker with a swift turn, sending his scarred, bearded head spinning away amongst the others.

SOMEWHERE BEHIND HIM he felt the sacrilegious powers of the standard flare and intensify, sending a fresh wave of burning rage through the stunned madmen. The wave of boiling anger passed through him and he shuddered, recognising the insidious touch of the Ruinous Powers.

The Chaos warriors howled and convulsed, invigorated anew. A swift and powerful blow smashed against his shield, followed by another and another. He turned and countered, parting a hand and its weapon from the wrist of the owner.

His ears began to ring with the maddened whoops and cries of the warriors as another blow landed heavily upon his shield, smashing the thick painted wood to splinters. He drove the remnants of the disintegrating wood into the bare neck of the attacker and then cried out as something large and heavy smashed the golden feline helm from his head. He was faltering again but he would not fail his gods.

A red rage descended over Ulgoth's eyes, a boiling and palpable anger that roared in his ears and shook his punished body. He was only dimly aware of the deep vibration of his breastbone as he unleashed a scream of utter fury, the terrible sound no more than white noise in his own ears.

He started forward into the storm of shifting flesh, swinging his sword around his head in a wide arc. Scraps of lank fur and body matter enveloped him as he advanced, using his own armoured forearm to parry the blows of the snarling warriors. His bare face was a rictus of fury, his teeth bared, his eyes wide and lost.

'Misbelievers! Heretics! Morr shall find your tainted souls waiting bloodied at his gates!'

He lost himself then for a moment, his eyes dimming as the rage building within him was unleashed. Screams of pain assailed his ears as he lunged on, striking and turning, swinging his sword about him in a wild, indiscriminate storm of retaliation. Blows rained against his armour and yet he was barely aware of them, lost as he was in undiluted rage.

The next thing he felt was the ground at his back, driving the breath from his lungs. The wet remains of the lunatic warriors lay scattered about him, little more than twisted and leaking sacks of angular flesh, broken, bloodied and done. As the anger began to drain away he became aware of his injuries, the dull pain gradually increasing as the buzzing in his ears dissipated.

Cries of disbelief rose up from the surviving Marauders, sounds that even now seemed distant and detached. A veil of blackness began to descend over his eyes, the bright sunlight streaming through the canopy dimming with the passing of each heartbeat. No matter how hard he tried, he found himself unable to lift even his head, let alone the sword still clutched in his hand.

The ground beneath him shook under the weight of the circling steeds, their bewildered riders still seemingly unsure of what to do next, hooves and dark sinuous legs flashing past his fading vision.

Beneficent goddess, healing mother, I call to you once more. Lend your strength to this punished knight. Dull his pain and wash away his fatigue. Breathe life into his ravaged form once more so that he may continue to champion your cause.

He flinched. Somewhere deep in his mind he could hear Reya's sweet voice once again, as soft and soothing as music and yet stronger than any other sound about him.

As she continued to pray he could feel the effects of her incantation begin to wash over his aching form like a warm treacle, dimming the pain that wracked his body. His blood became fire in his veins, a charged surge of invigorating warmth that seemed to ignite every muscle at once. He swore that he could feel the embrace of the goddess herself around him. Arms that were tender and yet stronger than any he had ever felt enveloped him and picked him up, lifting his buckled, blood-flecked form up from its prone position and onto its feet.

He opened his eyes and bared his teeth as he looked out upon the face of the astonished Marauder, the warrior's rusted axe barely an inch from his face. The mounted heretic reeled back in shock as Ulgoth raised his sword, thrust his arm forward and impaled him for his troubles, this sudden attack causing the shocked animal beneath him to rear up and throw the skewered body to the ground.

'Not one of you shall escape my wrath!' he raged, ignoring the brace of arrows that struck him even as he pulled his blade free.

'You will all answer to me! You had better pray to Shallya to grant you the mercy that I cannot!'

He watched as the panicked Marauders hauled at the reins, bringing their steeds about. Even as the standard bearer and the two archers made to leave he plucked the fallen axe from the hand of the dead warrior beneath him and hurled it, striking one of the unfortunate archers from the saddle.

'Your fates were sealed the moment you made war on the Empire! You will not escape retribution!'

Sword in hand he grabbed the reins of the black mount and hauled himself up onto its back, ignoring the pain that had begun to wrack his body once more. He heaved the creature around and dug his heels into its flanks, unstoppable now.

Within moments he had caught up with the archer and, his eyes fixed upon the blasphemous standard before him, he spun the sword in his hand and drove it through the man's neck as he passed, leaving the blade and its victim behind.

'Run to the ends of the world if you must, servant of filth! I will be at your heel!'

The surviving Marauder glanced behind him and gasped, his scarred face slackening. He turned back and began to shout and holler at his mount, urging it to pick up speed, the banner furled and laid across his shoulder.

Rider and mount had advanced no more than a few strides into the trees when something landed behind him, its cold, crushing weight pressed against his back.

Armoured fingers closed around his neck and he cried out, snatching at the sword fastened to his waist. Cold armoured fingers closed around his mouth, wet with blood.

A red mist descended over his eyes as he felt himself falling from the panicked mount, the dead Marauder in his grasp. A terrible guttural screaming filled his ears, shaking him to his very core. The air around him seemed to burn with black rage, the fallen standard at his side shuddering and flapping as it fought his desperate grasp. The canopy above seemed to shake and thrash, each branch a flailing fist of red rage. The skies beyond were red, the colour of spilled blood. The breeze became a gale, a flaying storm of hot, sulphured wind, howling as it tore at his exposed face. He felt his fingers close around the vibrating cloth and he began to tear, ignoring the sickening stench of his own burning flesh as the fingers of his gauntlets began to glow red-hot.

Warrior?

He flinched, the distant, soothing voice drifting through his mind.

Warrior? Open your eyes.

He did so and the light of the world flooded in, the excruciating pain following a heartbeat later. Everything was so bright, too bright to bear. The tops of the trees were now little more than black shadows, indistinct and ominous against the bright, blinding sunlight. The raging pain coursed through him, its cruel serrated fingers tight around his ravaged body.

With no little effort he lifted his gauntleted hands to his face, the stinging pain causing his lips to draw back over his teeth. They were blackened and burned, almost as if he had stood with them in a brazier, the metal and chainmail twisted and black with smouldering soot.

'Rest, brave warrior. You are victorious.'

The pain dulled almost at once and he turned his head to see the priestess kneeling beside him, her slight frame enveloped by the streaming sunlight. What remained of the foul standard lay beneath her, tattered and torn, its unholy influence banished. Reya ran her eyes slowly over his prone body, her hands hovering over the twisted and buckled mess of armour. She sighed softly.

'You tore the debased banner apart with your hands. This last act was too much to bear, even for you. You are dying.' With that she seemed to pause for a moment, turning to watch the children as they scurried up to her and began to drag the smouldering remnants of the blackened banner away to be disposed of.

Once she was sure that the children were out of earshot, she turned her attention back towards the dying man, her soft eyes filled with pity.

'The Foul Pantheon are jealous masters, warrior. In the end they will always betray those who serve them. Always.'

He felt a breath catch in his throat as Reya spoke. The treetops above seemed to shrink away into the skies around the scabrous face of the woman, her presence causing a sudden wave of revulsion to set his blood afire. The soothing calm that had dulled his pain started to drain away, dispelled by the mounting rage within his soul.

He tried to move his punished form but found that he could not, his injuries too severe.

'Rest now. It's all I can to halt the pain. Be at peace. Shallya shows mercy to all, warrior, even to those who are no longer able to recall how to practise compassion and empathy.'

Her words were little more than a buzzing in his ears and felt his heart pounding in his chest now, the events of the past peeling away in layers in his shattered mind.

He felt his emerging soul shuddering with revulsion as he recalled speaking the names of the gods, of Sigmar and Morr, of Ulric and Myrmidia. Gods he had once revered, long ago. Gods he had forsaken, renounced with all his heart and soul. The gods of the enemy.

Ulgoth, valiant Knight Panther did not exist. He had never existed.

Uulguth, Champion of the Dark Pantheon, lifted his head and looked down at his battered, dying body. Gone were the exotic furs that had covered his proud armour, replaced instead with the rotting skins of his enemies. His shining silver plate was a dull black, pregnant with trophies and totems dedicated to the four gods of Chaos. Even now, as the enchantment of the Shallyan witch slipped away, he still felt a tingle of revulsion in his soul as he looked upon his own debased form.

'Damn you, witch…' he whispered, fighting to lift his blackened, blood-slicked hands. Dark blood began to spray from his lips as he spoke, his voice a terrible, rattling rasp. 'I spit on your bitch goddess and her benevolent magicks. You will pay for what you made me do, Shallyan sow. By the Dark Gods, I swear this…'

Reya sighed and placed her hand upon his chest. There was no hatred or revulsion in her eyes, only pity.

'Please understand, I could not allow you or your warriors to hurt the children. I beseeched her mercy. She answered my prayer with you. The power and the purity of the herciful goddess can wash away the darkness from any soul, if even for only a short time.

'Do you see, lost one? You were purified, cleansed of sin. You were yourself again, if only for one last, glorious time.'

Uulguth began to shake and convulse, the light around him starting to grow dim. Reya shook her head slowly and hushed him, running a gentle hand across his scarred grey face. Even as he felt his body growing cold and his breath coming in ragged gasps he could not let go of the burning rage within his soul.

He had betrayed his gods while under this witch's spell. He had slaughtered his own men, filled with a zeal and rage not his own.

He began to snarl, his ruined gauntlets clattering as he raised them slowly towards the woman's neck.

'I die a servant of Chaos. I served the Ruinous Powers in life and I do so in death. Even your damned goddess cannot change that.'

Reya pushed his hands away softly and without effort. 'Faith,' Reya answered, her eyes still filled with forgiveness, 'is the most powerful weapon of all. It was faith, true faith that saved us. Before you die, warrior, ask yourself this. Where are your gods now? They have abandoned you. You will find neither comfort nor forgiveness in death.

'Shallya restored your honour and zeal. She washed away the filth and the sin within you. She brought the true warrior to the surface and you shone, lost one. You shone like the sun once again, if only for a moment.'

'Damn you, whore. I hope your death is a slow, lingering one. I hope you die screaming in agony. I hope the red pox sloughs the skin from your palsied bones and rots the little brats alive. Damn y–'

SHE MET HIS burning gaze for a moment and held it until the light finally left his eyes and his quaking body fell still.

'Go with peace,' Reya whispered, shedding a single glistening tear.

THE DAEMON'S GIFT
by Robert Baumgartner

'HERE THEY COME,' Aelfir said. He grinned, showing teeth filed to points. Rain lashed the night, drenching the cold stones that rose above the warband. Great fires burned despite the rain, the water sizzling as it fell on the burning wood. In the light of the fires twisted shapes of beasts could be seen, monstrous blends of man and animal with cruel horns that cast distorted shadows as they dashed among the stones, rushing up the sides of the ancient temple mound toward the waiting Orning warriors.

'Let us go and greet them,' said Khojin, resplendent in silver armour that gleamed even in the rain. 'Mugin, sound the charge.'

A bone whistle blew, a piercing blast that caused Aelfir's head to ache. Aelfir charged down the mound, rushing beside Khojin into the teeth of the beasts' advance. The shock of the Northmen's charge overwhelmed the beasts at first, but the men were swiftly surrounded. The darkness grew around them as the fires died and the beasts howled, thirsting for blood.

As the screams of the dying echoed in his ears, Aelfir called upon his god, 'Tchar. Tchar. Blood and souls for you. Blood and souls for the Old One of the Mound!'

Khojin roared aloud, 'Tchar! By my oath to you, send me the Fire of Transformation in my hour of need!'

Golden mouths opened in Khojin's dark skin and in his silver armour. The mouths sang a strange song in no tongue Aelfir knew, and from them a golden fire began to flow, spilling onto the earth around Khojin and rising about the embattled men. The strength of the beasts seemed to fail in the golden fire and the warband took new heart. Ulla the shieldmaiden laughed aloud, and recklessly ran to Khojin to embrace him.

Aelfir felt the eye of Tchar upon him in that place as men fell about him, and he cut down beast after beast. As the blood of man and beast mingled on the mound, he saw the souls of the beasts and of men shining forth like blue light under their skins. And he saw from the corner of his eye a dark shape moving among the slain, with mad blue eyes, crouching to chew upon the fallen before the souls flew from their flesh. A daemon walks among us, he thought.

The bone whistle shrilled again, and Aelfir winced in pain. From the summit of the mound Khojin's Tarkhal riders charged, plainsmen of the eastern steppes riding wildly down upon the beasts. Kitsa, Aelfir's beloved, rode at the head of the riders with her black hair flying like a flag, crashing into the beasts and scattering them, riding them down among the stones. As the golden fire faded and darkness fell over the battlefield, the Tarkhals screamed their triumph.

THREE DAYS LATER the warband gathered at the mouth of a great cave under high cliffs. A ramshackle wall of wood and bone, adorned with tattered banners of gold and blue, blocked the mouth of the cave. Dead men hung from the wall, their blond hair flowing with the banners in the breeze that drove a cold smell of rot against the banners of the warband. Overhead, eagles soared in the clear blue sky. Aelfir sat on his borrowed horse uneasily, tensing as the grey backed away from the wall, lifting its hooves high from the sucking mud of the track. He did not understand what had happened to his home.

'Aelfir,' Khojin said, 'when we left the south lands and followed the call of the gods to Middenheim, my people and I were lordless and landless. You called us to join you, here in the north, promising wide lands and a safe dwelling where we might gather our strength to go south again. You and I are blood brothers, and I have given you my sister, Kitsa, but I do not think I would have brought my people here had I known what was waiting.'

The two men turned their horses from the wall towards the waiting warband. The tribesmen sat on horseback, loosely gathered about their banners under the looming Tarkhal wagons. Chained behind the wagons slaves sat huddled in their misery, men and women dressed in rags with bare and bleeding feet.

Khojin cried aloud, 'Tarkhals! Hear me! Aelfir has brought us to this place, and Tchar has blessed his path! Though the hold here looks grim, we will find shelter from the winter with his father, Orn, and gather our strength again!'

The mass of the Tarkhal riders, young men with the broad faces and narrow eyes of the eastern steppes, screamed repeatedly, throwing back their heads and shrieking their approval of their chieftain. They wore black beards and greased their long black hair with fat, and red cloaks hung over their bare chests. The Ornings, sullen and pale, blond of hair and wrapped in furs, sat silently, unsure of the home they had sought for so long.

THE WARBAND ENTERED the city, passing through a gap in the wall. They grew grim as they heard strange cries echo among the longhouses. The staves that made up the house walls had been warped into strange shapes and the shingles on the roofs bore half formed faces. As they rode down the empty streets, Khojin peered at the runes scrawled upon the wooden buildings. 'Mighty magic was done here,' he said to Aelfir, 'but for good or ill I cannot tell. These runes should channel the raw power of the gods into the very city itself, but, why?'

A cry came from the Tarkhal scouts. A rider galloped up to Khojin. 'Lord, there are still men in the city! But they are strange, mad, and they show the touch of the gods upon their bodies.'

'Where?' asked Khojin.

'Did they speak?' asked Aelfir. 'Was there a winged man among them?'

'We saw no winged man,' said the scout. 'They were naked but for rags, even the women among them. They stood upon the roofs of the longhouses and spoke in words we could not understand. We feared them, so we fled.'

'Batu you dog!' Khojin shouted. 'Lead us to them!'

Khojin drove Batu before him, beating him with the flat of his sword. When they reached the other scouts they galloped down the dirt lanes of the city. Aelfir, a poor rider, was hard pressed to keep up.

'Khojin!' he cried realizing where they were. 'Beware! We draw near the river and the fields of the dead!'

The Tarkhals clattered to a halt before a narrow bridge over a dark, swift flowing river. As Aelfir forced his mount to stop beside them he saw on the far side of the water men and women he recognized as kin walking deeper into fields of bones. Scattered across the fields were corpses tied upright to stakes, adorned in armour and bright robes – the old lords of his tribe. Aelfir's kinsmen moved as if in a trance, wandering among the bones, singing in weird, high voices.

As the riders sat in silence, a harsh and grating voice spoke from behind them, 'Leave them, the gods have taken their minds.'

AELFIR LOOKED UP to his father in the high seat, masked and hooded, covered in great robes that hid all, and wondered what had gone so wrong. His father was speaking to Khojin about the runes he had scrawled on the longhouses.

'By the power of those runes and the storm of the gods I have joined to my city,' Orn said. 'I shall endure as long as it shall stand.'

'But Orn,' Khojin said, 'what has happened to your people?'

'The power of the ritual was too great,' Orn said. 'The storm destroyed their minds. I alone remain, but you shall be my new people. The Ornings and the Tarkhals shall join and my city will be full of life again. Khojin, take an Orning maiden and make her your bride. Aelfir, marry a Tarkhal maiden. I hear you have one already picked out.'

THE NEXT DAY Aelfir sat in a daze as the tribe feasted. He remembered the wedding ceremony that had taken place that morning, sanctified by the sacrifice of the nine gifts of Tchar. The corpses of the men who were the last and most important of Tchar's gifts sat at a table a little way from him, cleaned and arrayed in finery, a hearty spread of mead and food arrayed before them.

'As you clasp hands together above this fire,' Orn had intoned while Ulla and Khojin and Aelfir and Kitsa stood before him, 'remember your oaths to each other, spoken and sealed before this high seat, and this holy flame of Tchar.'

A sudden silence broke his reverie. A tall young man in a grey cloak with an unsheathed sword and glaring blue eyes was striding down the length of the hall. 'Orn!' the swordsman cried. 'Orn! I have come for you!'

None dared approach as the warrior stalked to the high seat. Aelfir, at the last moment, leapt up but was dashed aside. Orn stood in silence as the warrior ripped aside his robes, showing withering, discoloured flesh and deformed stumps where the wings Aelfir remembered had once stretched.

'Tchar's mercy is gone, and his judgment has come!' said the warrior. He turned to the staring tribesmen, saying, 'I give this gift to the one who can claim it,' and drove the sword into Orn's chest, leaving it there.

As the warrior strode away, the men rose from their seats to slay him, but they stopped in wonder and terror at the transformation that struck Orn. Orn's flesh grew warped and twisted, his bones and muscle straining at his stretching, tearing skin. Orn fell onto all fours and began to stumble about the room, moaning piteously.

Khojin said, 'The sword is a gift from Tchar. Back, all of you. I will take the sword from this spawn.'

But as Khojin approached the spawn suddenly tensed and lashed out with its forelegs, striking Khojin to the ground. The Tarkhals ran to aid their chosen, but none dared to take the sword until Aelfir approached.

As Aelfir drew near the spawn grew quiet. He stepped forward and laid his hand upon the hilt of the sword. He saw out of the corner of his eye a low, dark shadow that seemed to look on with malevolent approval. The sword seemed to fall out into his hand.

'How?' Khojin snarled in wonder, 'But, it is said the were know their own.'

The twisted shape shuddered. Orn's slack face, with its too-wide mouth began to mutter and mumble a continuous stream of noise that rose into a high wailing. The spawn forced its way through the doors of the great hall and fled, wailing, into the darkness of the city.

'AELFIR, WHAT PRICE would you ask for that sword?' Khojin demanded. 'Whatever it is, I can pay. Do you want gold? Slaves? Horses? Warriors for your warband?'

'I have what I want,' Aelfir said.

'As Tchar wills it,' Khojin sneered, limping to the high seat. His wounds were bandaged and a cup was set before him, but his eyes never left Aelfir. Ulla went to Khojin and embraced him, happily whispering into his ear, but his eyes remained cold as he absently stroked her golden hair.

The warriors of the Tarkhals and the Ornings gathered about Aelfir and Kitsa, admiring the blade and guessing about its origins.

'Daemon-forged,' a gaunt Tarkhal said.

'Yah,' said a badly scarred Orning. 'A blade out of the sagas of old.'

'I will make my own saga wielding it,' Aelfir declared.

'If I had a blade like that, I would never sell it,' said Mugin, 'but saying no to a chosen is a good way to end up dead.'

'With this blade,' said Aelfir, 'I can say what I want to anyone I want. Come, Kitsa, the old women have prepared an old hall for me near the river.'

'Let me say goodbye to Khojin and Ulla first,' Kitsa replied.

As Kitsa walked up the hall to the high seat, Khojin's eyes seized upon her. When she reached the high seat, Kitsa told Khojin and Ulla that she and Aelfir were leaving. 'So soon?' Ulla laughed. 'You're married now, you can do it all the time. Why hurry?'

Kitsa blushed, and laughed. Khojin asked Ulla for a moment alone with Kitsa. After Ulla went to find a drink and say goodbye to Aelfir, Khojin turned to Kitsa and whispered urgently, 'Kitsa, you must make him give me that sword!'

'Khojin,' she said. 'He never will.'

'Would you be a widow?'

'What do you mean?'

'I mean there cannot be two masters in a house, two chieftains in a tribe. The blade is a mighty sign of Tchar's favour. If I am to lead these people, I must have it. If he will not give me the blade I must take it and he must die.'

'Khojin,' she said. 'No. I swore an oath to him.'

'Yes,' he said, 'you are a Tarkhal, bound to me by blood and clan. I swore an oath, too, but he is an outsider. Already he has defied me. Tonight you must kill him and get me the sword. If you do not, there will be war between us, Aelfir and I, and your hands will not be clean of the blood that is shed.'

'Khojin, I cannot.'

'You must.'

Kitsa rejoined Aelfir at the door, her face downcast. 'Kitsa, don't look so joyous,' he said. 'The other girls will be jealous.'

She broke into tears.

THE OLD WOMEN of the tribe lit their way to Aelfir's hall with raised torches, singing bawdy songs until they ducked beneath the low lintel of his door. But when they were left alone, and the fire sank low in the hearth, Kitsa was inconsolable and Aelfir was unsure. They slept apart. He gave her the bed and slept on a bench next to the fire.

As the night drew on, Kitsa awoke. She crept from her bed silently and stood above Aelfir as he slept. The dying

light of the fire caught upon a gleam of steel in her left
hand. She raised the dagger, stopped, and raised it again.
She shook, put the dagger away, and paced before her
sleeping lover. The fire was only embers when she heard
harsh whispers at the door of the hall. She saw that Aelfir
stirred and with a look of fear took the sword from
where it lay by his side.

Kitsa turned to the door and put her hand upon the
latch. When she opened the door Khojin was there with
many Tarkhal tribesmen bearing torches. 'Khojin, what
are you doing?' she asked.

'What you fear to do,' he said.

'No. Here is the sword. Take it and go.'

At that moment, Aelfir awoke. He saw his sword being
passed through the door and leapt to his feet. 'Kitsa, no!'
he shouted, grabbing her by her black hair and throwing
her back from the door. Her head struck a corner of the
bed and she lay very still.

Khojin howled when he saw Kitsa pulled back from
the door. 'Orning, give me back my sister!'

'Give me my sword, thief!' Aelfir replied.

Aelfir heard Khojin speak to his men in the language
of the Tarkhals. He could not tell what was said, but
moments later a man's shadow darkened the door and a
Tarkhal warrior ducked under the low lintel. For a
moment the man was vulnerable and Aelfir brought his
fist down hard on the back of the man's head, knocking
him to the floor. Aelfir quickly took the man's sword and
slew him, crying out, 'Khojin, this one dies for Tchar!'

As he said it the room darkened and he felt a presence.
A low, dark shape seemed to stand in the farthest corner
from the fire. He caught the gleam of eyes and heard
whispering, malevolent, gleeful chattering at the edge of
hearing.

More men tried to force their way in through the low
door. In their rush they hindered each other, and four

more fell before his blade. The shape in the corner grew larger and more distinct and the chattering grew louder.

The Tarkhals tried again. Aelfir slew three more warriors in a rush, but was about to be overwhelmed when the Tarkhals turned in fear and fled. He struck down one last warrior and howled to Khojin, 'Nine gifts for Tchar!' In response torches were thrown in through the open door, setting the bedding alight. Aelfir ran to Kitsa, and crouching, gathered her into his arms.

Then he felt a presence at his side and turned. A gaunt and naked man with mad blue eyes crouched over the fallen Tarkhals, grinning with blood-stained fangs. Suddenly, Aelfir saw the shadow had taken temporary form in that body, and knew that a daemon had come to devour the souls of the slain.

'Who are you?' he asked.

'Some call me Jormunrekkr Ornsbane.'

'You were the one in the hall and on the mound.'

'Yes.'

The fire rose higher and the daemon laughed.

Aelfir shook Kitsa, trying to wake her, but she lay still. He felt the back of her head, finding blood. 'No,' he said. 'No. No. No.'

'Yes,' Jormunrekkr laughed, fading into a shadow, disappearing. 'You are a fool, Aelfir.'

The walls were burning. At the door he saw the Tarkhals moving, waiting for the chance to kill him when the smoke and heat forced him out. Aelfir pulled the bench he slept on to the hearth and picked up an axe from the fireside. Standing on the bench, Aelfir climbed onto the mantel of the hearth and stood up. Holding his breath against the smoke, he hacked repeatedly at the ceiling near the chimney, desperately trying to break out on to the roof.

Aelfir succeeded in breaking a hole through the roof, scattering the shingles to the street below. The stone of the mantel grew hot and Aelfir tried to force his way through the gap he had made. He became stuck with only one arm and his head through. As the fire rose inside the hall, he felt his clothes catch fire. In panic, he broke through and leapt, burning, to the roof of a nearby house.

AELFIR RAN, BURNING, along the roof of the empty house. His cloak and shirt were alight and across half his face the flames had seared his skin to crimson, closing one eye. He heard Khojin's men below him, the thud of their feet in the dirt of the lane and the clank of their armour kept pace with his flight. In desperation, he leapt to another roof, losing his footing and landing hard on the shingles.

He staggered up and continued running. He heard shouts and the sound of men climbing around him. In his pain there was room in him for only one thought. 'The river,' he gasped through scorched lips as he ran across the roof tops.

Ulla swung up to the roof, blocking the way, shouting, 'Aelfir! Kitsa is dead! Stay and pay the blood debt you owe!'

She stood before him with a sword in her hand, but the pain of the flames drove him blindly on. At the last moment he saw the blade and threw himself to one side, dodging her blow but crashing into her and in his haste carrying her off her feet. For a moment they hung in the darkness, burning like the daemons themselves, and then suddenly they were gone, crashing into the icy black water of the river that flowed between the houses of the living Ornings and the tombs of their dead fathers.

When Aelfir's head at last arose above the rushing surface of the river he found he was not alone, something clung to him under the black water. He howled in fright, briefly lost in childhood tales of the clutching things that made the river their home. Then in the pain of his burns he remembered his flight from Khojin and Ulla barring his way and he realized what he must do.

He knotted his fingers in the silky hair he found floating just below the river's surface and kept her head down. Her hands clawed at him, raking his face. He did not know how long in the blackness he held her under before her struggles stilled and he freed himself of her grip.

As she slid away from him in the dark he saw witchlights rising from the depths toward them, illuminating the terror on her face. In panic, he thrashed to the shore, hauling himself out of the black water among the bones scattered about the tombs on the far side of the river.

He crawled away from the river. In the water he had lost most of the rags the fire had left him. He was naked and covered with burns. He shook with cold and he could not stand. He knew that he was dying. He saw a fire before him, bones burning among the tombs and he crawled towards it.

Reaching the fire, he rolled on to his back, gasping, unable to continue. When he looked about him he recognized the twisted faces of the Ornings driven mad by his father's ritual looking down at him, and among them he saw the ice-blue eyes of his father's slayer.

'You ARE WEAK, Aelfir,' Jormunrekkr said, 'weak and a fool. And you are dying. It is fitting. You are the last of a house that failed.'

'We failed in nothing,' Aelfir gasped. 'Always we kept the rites, always in our land Tchar's words were spoken and the eagles were fed. Where did we fail?'

'When the storm raged and the powers called the men of the north down to rend the world the Ornings betrayed their master. Where was Orn when the armies of the gods met at the southland city?'

'I was there!' Aelfir said. 'I led men to the Wolf City for Tchar!'

'You were not chosen. Until that time you had lived your life out of the sight of the gods. How could you take the place of your father? And yet he sent you south to die. He heard whispers in the sea of souls, voices that promised him immortality if he could bend the power of the storm to his will. Tchar promised him only death on the walls of the Wolfburg. He made his choice. Now he will have immortality, running with the spawn.'

'Why did Tchar want my father to die? Why does the Eagle kill his chosen?'

Jormunrekkr's eyes flashed. 'Look into the fire, Aelfir.'

Painfully, Aelfir turned toward the fire. It grew until he saw nothing else for a time, and then he saw the hound, a hound the size of a mountain, running ceaselessly, drawing ever nearer, over a field of corpses. Next he saw the carrion crow, a rotting thing greater than a longhouse, digging in the world's grave for the flesh of men. Last he saw the serpent, coiling in the depths of the sea, rising to devour the land. From these visions Aelfir recoiled in horror.

'Now you see,' Jormunrekkr said, 'against these the Eagle raises his chosen, and bids them live or die according to his need.'

'You came for my gifts on the mound, and in the burning hall,' Aelfir said. 'Give me a chance to win back Tchar's favour. Let me serve the Eagle once more.'

'Will you keep the faith your father forsook?' Jormunrekkr demanded. 'Can you?'

'Give me strength. I will do it.'

'Your father feared to die. Show me you are unafraid. You know the pain of burning, here is a fire. Would you be chosen? Go into it.'

Aelfir struggled to raise himself from the earth. 'I am too weak to stand.'

'Crawl.'

'I will die.'

'Tchar does not promise long life to his chosen.'

Aelfir struggled to his knees, feeling burned skin stretch and crack. He swayed, too weak to hold himself up, and a low moan escaped his lips. He grew quiet, closed his eyes, and fell forward into the fire.

His hair caught fire. A shriek burst from his lips. The pain from his burns returned a hundredfold. He cried out, 'Tchar! Tchar!' and the fire felt like cool water on his skin. He opened his eyes, and he saw that the flames were blue. He looked for Jormunrekkr and saw a vast dark shape with many blue eyes, eyes that burned like stars.

A great weariness came upon him. He lay down peacefully. He looked for his mad kinsmen and saw them standing about in reverent silence, their souls shining through the veil of the flesh. It seemed to him that they wore crowns of flame. And then the crowns warped, and the colours multiplied, and he saw the horrors of Tchar unfolding, rising like alien flowers from the heads of his kinsmen.

He fell into a dreamless sleep.

AELFIR AWOKE FILLED with new strength. He rose lightly to his feet, marvelling at the strange new gold-flecked skin that had grown during his sleep to replace his burned flesh, the new thickness of his arms and legs, and the width of his chest. Out of the litter of the dead he pulled some blue rags and bound them about his waist as a kilt.

A short distance away he saw his mad kinsmen playing with the fire and knew them for what they were, daemonhosts, blessed for a time with the companionship of the children of the uttermost north, the daemons of Chaos.

AELFIR APPROACHED THE fire. The daemonhosts turned to watch him and withdrew from the flames. He saw both the daemons and the spirits of his kin, and also their shared flesh. The daemons began to show their shapes in the flesh they wore, growing claws and tentacles, opening new eyes and mouths.

Aelfir stopped at the fire and made a torch out of rags and bones. He lit it, and raised it above his head. 'Hear me,' he called, 'my kinsmen. Hear me you Shining Ones, you Blessed Ones. You wander lost. Come to the halls of my people. I invite you in. Once you got offerings, now there will be red blood, and fire, and the walls of the world will thin.'

He turned and walked with firm strides back towards the city of the Ornings. Drawn like moths to a flame, the blessed ones followed.

He crossed a narrow bridge over the swiftly flowing river and thought for a second he saw his father's ruined form running in the lanes between the longhouses. He paused only for a moment, then set fire to the nearest house. The blessed ones capered madly about the blaze and made torches of their own from the trash in the silent street. With unnatural, shrill voices they piped a song he could almost understand, then scattered, running madly through the city.

The fire quickly spread. Stave and shingle burned as the fire leapt from house to house, but always in the wake of Aelfir and the daemonhosts. The Tarkhals and the remaining Ornings fled from their burning long-houses only to be pulled down and slain, or cast back into the fires. Smoke laden with the stench of burning flesh rolled through the streets. The roar of the flames and the screams of the dying were loud in Aelfir's ears when at last he came to Orn's great hall.

Before the open doors Khojin stood alone as the last of his people fled and died under the claws of the daemonhosts. The flames roared on the shingles and roof beams crashed within the hall. Daemonhosts capered about Khojin, mocking him in piping tones. His silver armour gave back the flames in reflection. He seemed like a man on fire. In his hand was the sword Ornsbane.

The daemonhosts parted to let Aelfir through. 'Now, Khojin of the Tarkhals,' he cried. 'Tchar has turned against you and your life is at its end. You betrayed me but could not slay me, I won free of the burning hall, and now I have returned out of the darkness to claim my sword.'

'As Tchar wills it,' said Khojin, 'but I will never submit to you and I may yet have my revenge for my sister and my bride. Die!' Red fire leapt from his outstretched hand, engulfing Aelfir for an instant before disappearing, leaving Aelfir unmarked.

Aelfir laughed, 'No fire of yours can harm me now.'

Aelfir leapt forward, catching Khojin's wrist as he attempted to swing his sword and punching him twice in the breastplate of his armour, breaking ribs.

Khojin fell to his knees and crawled away from Aelfir, fighting for breath and trying to remove his damaged armour.

Aelfir picked up the sword. Despite the fire, a darkness grew about him. He heard daemonic voices calling for Orn, his father, and knew they must be satisfied. Using the sword as a conduit, he reached out to his father, compelling him to come forth out of the burning city and obey the blade that made him a spawn.

Orn's twisted form appeared. Lurching out of the flames, Orn fell upon Khojin, devouring him.

In the burning door of the great hall a shape of shadow waited, watching with ice-blue eyes. Aelfir saw the daemonhosts gather about Orn as he fed, and saw Orn drawn, howling, into the flames. He heard Jormunrekkr's sardonic voice say, 'Ready the benches and measure the mead, for a hero comes to the Daemon's Hall.'

DEATH'S COLD KISS
by Steven Savile

I

THE OLD PRIEST fled the castle.

Lightning seared the darkness, turning night momentarily into day. The skeletal limbs of the trees around him cast sinister shadows across the path that twisted and writhed in the lightning. Thunder rolled over the hills, deep and booming. The rain came down, drowning out lesser sounds.

The primeval force of the storm resonated in Victor Guttman's bones.

'I am an old man,' he moaned, clutching at his chest in dread certainty that the pain he felt was his heart about to burst. 'I am frail. Weak. I don't have the strength in me for this fight.' And it was true, every word of it. But who else was there to fight?

No one.

His skin still crawled with the revulsion he had felt at the creature's presence. Sickness clawed at his throat. His blood repulsed by the taint of the creature that had entered Baron Otto's chamber and claimed young

Isabella. He sank to his knees, beaten down by the sheer ferocity of the storm. The wind mocked him, howling around his body, tearing at his robes. He could easily die on the road and be washed away by the storm, lost somewhere to rot in the forest and feed the wolves.

No.

The temple. He had to get back to the temple.

He pushed himself back up and lurched a few more paces down the pathway, stumbling and tripping over his own feet in his need to get away from the damned place.

There were monsters. Real monsters. He had grown numb to fear. A life of seclusion in the temple, of births and naming days, marriages and funeral rites, such mundane things, they somehow combined to turn the monsters into lesser evils and eventually into nothing more than stories. He had forgotten that the stories were real.

Guttman lurched to a stop, needing the support of a nearby tree to stay standing. He cast a frightened look back over his shoulder at the dark shadow of Drakenhof Castle, finding the one window that blazed with light, and seeing in it the silhouette of the new count.

Vlad von Carstein.

He knew what kind of twisted abomination the man was. He knew with cold dark certainty that he had just witnessed the handover of the barony to a daemon. The sick twisted maliciousness of Otto van Drak would pale in comparison with the tyrannies of the night von Carstein promised.

The old priest fought down the urge to purge his guts. Still he retched and wiped the bile away from his mouth with the back of his hand. The taint of the creature had weakened him. Its sickness was insidious. It clawed away at his stomach; it tore at his throat and pulled at his mind. His vision swam in and out of focus. He needed to distance himself from the fiend.

His mind raced. He struggled to remember everything he knew about vampires and their ilk but it was precious little outside superstition and rumour.

The oppression of the pathway worsened as it wound its way back down toward the town. The sanctuary of rooftops and the welcoming lights looked a long, long way away to the old man. The driving rain masked other sounds. Still, Guttman grew steadily surer that he was not alone in the storm. Someone – or something – was following him. He caught occasional glimpses of movement out of the corner of his eye but by the time he turned, the shadow had fused with deeper shadows or the shape he was sure was a pale white face had mutated into the claws of dead branches and the flit of a bat's wing.

He caught himself looking more frequently back over his shoulder as he tried to catch a glimpse of whoever was following him.

'Show yourself!' the old priest called out defiantly but his words were snatched away by the storm. The cold hand of fear clasped his heart as it tripped and skipped erratically.

A chorus of wolves answered him.

And laughter.

For a moment Guttman didn't trust his ears. But he didn't need to. It was a man's laughter. He felt it in his gut, in his bones and in his blood, the same revulsion that had caused him to black out at the feet of von Carstein when the man first entered van Drak's bedchamber.

One of the count's tainted brood had followed him out of the castle. It was stupid and naïve to think that von Carstein would be alone. The monster would have minions to do his bidding, lackeys who still clung to their humanity and servants who had long since given it up. It made sense. How could a creature of the damned hope to pass itself off among the living without an entourage of twisted souls to do its bidding?

'I said show yourself, creature!' Guttman challenged the darkness. The rain ran down his face like tears. He wasn't afraid anymore. He was calm. Resigned. The creature was playing with him.

'Why?' A voice said, close enough for him to feel the man's breath in his ear. 'So your petty god can smite me down with some righteous thunderbolt from his shiny silver hammer? I think not.'

Brother Guttman reeled away from the voice, twisting round to face his tormentor but the man wasn't there.

'You're painfully slow, old man,' the voice said, behind him again somehow. 'Killing you promises to be no sport at all.' Guttman felt cold dead fingers brush against his throat, feeling out the pulse in his neck. He lurched away from their touch so violently he ended up sprawling in the mud, the rain beating down around his face as he twisted and slithered trying to get a look at his tormentor.

The man stood over him, nothing more than a shape in the darkness.

'I could kill you now but I've never taken a priest. Do you think you would make a good vampire, old man? You have a whole flock of dumb sheep to feed on who will come willingly to you in the night, eager to be fed on if your holy kiss will bring them closer to their precious Sigmar.' The man knelt beside him, the left side of his face lit finally by the slither of moonlight. To Guttman it was the face of ultimate cruelty personified but in truth it was both beautiful and coldly serene. 'What a delicious thought. A priest of the cloth becoming a priest of the blood. Think of the possibilities. You would be unique, old man.'

'I would rather die.'

'Well, of course. That goes without saying. Now, come on, on your feet.'

'And make your job easier?'

'Oh, just stand up before I run out of patience and stick a sword in your gut, brother. You don't have to be standing to die, you know. It isn't a prerequisite. Swords are just as effective on people lying in the mud, believe me.' He held out a hand for the priest to take but the old man refused, levering himself up and stubbornly struggling to get his feet beneath himself.

'Who are you?'

'Does it matter? Really? What's in a name? Truly? Turned meat, cat's urine and mouldy bread by any other names would still smell repugnant, wouldn't they? They would still stink of decay, rot, so why this obsession with naming things? There is no magic in a name.'

'What a sad world you live in,' Guttman said after a moment. 'Where the first things that come to mind are riddled with corruption. Give me a world of roses and beauty and I will die happily. To live as you do, that is no life at all.'

'Do not be so hasty to dismiss it, priest. They have an old saying in my hometown: Die reinste Freude ist die Schadenfreude,' the man said in perfect unaccented Reikspiel. 'The purest joy is the joy we feel when others feel pain. Now I believe it is the only genuine joy we feel. The rest is transitory, fleeting. Soon the darkness will be all you have left, and the light and your precious roses and everything else you think of as beautiful will be nothing more than memories. The knowledge of this gives me some slight happiness I must confess. When you've been reduced to nothing, then let us see how much of the so-0called beautiful you choose to remember. My name is Posner. Herman Posner. Say it. Let it be the last thing you say as a living creature. Say it.'

'Herman Posner,' Brother Victor Guttman said, tasting the name in his mouth. The words were no more evil than any others he had said. There was nothing unique about them. They were not tainted with vile plague or ruined by undeath. They were just words, nothing more.

'A rose or rot, priest? You decide,' Posner said. His hand snaked out grabbing the old man by the collar and hauling him up until his toes barely touched the floor. Guttman struggled and fought, kicking out as Posner drew him in close enough for the priest to taste the redolent musk of the grave on his breath. The creature's touch was repulsive.

It didn't matter how much he kicked and twisted against Posner's grip; it was like iron.

He felt the teeth – fangs – plunge into his neck, biting deep, hard. The old man's body tensed, every fibre of his being repulsed by the intimacy of the kill. He lashed out, twisted, flopped and finally sagged as he felt the life being drained out of him.

And then the pain ended and Posner was screaming and clutching his own chest.

Guttman had no idea what had caused the vampire to relinquish his hold. He didn't care. His legs buckled and collapsed beneath him but he didn't pass out. He lay in the mud, barely able to move. He was sure his tripping heart would simply cease beating at any moment and deny the vampire its kill. There was a delicious irony to the thought, the beast gorging itself on dead blood, only realising its mistake when it was too late.

Posner lifted his hand. The skin beneath was burned raw with the mark of Sigmar's hammer.

For a moment the old priest thought it was a miracle – that he was saved. Then the cold hard reality of the 'miracle' revealed itself. The silver hammer he wore on a chain around his neck had come loose from his clothing and as the vampire leaned in the silver had burned its mark on the beast. Silver. At least that part of the stories was true. The metal was anathema to the lords of the undead. He clasped the talisman as though it might somehow save him. It was a feeble gesture. Posner leaned over him and grasped the silver chain, ignoring the hiss and sizzle of his own flesh as he yanked the holy symbol from around Guttman's throat, and tossed it aside.

The stench of burned meat was nauseatingly sweet.

'Now let's see how you fare without your pretty little trinket, shall we?'

Before Guttman could scramble away Posner had him by the throat again, fingernails like iron talons as they sank mercilessly into his flesh. The pain was blinding. The priest's vision swam in and out of focus as the world tilted away and was finally consumed in an agony of black. The last sensation he felt as the pain overwhelmed him was the vampire's kiss, intimate and deadly, where his fluttering pulse was strongest. Guttman's eyes flared open and for a fleeting moment the world around him was intense, every colour more vibrant, more radiant, every scent more pungent, more aromatic, than they had been through his whole life of living with them. He was dying, drained of life and blood, and this intensity was his mind's way of clinging on to the memories of life, one final all-consuming overload of the senses. Victor Guttman let it wash over him. He felt his will to live fade with his thoughts as he succumbed to Posner. He stopped struggling, the fight drained out of him.

Posner yanked his head back better to expose the vein and sucked and slurped hungrily at the wound until he was sated. Grinning, he tilted the old man's head and dribbled blood into his gaping mouth. Guttman coughed and retched, a ribbon of blood dribbling out of the corner of his mouth. His entire body spasmed, rebelling against the bloody kiss and then he was falling as Posner let go.

The vampire walked away, leaving the old man to die.

To die, Guttman realised sickly, and become one of their kind. An abomination. No. No. It cannot happen. I will not kill to live. I will not!

But he knew he would.

In the end, when the blood thirst was on him and his humanity was nothing but a nagging ghost he would feed.

Guttman clawed at the mud, dragging himself forward a few precious inches before his strength gave out. His erratic breathing blew bubbles in the muddy puddle beside his face. His hand twitched. He felt himself slipping in and out of consciousness. Every breath could easily have been his last. He had no idea how long he lay in the mud blowing bloody bubbles. Time lost all meaning. The sun didn't rise. The rain didn't cease, not fully. He tried to move but every ounce of his being cried out in pain. He was alone. No passing carters would save him. He had a choice – although it was no choice at all: die here, now, and wake as a daemon, or fight it, grasp on to the last gasp of humanity and hope against hope that something in the temple could stave off the transformation and buy him precious time. Death was inevitable, he had always known that, accepted it. He would meet Morr, every man, woman and child would eventually; it was the way of the world. He promised himself he would do it with dignity. He would die, and stay dead. Judge me not on how I lived but how I die… who had said that? It made a grim kind of sense.

On the hillside around him the cries of the wolves intensified. It was a mocking lament. He knew what they were, those wolves. He knew how the beasts could shift form at will. He dreaded the moment their cries made sense to him, for then his doom would be complete.

He dragged himself another foot, and then another, almost blacking out from the sheer exertion. His face held barely inches above a muddy puddle, he stared at his own reflection in the water, trying to memorise everything he saw. He knew the image would fade, knew he would forget himself, but it was important to try to hold on to who he was. Another foot, and then another. The old priest clawed his way down the long and winding road. He felt the steel breeze on his face as he craned his neck desperately trying to see how far away the city lights were.

Too far, they taunted him. Too far.

He would never make it.

And because of that he was damned.

Desperately, Victor Guttman pushed himself up, stumbled two unsteady steps and plunged face first into the mud again. He lay there, spent, cursing himself for a fool for coming to the castle alone. The chirurgeon was long gone, probably safely at home in his bed already, tucked up beside his shrew of a wife while she snored. Or he's lying dead in a ditch somewhere. He was just as alone when he left the castle. Just as vulnerable. And probably just as dead. Guttman thought bitterly.

Again he stumbled forward a few paces before collapsing. Five more the next time. He cried out in anger and frustration, willing someone to hear him and come to his aid. It was pointless, of course. The only people abroad at this ungodly hour were up to no good and would hardly come to investigate cries on the dark road for fear of their own safety. Thieves, robbers, bandits, lotharios, debauchers, drunks, gamblers and vampires, children of the night one and all. And not a Sigmar fearing soul amongst them. He was alone.

Truly alone.

II

MEYRINK AND MESSNER were passionately arguing an obscure point of theosophy, the older man being driven

to the point of distraction by the younger's sheer bel-
ligerence. He was impossible to argue with. There was
no reasoning, only absolutes. The arguments were black
and white. There was no room for the grey spaces of
interpretation in between. Normally there was nothing
Meyrink enjoyed more than a good argument but the
youth of today seemed to have abandoned the art of
reason in favour of passion. Everything was about passion. Meyrink laid aside the scrimshaw he had been
carving and rolled his neck, stretching. The carving was
therapeutic but his eyes weren't what they had been
even a few years ago and the close detail gave him a
headache from straining. He felt every one of his years.
Brother Guttman would return soon. Perhaps he could
make young Messner see reason.

'Perhaps, perhaps, perhaps,' Meyrink muttered
bleakly. He didn't hold out a lot of hope.

'Ah, is that the sound of quiet desperation I hear leaking into your voice, brother?'

'Not so quiet, methinks,' Meyrink said with a lopsided
grin. He liked the boy, and was sure with the rough
edges rounded off his personality Messner would make
a good priest. He had the faith and was a remarkably
centred young man.

'Indeed. I was being politic. Come, let's warm our
bones beside the fire while we wait for Brother
Guttman's return.'

'Why not.'

''Tis a vile night out,' Messner remarked, making himself cosy beside the high-banked log fire that spat and
crackled in the hearth. He poured them both cups of
mulled wine.

'For once I'll not argue with you lad,' Meyrink said
wryly.

The night stretched on, Meyrink too tired to debate.
He looked often at the dark window and the streaks of

rain that lashed against it. Messner was right: it was a vile night. Not the kind of night for an old man to be abroad.

They supped at their cups, neither allowing the other to see how much the old priest's lateness worried them until a hammering on the temple door had them both out of their seats and almost running through the central aisle of the temple to answer it. Meyrink instinctively made the sign of the hammer as Messner threw back the heavy bolts on the door and raised the bar. It had been many years since they had left the temple open through the night. It was a curse of the times. He didn't like it but was sage enough to understand the necessity.

Messner opened the door on the raging storm.

The wind and rain ripped at the porch, pulling the heavy door out of the young priest's hands.

For a heartbeat Meyrink mistook the shadows on the threshold for some lurking horror, distorted and deformed as they were by the storm, but then the wine merchant Hollenfeuer's boy, Henrik, lumbered in out of the driving rain and dark, a bundle of rags cradled in his arms. It took Meyrink a moment to realise that the rags weren't rags at all, but sodden robes clinging wetly to slack skin and bones, and that Henrik had brought Brother Guttman home. The old priest's skin had the same blue pallor as death. His eyes rolled back in his head and his head lolled back against the boy's arm, his jaw hanging loose.

'Found 'im on the roadside a couple of miles back. Carried 'im 'ere.' Henrik grunted beneath the strain. He held the old man in his straining arms like a sack of coals. 'No idea how long 'e'd been there. 'E's still breathing but 'e's not in a good way, mind. Looks like 'e's been attacked by wolves or summink. 'E's got some frightenin' wounds where 'e's been bitten round the throat.'

'Put him down, put him down,' Meyrink flapped. 'Not here, no, no, not here. In his room. In his room. Take him to his room. What happened? Who did this to him?'

'I dunno,' Henrik said, tracking the storm into the temple. Behind him, Messner wrestled with the door. Meyrink moved in close, feeling for the old priest's pulse. It was there, faint for sure, but his heart was still beating and his blood was still pumping.

They carried the broken body of Victor Guttman up the winding stairs to his bare cell and laid him on the wooden pallet he called a bed, drawing the blanket up over his chest to his chin. The old man shivered. Meyrink took this as a good sign – there was still life enough in him to care about the cold.

He sent Henrik on his way, urging him to summon Gustav Mellin, the count's chirurgeon. He pressed a silver coin into his palm. 'Be convincing, lad.' The wine merchant's boy nodded and disappeared into the storm.

Meyrink went back to the old priest's cell where Messner was holding a silent prayer vigil. He cradled Guttman's fragile hand in his, whispering over and over entreaties to Sigmar, begging that His divine hand spare the old man from Morr. It was odd how the young man could be so adamant in the face of theory and yet so devout in the face of fact. His blind faith was as inspiring now as it had been annoying a few hours ago. Meyrink hovered on the threshold, looking at the young man kneeling at the bedside, head bowed in prayer. Guttman was clinging to life – a few words, even to the great and the good, wouldn't save him. It was down to the old man's will and the chirurgeon's skill, if he arrived in time. When it came down to it that was their prime difference: Meyrink was a realist, Messner an idealist still waiting for the brutality of the world to beat it out of him.

Meyrink coughed politely, letting Messner know he was no longer alone.

'How is he?'

'Not good. These wounds...'

'The bites? If that is what they are.'

'Oh that is what they are, without doubt. Whatever fed on him though, it wasn't wolves.'

'How can you be sure?' Meyrink asked, moving into the cell.

'Look for yourself. The first set of puncture wounds are precise and close together, suggesting a small mouth, certainly not a wolf. And there are nowhere enough teeth or tearing to match the savagery of wolves. If I didn't know better I'd say the bite was human.'

'But you know better?'

Messner shook his head.

'Then let us content ourselves with the fact that the world is a sick place and that our dear brother was set upon by one of the flock. It makes no difference to the treatment. We must staunch the blood loss and seal the wounds best we can, keeping them clean to keep out the festering. Other than that, perhaps you are right to pray. I can think of nothing else we can do for our brother.'

They did what they could, a mixture of prayer, medicine and waiting. Mellin, the chirurgeon arrived at dawn, inspected the wounds clinically, tutting between clenched teeth as he sutured the torn flesh. His prognosis was not good:

'He's lost a lot of blood. Too much for a man to lose and still live.'

'Surely you can do something?'

'I'm doing it. Cleaning up the wounds. If he deteriorates, my leeches will be good for the rot, but other than that, he's in the hands of your god.'

Guttman didn't wake for three straight days. Mostly he lay still, the shallow rise and fall of his chest all that distinguished him from the dead, though he did toss and turn occasionally, mumbling some incoherent half words while in the grip of fever dreams. The sweats were worst at night. In the darkest hours of the night the old priest's breathing was at its weakest, hitching and sometimes stopping for long seconds as though Guttman's body simply forgot how to breathe. Messner only left his bedside for a few moments at a time for daily ablutions. He ate his meals sitting against the bed frame and slept on a cot in the small cell, leaving Meyrink to oversee the day-to-day running of the temple and lead the congregation in prayers for Brother Guttman's swift recovery.

The fever ran its course and on the fourth day Victor Guttman opened his eyes.

It was no gentle waking: he sat bolt upright, his eyes flew open and one word escaped his parched mouth: 'Vampire!' He sank back into the pillow, gasping for breath.

The suddenness of it shocked Meyrink. He thought for a moment that he had misheard, that the dry rasp had been some last desperate plea to the gods for salvation before the old priest shuffled off the mortal coil, but it wasn't. He had heard correctly. Guttman had cried vampire.

Meyrink stared at the sutured wounds in the old man's throat, his mind racing. Could they truly be the mark of the vampire? The thought was ludicrous. It hadn't even crossed his mind. Vampires? But if they were... did that mean Victor Guttman is one of them now? Tainted? He was a priest of Sigmar surely he couldn't succumb to the blood kiss...

Meyrink took the old man's hand and felt none of the revulsion he was sure he should if Guttman had been born again into unlife.

'It's not too late, my friend,' he said, kneeling at Guttman's bedside. 'It's not too late.'

'Kill… me… please,' the old man begged, his eyes rheumy with pain. The chirurgeon had left nothing to dull the pain and Meyrink was loathe to let the man loose with his leeches. 'Before I… succumb… to it.'

'Hush, my friend. Save your strength.'

'I will not… kill. I will… not.'

III

REINHARDT MESSNER TURNED the brittle pages of the dusty old tome. He was tired, his enthusiasm for the search long since gone and the ink on the paper was a degree less intelligible than a spider's scrawl. The words had long since begun to blend into one. Beside him Meyrink grunted and shifted in his chair. It had been three days since Brother Guttman's return to the land of the living. During that time he had faded in and out of consciousness. He refused food, claiming he had no appetite. He drank little water, claiming he had no thirst. This disturbed the young priest. No hunger, no thirst, it was unnatural. It added a certain amount of credence to the old man's story of vampires but Messner refused to believe there was any real truth to it. Still, he studied the old tomes looking for some kind of geas that might be used to seal Guttman in the temple. It was useless. There was nothing.

The few references to the vampiric curse he had found revolved around fishwives' gossip and stupid superstitions about garlic and white roses. The only thing of any use was a single line about silver being anathema to the beasts. Other than that there was nothing of substance. One had ideas of how to keep a vampire out of a building, not keep it trapped within one – though for a while he hoped the solution might be one and the same.

'This is out of our province,' he admitted grudgingly, closing the book in a billow of dust. 'Short of sealing Brother Guttman in a silver lined vault, which is both impractical and impossible given the cost of the metal, I have found nothing. I hate to say it, but this is useless. We are wasting our time.'

'No, it has to be in here somewhere,' Meyrink objected, for once their roles of donkey in the argument reversed. Meyrink was being the stubborn ass refusing to see the impossibility of their situation. If Guttman had been infected – and that was how he thought of it, a disease – then the best thing they could do for the old man was drive a stake through his heart, scoop out his brains and bury him upside down in consecrated ground.

If…

'You know it isn't, brother. This is a wild goose chase.'

'What would you have us do? Slay our brother?'

That was a question he wasn't prepared to answer. 'Nothing good comes of death,' he said instead, hoping Meyrink would take it as his final word.

'Yet we cannot stand guard over him night and day, it is impossible. There must be a way.'

A thought occurred to him then: 'Perhaps magic runes…?' They could place runes on the doors and windows to act as locks barring Guttman's ingress and egress, thus confining the vampire to the crypts.

Meyrink spat. 'Would you consort with the servants of Chaos?'

He was right, of course. The practice of magic was outlawed – it would be next to impossible to find anyone to craft such magic, and even if they could, for how long would the magic remain stable? To rely on such a warding was to court disaster, for certain, but Messner knew there was hope in the idea. Could such a series of runes be created to turn the old temple into a sanctuary for Guttman?

'The count would have access…' and then he realised
what he was saying. The count.

Von Carstein.

The vampire count.

He made the sign of Sigmar's hammer.

There would be no going to the castle for help.

IV

THE DOORS AND window frames of the temple had been
inlaid with fine silver wire; bent into the shape of the
runes the mage had sworn would keep the undead at
bay. Meyrink had had no choice but to employ the man,
despite his deep-seated distrust of magicians.

Meyrink studied the silver swirls.

There was nothing, as far as he could tell, remotely
magical about the symbols that had cost the temple an
Emperor's ransom. The man had assured the priests that
the combination of the curious shapes and the precious
metal would turn the confines of the temple into a
prison for any of the tainted blood. He had sworn an
oath, for all the good it did them now.

Like the windows and doors, the entrance to the crypt
itself was protected by a serious of intricate metal swirls
that had be laid in after Victor Guttman had been led
below. Together, the mage had promised, these twists of
metal would form an impenetrable barrier for the dead,
keeping those without a soul from crossing. Again,
Meyrink had no choice but to believe the man, despite
the evidence of his own eyes.

Meyrink descended the thirteen steps into the bowels
of the temple.

The crypt was dank, lit by seven guttering candles that
threw sepulchral shadows over the tombs, the air fetid.
Guttman had refused the comforts of a bed and slept
curled up on a blanket in a dirty corner, ankles and
wrists chained to the wall like some common thief.

It hurt Meyrink to see him like this: living in the dark, hidden away from the world he so loved, shackled.

This was no life at all.

'Morning, brother,' he called, lightly, struggling to keep the grief out of his voice.

'Is it?' answered the old man, looking up. The flickering candlelight did nothing to hide the anguish in his eyes or the slack skin of his face. 'Time has lost all meaning underground. I see nothing of light and day or dark and night, only candles that burn out and are replenished as though by magic when I finally give in to sleep. I had the dream again last night...'

Meyrink nodded. He knew. Two more girls – they were no more than children in truth – had succumbed to the sleeping sickness and died during the night. Two more. They were calling it a plague, though for a plague it was a selective killer, draining the very life out of Drakenhof's young women while the men lived on, seemingly immune, desperate as those they loved fell victim. It was always the same: first they paled, as the sickness took hold then they slipped into a sleep from which they never woke. The transition was shockingly quick. In a matter of three nights vibrant healthy young women aged as much as three decades to look at and succumbed to an eternal sleep. Meyrink knew better: it wasn't a plague, it was a curse.

'Did I...? Did I...?'

He nodded again.

'Two young girls, brother. Sisters. They were to have been fifteen this naming day.'

Guttman let out a strangled sob. He held up his hands, rattling the chains in anger and frustration. 'I saw it... I...' But there was nothing he could say. 'Have you come to kill me?'

'I can't, brother. Not while there is hope.'

'There is no hope. Can't you see that? I am a killer now. There is no peace for me. No rest. And while I live you damn the young women of our flock. Kill me, brother. If not for my own sake, then do it for theirs.' Tears streaked down his grubby face.

'Not while you can still grieve for them, brother. Not while you still have compassion. When you are truly a beast, when the damned sickness owns you, only then. Before that day do not ask for what I cannot do.'

V

'HE HAS TO die!' Messner raged, slamming his clenched fist on the heavy oak of the refectory table. The clay goblets he and Meyrink had been drinking from jumped almost an inch, Meyrink's teetering precariously before it toppled, spilling thick bloody red wine into the oak grain between them.

'Who's the monster here? The old man in the dungeon or the young one baying for his blood?' Meyrink pushed himself to his feet and leaned in menacingly. It was rapidly becoming an old argument but that didn't prevent it from being a passionate one.

'Forty-two girls dead, man! Forty-two! What about the sanctity of life? What is the meaning of life, brother, if you are willing to throw it away so cheaply?'

'We don't know,' Meyrink rasped, his knuckles white on the tabletop. 'We just don't know that it is him. We have no evidence that he gets out. He's chained up in there. There are wards and sigils and glyphs and all sorts of paraphernalia aimed at keeping him locked up down there, helpless… harmless.'

'And yet every morning he feeds you stories of his dreams, talks of the young ones he has seen suffering at the hands of the monstrous beasts. He regales you in glorious detail, brother. The creature is taunting you and you are too stupid to realise it.'

'No. Not too stupid. It is compassion. The old man raised you as he would his own son, from when the temple took you in fifteen years ago. He cared for you. He loved you. He did the same for me in my time. We owe him–'

'We owe him nothing anymore. He isn't Victor Guttman! He's a daemon. Can't you get that into your thick skull, man? He barely touches the food we take down for him for a reason, you know. It doesn't sustain him. Blood does. Blood, Brother. *Blood.*'

'Would you do it? Would you turn murderer and kill the man who might as well have been your own father, everything he did for you? Would you? Take the knife now, go down into the crypt and do it, cut his heart out. Do it, damn you! If you have so little doubt, do it…'

'No.'

'Well I am not about to.'

'I know men who could,' Messner said softly, wriggling around the impasse with a suggestion neither man really wished to consider. Bringing in outsiders. Part of it was fear – what would happen if people realised the priesthood of Sigmar had been infected with the tainted blood of vampires? Another part was self-preservation. The streets had been rife with rumours for days. Two witch hunters were in Drakenhof, though from what little Messner had managed to learn they were not church sanctioned Sigmarite witch hunters, and were barely in the employ of the elector count of Middenheim. Their charge had been issued nearly a decade ago, now their hunt was personal. They had come to town a week ago, looking for a man by the name of Sebastian Aigner, who, if the gossips were to be believed, they had been hunting for seven years. He was the last of a bunch of renegade killers who had slaughtered the men's families, burning them alive. Skellan and Fischer, the witch hunters, had found the others and extracted their blood debt. They had come to Drakenhof looking to lay their daemons to rest, and perhaps, Messner thought, they could purge the temple of its daemon in the process. 'They could tell us for sure. This is what they do.'

Meyrink looked sceptical.

'Forty-two young women, forty-two. Think about it.'

'That is all I have been doing, for weeks. Do you think I don't lie awake at night, imagining him out there, feasting? Do you think I don't sneak down into the crypt at all hours, hoping to catch him gone, so that I know beyond a shadow of a doubt that he is the killer my heart tells me he isn't? Always I find him there, chained to the walls, barely conscious, looking like death itself, and it breaks my heart that he is suffering because of me!'

'Forty-two,' Reinhardt Messner said again, shaking his head as though the number itself answered every objection Brother Meyrink voiced. And perhaps it did at that.

'Talk to them if you must, but I want no part of it,' Meyrink said, finally, turning and stalking out of the room.

Alone, Messner righted the spilled goblet and began mopping up the mess. It was, it seemed, his destiny to clean up after Meyrink.

VI

MESSNER GREETED THE younger of the two with a tired smile and held out a hand to be shaken.

Skellan ignored it and didn't return the smile. There was something distinctly cold about the man, but given his line of work it was perhaps unsurprising. The older man, Stefan Fischer, nodded and followed Skellan into the temple. He, at least, had the decency to bow low before the statue of Sigmar Heldenhammer and make the sign of the hammer whereas the other just walked down the aisle, toeing at the seats and tutting at the silver runes worked into the window frames. His footsteps echoed coldly.

Messner watched the man, fascinated by his confidence as he examined every nook and cranny of the old temple. Skellan moved with authority. He lifted a thin glass wedge from the front table, beside the incense burner, and tilted it so that it caught and refracted the light into a rainbow on the wall.

'So tell me,' Skellan said, angling the light up the wall. 'How does this fit with your philosophy? I am curious. The taking of a human life... it seems... alien to my understanding of your faith. Enlighten me.'

Behind Messner, Meyrink coughed.

'Sacrifice for the good of mankind, Herr Skellan. Sacrifice.'

'Murder, you mean,' Skellan said bluntly. 'Dressing the act up in fancy words doesn't change it. You want me to go down into the basement and slay a daemon. I can do this. It is what I do. Unlike you I see no nobility in the act. For me it is a case of survival, plain and simple. The creatures would destroy me and mine, so I destroy theirs. So tell me again, why would you have me drive a stake into the heart of an old man?'

'He isn't an old man anymore. Victor Guttman is long gone. The thing down there is a shell, capable of ruthless cunning and vile acts of degradation and slaughter. It is a beast. Forty-two young women of this parish have suffered at the beast's hands, witch hunter. Forty-two. I would have you root out the canker by killing the beast so that I do not find the words forty-three coming to my lips.'

'Good. Then we understand each other.'

'So we kill to stop more killing?' Brother Meyrink said, unable to hold his silence. 'That makes as much sense as going to war to end a war.'

'We love to hate,' the witch hunter said matter-of-factly. 'We love to defeat and destroy. We love to conquer. We love to kill. That is why we love war so much we revere a killer and make him a god. In violence we find ourselves. Through pain and anger and conflict we find a path that leads us to, well, to what we don't know but we are determined to walk the path. It has forever been so.'

'Sigmar help us all,' Meyrink said softly.

'Indeed, and any other gods who feel benevolent enough to shine their light on us. In the meantime, I tend to help myself. I find it is better than waiting for miracles that will never happen.'

'How do you intend to do it?' Meyrink asked.

Messner paled at the question. Details were not something he wanted.

The witch hunter drew a long bladed knife from his boot. 'Silver-tipped,' he said, drawing blood from the pad of his thumb as he picked himself on the knife's sharpness. 'Surest way to do it. Cut his heart out of his chest, then burn the corpse so there's nothing left.'

Messner shuddered at the thought. It was barbaric. 'Whatever it takes,' he said, unable to look the witch hunter in the eye.

'Stay here, priest. I wouldn't want to offend your delicate sensibilities. Fischer, come on, we've got work to do.'

VII

THEY DESCENDED IN darkness, listening to the chittering of rats and the moans of the old man, faint like the lament of ghosts long since moved on. His cries were pitiful

The candles had died but tapers lay beside fresh ones. Skellan lit two. They were enough. Death was a dark business. Too much light sanitised it. His feet scuffed at the silver wrought into the floor on the threshold. It was nothing more than mumbo-jumbo. There was no magic in the design. Some charlatan had taken the temple for all it was worth. It was amazing what price people would pay for peace of mind.

The fretful light revealed little of the dark's secrets.

Carefully Skellan moved through the crypt, Fischer two steps behind him, sword drawn in readiness for ambush. Skellan had no such fear. The only things alive down in the crypt were either too small or too weak to cause any serious harm. There was no sense of evil to the place. No taint. He raised the candle, allowing the soft light to shed more layers of pure black in favour of gentler shadows.

The old priest was huddled in the corner, naked and emaciated, his bones showing stark against the flaked skin. He barely had the strength to lift his head but defiance blazed in his eyes when he did so. Suppurating sores rimmed his mouth. There were dark scars where he had been bitten. Skellan had no doubt about the origin of the wound. It was the cold kiss of death: a vampire's bite. The old man had been fed on, of that there was no doubt. But that didn't mean that he had been sired into the life of a bloodsucking fiend.

Again, there was no residual evil that he could discern, only a frightened old man.

He trod on a plate of food that lay untouched at Guttman's feet, the plate cracked and mouldy cheese smeared beneath his boot. A nearby jug of water was nearly empty.

'Have you come to kill me?' The old man said. It sounded almost like a plea to Skellan's ears. The poor pathetic wretch had obviously tortured himself to the point of madness with the dreams of blood feasts. It was natural, having been fed upon to dream of feeding in the most feverish moments of the night when the kindred vampires were abroad. But dreams were not deeds. A true vampire would feel no remorse. There would be no tortured soul beginning for slaughter. There would be only defiance, arrogance, contempt, as the love of hatred boiled away all other emotions.

'Yes.'

The fear seemed to leech out of Guttman, the puzzle of bones collapsing in on themselves as his body slouched against the cold crypt wall.

'Thank you.'

'It will hurt, and there will be no remains for loved ones to come cry over, you understand? It can be no other way. The curse is in you, whether you killed these women or not.'

'I killed them,' Guttman said forcefully.

'I doubt it,' Jon Skellan said, drawing the silver dagger from his boot. 'Does this scare you, priest? Does it make your skin itch and crawl?'

Guttman stared at the blade as it shone in the candlelight. He nodded.

'Make your peace with Sigmar,' Stefan Fischer said from behind Skellan. He turned his back on the murder.

A litany of prayers for forgiveness and for the safe passage of his soul tripped over Victor Guttman's lips, not stopping even for a moment as Skellan rammed the silver knife home, between third and forth rib, into the old man's heart. His eyes flared open, the truth suddenly blazing in his mind. His screams were pitiful as he succumbed to death's embrace. He bled, pure dark blood that seeped out of the gaping wound in his chest and pooled on the floor around him.

Skellan stayed with the old priest as he died, a pitiful old man in chains.

He hung there, limbs slack, body slumped awkwardly, head lolling down over his cadaverous ribs, where the knife protruded from his chest cavity.

'It's over,' Fischer said, laying a hand on his friend's shoulder. 'Come, let's leave this place. Bringing death to a temple leaves me cold.'

'In a moment my friend. Go to the priests, tell them the deed is done, and fetch the paraffin oil from the cart. This place needs cleansing of the stench.'

'But–'

'No buts, old friend. The place must be purged. The priests can find more walls to praise their god. But not here. Now leave me for a moment with the dead, would you? I need to pay my respects to a brave old fool.'

He sat alone for an unknowable time, the candle burning low in his hand, unmoving, waiting, alone with the dead priest.

The pungent reek of paraffin drifted down from above. It was a sickening, stifling smell. Disembodied voices argued, Fischer's the loudest as he continued to douse the temple in oil. The place would burn.

Victor Guttman's eyes flared open in the dying light and his hand flew to the silver blade still embedded in his heart. He screamed as he yanked it out and sent the knife skittering across the crypt floor. The flesh around the wound was seared black.

'I tasted his blood,' Victor Guttman rasped, his head jerking up as he strained against his chains, all trace of the man gone. 'I want more!'

Guttman twisted and jerked, tugging at the chains that bound him, but there was no escape.

'No,' Skellan said softly. 'I told you I was here to kill you, consider this my promise delivered.' With that he stood, collected his silver knife and slipped it into the boot sheath, the gesture itself a mocking bow to the beast chained to the cold stone wall.

He walked slowly up the stairs, the creature raging in the darkness he left behind.

Fischer was waiting at the crypt's entrance, his face grim. He held a bottle in his hand, a rag stuffed into its mouth. He passed it to Skellan who lit the end with the last of his candle's dwindling flame.

Together they stood at the huge wooden door, the cocktail of lamp oil and fire burning in Skellan's hand. He tossed it deep into the body of the temple where the glass shattered off the statue of Sigmar. Flames licked at the stonework, tongues of blue heat lashing out to consume the wooden seats. Skellan and Fischer backed out from the intense heat as the conflagration took hold and consumed the temple.

He turned to the younger priest, Messner, who had begged his help.

'The beast is dead.'

'But…'

'There are no buts, the beast's evil cannot survive the fire. It is done. Deliver payment to Herr Hollenfeuer's wine cellar.'

'How can we pay? We have nothing left. You've destroyed everything we ever had!'

Skellan shook his head sadly. 'No, young sir, you did that. I am merely the tool you chose for its destruction. Do not blame the sword for the soldier's death, blame the man wielding it.'

VIII

HIGH ABOVE THE blaze, three men stood watching the towering inferno with perverse delight.

Vlad von Carstein, the vampire count of Sylvania, watched the flames intently. Beside him, Herman Posner turned to his man, Sebastian Aigner: 'Go out and feed. Make sure the fools down there know that they killed an innocent man. I want the knowledge to tear them apart.'

Aigner nodded. 'It will be as you wish.'

'Poor, stupid, cattle,' Posner said, a slow smile spreading across his face. 'This place promises a lot of sport, my lord.'

Von Carstein said nothing, content to watch the Sigmarite temple turn to ashes and smoke.

ABOUT THE AUTHORS

Robert Allan lives and has been accused of trying to work in Barnsley, UK where he spends most of his time dreaming up ways to rock the Black Library universe.

Robert Baumgartner works as an attorney in corporate and employment law. He lives in Tennessee, USA.

Richard Ford works as an editor for role-playing and miniature games company Mongoose Publishing. He originally hails from Leeds but currently lives in Wiltshire, UK.

Graham McNeill hails from Scotland and works in Games Workshop's Games Development team. He has written seven novels for the Black Library and a host of short stories for *Inferno!* magazine.

Nick Kyme hails from Grimsby, a small town on the north-east coast of England known for its fish (a food which, ironically, he dislikes profusely). Nick moved to Nottingham in 2003 to work on *White Dwarf* magazine.

Matt Ralphs lives and works in Nottingham. His previous writing credits include three background books, *The Imperial Infantryman's Uplifting Primer*, *Blood on the Reik* and *The Life of Sigmar*.

Steven Savile has written a wide variety of sf, fantasy and horror stories. He won the L Ron Hubbard 'Writers of the Future' award in 2002, and has been nominated three times for the Bram Stoker award. He currently lives in Stockholm, Sweden.